In the Land of Eternal Spring

A novel

by

Alan Howard

Harvard Square Editions
New York
2017

ISBN 978-1-941861-39-4
Printed in the United States of America
Published in the United States by
Harvard Square Editions
www.harvardsquareeditions

For Rosa, Diana, John, Ella and Felix

Ah, what an age it is
When to speak of trees is almost a crime
For it is a kind of silence about injustice!

—Bertolt Brecht

I

Guatemala City

ONE

IF ANYONE HAD ASKED, I would have honestly replied I
hardly ever think of her anymore, but sitting in front of
the fire the other night in this little house above the sea,
I noticed the orange flare of the pine sprigs that
sometimes get mixed into the kindling, and as happens
whenever I am in a certain mood and see this
incandescent glow in the black fireplace, I see those
mysterious orange lights on the mountainside that
night in Santa Cruz del Quiché, the lights that Laura
said made her feel closer to God, and I am reminded
with a gentle shock that I have felt her there inside me
every day of my life for the past 50 years.

The long winter is coming to an end. The first
bluebells have sprouted and a dense fog drifts across
the dunes. Soon I will be swimming early in the
morning along the deserted beach and then through a
cut in the sandbar that runs for miles out to sea,
conversing with the gulls and terns and a family of
brown pelicans that have taken up residence. I swim
until I am almost delirious in this ceremony of light
and water and air.

Here my ashes will be scattered and the pain will end. But before that happens, I must tell this story.

I was a journalist by trade and therefore will try to stick to the facts. I have my idiosyncrasies, like everyone else, which necessarily shape this record. For one, I have come to believe that happiness and freedom are built on the hard foundation of human solidarity and all the rest is fluff. That isn't the way I would have put it back then, but the fuse was lit and all kinds of official myths, including a few I subscribed to myself, were about to go up in smoke.

She came from a place called Prairie Village, a town resembling neither prairie nor village but typical of the more charming suburbs that surround the cities of the American heartland. I know this because many years ago—not long after the events I am about to relate—I took a detour off Interstate 70 on a trip cross country to see if I could find her house, which I did, on a safe suburban street much like those of my own childhood. It reminded me of a remark Manolo once made, about Americans thinking we were such unique individuals when with our TV addiction and the rest of the mass media we were probably one of the more homogenized people on earth.

But driving past her house that day, thinking of the ways I might have come to know her, I tried to imagine her as a little girl and could not; or as the teenager in her high school yearbook photo I once saw, the frilly dress and the rope of pearls high on her throat and that extraordinary smile before it bloomed, and I could not imagine that person either.

Contrary to everything I know to be true, it was as if our lives had begun only after we left the States for Guatemala City in the late spring of 1963.

I met her there in a house that looked like a new triple-decker motel—down to the diagonal parking lines out front. The interior was somehow both stark and garish, cold institutional marble floors and mirrored walls the setting for plush white sofas and matching chairs and a chandelier the size of a small boat. The hills above the city were studded with homes like this.

"Peter is our new Fulbright Scholar," Robert Thornby said, introducing me to our hostess, a sleek older woman with a deep tan and a very large glass of white wine. Thornby had a drink in his hand too. He was a big man with big hands and had been a nose guard on Purdue's 1952 Big Ten championship team. He was now the Junior Cultural Affairs Officer at the American Embassy and thought my social life would benefit from meeting more young people like myself. The party that night was for the teenage daughter of the lady with the nice tan.

"Oh, the fellow doing that marvelous study about teaching people how to read and write," she said now. "Someone at the embassy said it was *brilliant*."

"I wouldn't go quite that far," I said.

I am always surprised and a little suspicious when anyone describes my work in such superlatives. I get a lot of satisfaction when I've done something well, which isn't that often, but the results are at best a high degree of competence and would never be confused as *brilliant* by anyone who knew anything about the subject.

In this particular case the remark was bizarre. From the very beginning the embassy had seemed oblivious to my study of the Great National Literacy Campaign, then in its fifth year without visible impact on the masses. The State Department was financing the study and had adopted the campaign as one of the jewels in its Alliance for Progress—another example of the many good deeds that America did in the world. It was as if there had been no communication between the embassy and whoever in Washington had approved the grant.

Nor did our hostess have any interest in discussing the Great National Literacy Campaign.

Thornby left me in the company of a bubbly young woman in a tight white dress with a dainty waist bow who informed me that the frenzied movement in the center of the enormous room was a dance called the Mashed Potato, "the latest from the States," she said. It was near the beginning of the solo performance dance steps that seemed to obliterate the physical intimacy I had thought to be the whole purpose of dancing.

"I'm not much of a dancer," I said quite accurately.

She invited me to her church, the Union Church in Zone 10, "where all the Americans go," she added helpfully. "You could come this Sunday."

"Well, I really don't get along so well with churches," I said.

"But you'll like this one. It's really gassy."

"I'll try to make it," I lied.

I could not even begin to explain to this girl my hostile indifference to any church, how my notion of the divine was hopelessly bound up with an unpredictable variety of worldly phenomena: the spheres and dark corners of the female body, rare sunsets, the poetry of Keats; in sum, anything even remotely ecstatic. I was saved when a tall boy in a red blazer swept her away.

Thornby was talking to some Peace Corps volunteers. They looked as frazzled and dislocated as ever, the guys in boots and jeans and denim shirts, the women in sandals and shapeless dresses. They didn't seem any happier about being at the party than I was. These were the early volunteers, fascinated with the Kennedy rhetoric but too smart to swallow it whole. I'd met a few and suspected they saw me as part of the embassy crowd and therefore not quite as virtuous as themselves. It didn't bother me that much, except like most people I don't like being pegged for something I'm not.

I got myself a rum and Coke and wandered out to the balcony to take in the view and inhale the oxygen of solitude.

The air was cool and cleared my head. I could see the lights of the city far below, dim and puny against the intense starlight. I tried to get my bearings in the immense void of black sky and the vast unelectrified mountain darkness surrounding the city, but there was no visible horizon. The impression was one of a void, confused and confusing space. The faint lights of the city might have been a distant galaxy or some awry reflection of the bright stars. *You are a long way from home*, I said to myself, yes, but carrying the torch that had been passed to a new generation of Americans, ready to pay any price, bear any burden, for those people in the huts and villages and teeming cities across the globe struggling to break the bonds of mass misery, and then I thought about my old man and how he would have loved this big house, my old man who had eaten out his heart for this kind of dough. It was a rotten dream, of that I was convinced, but it kept him going most of his life and though it broke him in the end, I wondered if anything on earth could latch on to my own heart like that, infect my own blood, with its compulsive vision of Paradise on Earth.

"Come on, shy one. You can dance with an old lady at least!"

Our hostess, who it turned out was too drunk to dance, deposited me back inside where I stumbled into an argument with three sons of the local aristocracy, handsome young men in expensive suits.

We chatted about their trips to Miami and New York. They suggested places I should visit in Guatemala and complimented me on my Spanish. One of them invited me to his family's *finca* in Retalhuleu. He asked me what I was doing in Guatemala and I told him.

"The Alliance for Progress is the work of reds in the State Department," he said.

"It's obvious," added another.

Thornby was listening a little off to the side with one of the Peace Corps women.

"You don't really believe that, do you?" I said.

"Look, we went to school in the States and know the score," said the guy who had invited me to his family's estate.

I tried to reason with them, about the need for land reform, education, maybe even elections. It had been five months since the military coup that had again postponed the long-awaited elections and resistance was growing. How long did they think the army could keep the lid on? Then I heard the venom in their voices.

"The Americans are stupid and hypocritical."

"You don't understand that *our* peasants are *happy*," chimed in another one. "You can't even speak Spanish."

This last charge was obviously absurd. We had been conversing in Spanish for the past twenty minutes — and the guy had even complimented me on my fluency. I got angry, but that didn't help either. They were relentless. "You have your Negroes and we have our Indians," one of them said.

"At least *we* still have a few Indians left," said one of his pals. "The Costa Ricans didn't even leave enough for the tourists!"

They laughed and I turned away — smack into Thornby waiting to introduce me to the Peace Corps volunteer. They had been there the whole time and never said a word.

"Laura Jenson," Thornby said, his open hand presenting her and then me. "Peter Franklin."

"How do you do?" I said.

"Oh, you're an American," she said, surprised and bemused and finally, I thought, disappointed.

She had that casual naturalness that would become fashionable in a few years. Her honey brown hair fell across the side of her face, clipping an eye and curling around her throat like an expensive fur. Her mouth was large and tender. It was not a classically beautiful face but had an openness and intensity that made you pay attention.

"Have you been here long?" she asked.

Her voice had the rounded softness of the Midwest that sounded exotic to my parochial Easterner's ear.

"About an hour," I said.

She also had a smile that came from deep inside and knocked you out without half trying.

"I mean in the country," she said.

"Oh. A few months."

"I liked what you were saying to them."

"They weren't overwhelmed by my logic."

"Do you like it here?" she asked.

"It's interesting."

She tilted her head quizzically and tucked a strand of hair into place behind her ear.

"What does that mean?"

"I'm not sure." We both laughed. "What about you?"

"I like it," she said.

"I do too."

"But you're not sure."

"I'm not sure *what* I like," I said, "but I like being here."

"Maybe you'd like being anywhere," she suggested.

It was an agreeable thought that had not occurred to me.

"Maybe I would."

"What do you do here?"

I never turned down an opportunity to talk about the Great National Literacy Campaign. Most of the time people weren't interested, like our hostess, but Laura had this way of listening that kept me going.

I did believe the work was important, though not in the way I had anticipated. A country of five million people, three quarters of them illiterate, and the entire campaign, I had quickly learned to my chagrin, exactly two secretaries, a colonel at the Ministry of Education and an unknown number of volunteer teachers around the country. The secretaries sent out diplomas to any teacher who asked for them while the colonel performed most of his duties from his beach house in San José. The embassy threw in a few bucks to cover the secretaries' salaries and donated sacks of powdered milk that were supposed to be distributed free to literacy centers but more often than not ended up in the Central Market for sale.

It made me angry, but the whole country had been run this way since the coup in '54 when the CIA and United Fruit disposed of the popularly elected but dangerously independent Jacobo Arbenz and replaced him with a friendly dictator, one of whose first official acts was to take away the right to vote for illiterates.

I went on for a while, as I tended to do, until Laura stopped me.

"I've organized some literacy classes," she said.

She lived in Santa Cruz del Quiché, a town in the *Cordillera Central* about a six-hour drive north of the city. She knew about the questionable diplomas but didn't think that was so important. "People are so poor and have so many other problems," she said, "it's amazing they learn as much as they do." We disagreed on something about Paulo Freire and his *Pedagogy of the Oppressed*, with Laura defending his political approach and me questioning its effectiveness. The difference didn't seem important at the time, but I liked the friction of this little argument.

"How long are you in the city?" I asked.

"Just a few days."

"Let me take you to dinner tomorrow night."

"I have meetings all day. I don't know when I'll be done."

"Where are you staying?"

"*Pensión* San Francisco."

"How about I come by at seven. If you're not there, we'll do it another time."

"Hey, you two!" It was Jacob Stein, herding some of the Peace Corps toward the door. Jacob was in Guatemala on a post-graduate fellowship from Harvard. "Thornby's giving us a ride into town."

He steered me aside and squinted across the room, his dark eyes quick and hungry.

"Your babe's the only good-lookin' one," he said.

"She's not mine."

He nudged me.

"Don't give me that, you bum. I see that look in your eye."

He shook his head.

"I thought there'd be some tail here tonight. You know how long it's been since I got laid? Do you have any idea what happens to an unused pecker in *eleven weeks*!"

"What about 17th Street?"

"I wouldn't touch that stuff with a ten-foot pole," he said. "Come on," his eyes feinting toward the door, "you can't let her get away now."

Laura was waiting there with two other volunteers and Manolo Ortiz, who was in his last year of medical school and did some work with the embassy. On our way down to the car, Thornby looked back at the gleaming mansion we had just left. He had grown up on an Indiana farm and hated ostentation of any kind. I liked that about him.

"It's too much for Guatemala," he said. "Gives people communist ideas."

TWO

Thornby dropped us off at the fried chicken joint on Sixth Avenue. Street kids cruised the tables picking off chicken bones and leftover Cokes until a waiter chased them off. Not for long though; the kids regrouped in the parking lot, probed the perimeter of the open-air establishment, then moved in for another foray—and so on into the night.

We sat at a long wooden table near the sidewalk. The grill was at the far end of the large space, a warm light breeze clearing out the greasy smoke. The avenue at this hour was almost empty. Now and then an Indian padded along the sidewalk with a loaded sack over his shoulder, his feet covered with dust or mold or nature's leathery compensation for shoes, oblivious, apparently, to the abundance of shoe stores that, along with the beauty salons, seemed to occupy more than their share of retail space in this city.

This lone fried chicken joint was all that remained of one of those elaborate schemes the boys from the Rand Corporation or the Ford Foundation were always dreaming up. Build a chain of these restaurants throughout the country, which would expand the national poultry industry, reduce malnutrition and not incidentally create a market for U.S. feed grain companies. The scheme went bust when the local chickens kept dying and Purina or the Ford Foundation or whoever it was cut their losses and left.

"Warm tea," Jacob muttered, dipping his pinky into the cup. "If there's one thing I can't stand, it's warm tea. Do you believe it? People who can screw up *boiling water!*"

I knew what was coming next. The *Chapín* mentality. *La Hora Chapina* and *La Hora Inglesa.* Nobody did anything on time. Everyone lied. All the women were either virgins or whores and all the men cheated on their wives. The poor were hopeless, the rich oblivious, the government a disaster. It pained him to say this, but you could see they didn't have a clue.

This got him onto the subject secondary in importance only to his sexual deprivation, of how the country could be saved—the celebrated cycle of new capital, new markets and a growing middle class leading to prosperity, stability and democracy. It sounded logical and sometimes I believed it myself. One of the Peace Corps disagreed.

"The little guy never gets a fair shake," he said. "The big landowners get all the goodies and the little farmers get squat."

"So we're not perfect," Jacob said. "We make mistakes."

"Mistakes," Laura said. "You think that's all it is?"

"Look," Jacob said. "We try. Do you realize how many millions we give away every year in surplus food? That's one thing you have to admit. We're generous. You can't deny that."

Manolo Ortiz was astonished.

"What's so generous about giving away something you don't want?"

Manolo liked to make his points with questions. Thornby had introduced us shortly after I arrived in Guatemala. Manolo loved the philosophical play of ideas. A provocative guy, but we'd gone on a few good drunks together and I was fond of him.

"It helps a little," I said.

Manolo laughed. He had a kind of conspiratorial chuckle that carried you along and set you up for the kill.

"Come on," he said. "We have 60,000 children who die of malnutrition every year. You mean without your surplus food maybe there'd be 61,000?"

"That's a thousand kids," I said.

"But there's still 60,000 who die, right? Along with your few sacks of wheat and powdered milk comes a whole *structure*" — he gave the word a lethal resonance — "that prevents them from getting the nourishment they need."

"You can't get so emotional," Jacob said. "That's why we have these nuts with their bombs."

The bombs went off at night, the big ones with a thump and echo like a plane breaking the sound barrier. The next day there'd be nothing in the papers. The closest I ever heard to an explanation was Thornby joking about perennial revolutionaries or student demonstrations getting too frisky.

"Some people don't think they're nuts," Manolo said.

"I don't believe in violence," Jacob said.

"It's a pity that more of your compatriots don't think the same way."

Jacob strummed the table.

"You sound like those students at the university," he said.

Manolo laughed. "I *am* a student at the university."

"You know what I mean. Everything's our fault. I suppose you think we're *imperialists*."

"He didn't say that," Laura said.

"Look, I don't like the way we support these military characters either," Jacob said, "but we do a lot of good things too. You can't lose perspective."

"Like what?" Laura asked. "What good things?"

It wasn't a hostile question, but that's the way Jacob heard it.

"You sound bitter," he said to her. "It must be rough out there in the boondocks all by yourself. I can understand that."

"I'm not bitter," she said softly. "And I'm not all by myself."

"Show him the newsletter," the woman sitting next to her said. "We get it out once a month."

Laura dug into her big bag. It was a coarsely woven shoulder bag you saw Indian men with all the time but not the women. She pulled out an 8.5 by 11 mimeographed sheet and gave it to Jacob who examined it.

"Not bad," he said, handing it to me.

He couldn't have cared less about literacy centers. Jacob had come to Guatemala to study the feasibility of setting up a national stock market. It had taken him two weeks to conclude it was impossible and he had been bored out of his mind ever since.

As I looked over the newsletter, I was reminded of another big problem with the literacy campaign. Students would learn to put together the right sounds with the right letters and if you listened to them, as they moved a finger slowly along the line of print and pronounced a word, it would seem that they were reading when in fact they were only uttering the sound of the word. They didn't make the connection between the words and the reality they knew that the words symbolized.

There were degrees to this lack of comprehension, with some students understanding a good deal and others remaining functionally illiterate. Teachers had to be made aware of the problem and given exercises to address it, and students needed a regimen of complementary reading material—newspapers, other booklets, anything that drew them deeper into the literate world.

This newsletter from Santa Cruz did exactly that. It was drenched in the juices of everyday village life: riddles, jokes and recipes, stories on vaccinations and the town's renowned marimba band. Laura and another volunteer from a nearby village put it out for their literacy classes.

"It's exactly what the Great National Literacy Campaign needs," I said to her.

"We have a lot of fun doing it," she said, as if that somehow qualified my praise.

"You know what else it needs? A teacher's guide."

"What do you mean?"

"You two more or less know what you're doing. You have college degrees. Have you ever seen who is typically teaching one of these classes?"

"I know."

"Half of them haven't gotten beyond primary school themselves, and some not even that."

A kid under the table who I didn't even know was there began tugging at my leg. He held up a dry, meatless chicken bone and whispered, "*Señor*, could you put a little sauce on it please?" His Spanish was quite clear. I reached for the bottle of Tabasco, thinking there was something dead wrong about this act, when he added, "and some for my brother?" Another even smaller kid crouched behind him.

I couldn't do it.

"*Dónde vives*?" I asked the kid.

"In *La Chacarón*. Down the road a way is my church. Near where the Number 11 bus passes? You know where that is?"

"I know it. How many brothers do you have?"

"Two. Julian here, and the little one."

"How old is the little one?"

He glanced around nervously.

"You ask a lot of questions, *Señor*. I don't know that. No one ever told me."

"Do you live with your mother and father?"

"No. Only my mother. I don't know where my father is. He's dead."

A waiter came charging over and chased the two of them away. I realized now that everyone at the table had been taking in this exchange.

"Peter likes the local color," Jacob said. "But it's really a shame the way they let them roam around this place."

When we got up to leave, Manolo tapped Jacob's arm and nodded toward a roll left on the table.

"Let's be generous," he said cheerfully. "Let's ask one of those kids if he'd like our bread."

Jacob gave Manolo a dirty look, said goodnight to the rest of us and left. Manolo and I walked Laura and the other two volunteers out of the place. Laura stopped in front of me.

"See you tomorrow at seven," she said.

I watched the little band of Americans go straggling down the sidewalk. Laura was the tallest. She had an awkward, swaying gait, leaning forward like she was walking into a stiff wind with that big bag over her shoulder. Manolo was watching them too. He chuckled to himself and patted me on the arm.

"Come on," he said. "I think we need a drink."

THREE

We headed up Sixth Avenue and walked five blocks to the Roxi on 18th Street. I liked the Roxi. The loud marimba band had a lot of brass and a strong beat and the girls weren't bad either. We got a table and a bottle of local rum and watched the couples dancing in the red and blue neon lights: chunky women with big fat valentine asses and fragile women with skinny legs under stiff petticoats and interchangeable men with shirts open and chests gleaming. After two shots of the rum, all the women had a beautiful glow.

"So what do you think of her?" Manolo asked.

"Who?"

"Miss Peace Corps."

"Very nice. Do you think she has any prejudices?"

He smiled at his own expression for a woman who wouldn't sleep with him, which I took to be unusual. He had gone to the University of Wisconsin for two years where he could not have been happier with our custom of dating without chaperones and so many girls with a weakness for this intellectual Latin with the dark olive eyes and light olive skin. He had come back when his funds ran out, but it was also the hostile winters and rude alien manners and one of those girls in Madison—"the Eastern Jews impressed me"—who broke his heart.

But he was not going to venture an opinion on Laura Jenson.

"You seemed nervous," he said now. "You're going to see her tomorrow."

"For dinner."

"Be careful."

"I try."

"It's not *always* a virtue, you know. I think she likes you."

"How do you know?"

He laughed with that amused, off-key chuckle.

"I can't tell you all my secrets, man." He sipped at his drink and looked around the room. "You have to notice little things," he said, "live every minute," and remarked on one girl's hands and another's teeth. I knew he had been reading Sartre, which he admitted now had something to do with this comment. We picked up the thread of a running argument on Sartre and Camus and the Algerian Revolution.

"It's his country," I said. "Camus doesn't have the luxury of a Paris intellectual—to see everything with such perfect detachment."

"Now what the hell does that mean? *Perfect detachment.* Are you defending Camus' position or not?"

"I'm defending the way he expresses it."

"You mean you can say the stupidest, most reactionary things as long as you say them eloquently. Come on!"

We both laughed. Manolo reminded me of an English professor I had in college whose humor made learning feel effortless.

"Something like that," I said.

"You may be hopeless," he said affectionately. "Did you read that book I lent you?"

It was William Appleman Williams' *The Tragedy of American Diplomacy.* Manolo had taken one of his courses in Madison.

"Most of it."

"Did you learn anything?"

"I did as a matter of fact."

"Maybe there's still hope for you."

A woman in a red sweater and tight skirt sitting at the bar kept looking my way. A few minutes earlier she had strolled past our table with the casual sensuality that could make me forget the commercial core of these encounters. Now she came over and sat down directly in front of me, crossing her bare legs. She had a nice face with sad brown eyes and pale chalky skin that you wanted to restore.

"My name's Esperanza," she said. "What's yours?"

"Pedro."

She leaned close and I felt her hand under the table moving confidently along my thigh.

"Pedro," she said. "You're going to be mine tonight."

She hailed a waiter and ordered a cognac with Coca-Cola and ice. I poured another rum and admired Esperanza's firm legs. Manolo seemed to be enjoying the show.

"I like her," he said. "She looks like that Never-On-Sunday, what's her name?"

"Melina Mercouri."

"Melina Mercouri," he said. "She looks a little like her."

Esperanza rocked her head back and laughed like Melina Mercouri, her throat begging to be kissed, which I did.

"Oh, my," she said. "Such a romantic man."

Her hand had now found its destination under the table and my brain was mesmerized by the harmony of that hand and the hard prick it had sculpted. In my dawning drunkenness I could certainly see the resemblance with the enchanting Melina. You couldn't beat the Roxi for cheap euphoria.

"You're very beautiful," I said.

"Do you really mean that?"

She laughed.

"You have really nice teeth," I said, which was true.

"I like yours too."

She eyed me over the glass she held to her lips, then lowered the glass and kissed me. It started out like a normal nice wet kiss and then I was astonished by the ice cube that secretly slithered from her mouth to mine. Hot and cold and warm again. You never know what can happen in this life, I thought.

"I'll be right back," she said, rising with a little shimmy and tug at her skirt and then slipping into a room next to the bar.

"I hope you can afford this," Manolo said.

"I don't know how much it's going to cost yet."

"You'll find out soon enough," he said, punctuated with that goddamn chuckle.

We worked on the rum and watched the dancers. Manolo was very quiet now. The flashing lights were turned off while the band took a break and a slow ballad played on the jukebox. The boss lady was dancing with a guy with a felt hat down over his eyes. Other couples joined at the hip went through their steps, their faces gray and grim under the bare electric bulbs. There was an older man with a girl whose head barely reached his chest. Her face was dark and blank, her arm awkwardly stretched the length of his. She looked about ten years old, but there was a vague form to her chest, a hint of maturity in the full hips.

"It depresses me," Manolo said, nodding toward the dance floor. "Maybe you're too far away from it, but this is the way I grew up. I was like this."

"You've told me a little."

"Very little." He looked at me now. "Sometimes I wonder why we've become such good friends. My *compañeros* in the student association think you're a CIA agent."

"That's pretty funny."

"But not illogical. They look at what you do, traveling around the country, talking to all kinds of people. It's a perfect cover. We've been flooded with American agents here for the past ten years. Personally, I think the *compañeros* are wrong in your case. *Le tengo cofianza.* It's a Latin trait. We meet someone, we like them, we talk freely. Unfortunately a defect in these times."

"Manolo, I'm studying the literacy program. Maybe if we understand why it doesn't work, we can fix it."

He took a long drag on his cigarette and crushed it cold.

"Nothing is going to get fixed in this country until the twenty families who run it are lined up against the wall." He poured us what was left of the rum and nodded toward the bar behind me. "Your friend is back."

Esperanza was sitting at the bar. I went over and tapped her on the shoulder, which she ignored. I had walked into an erupting argument. She was glaring at another woman a few stools away and soon they were swearing under their breath at each other. The bartender tried to mediate but got nowhere. Then Esperanza said in a loud voice, "You filthy whore, how low can you sink?" When the woman didn't respond, my charming Esperanza picked up the beer bottle in front of her and smashed it against the edge of the bar. Now she had everyone's attention. She started toward her antagonist with the jagged neck of the bottle aimed at the other woman's face.

They dragged Esperanza away, crying hysterically, shouting and swearing. I went back to the table.

"I can't take you anywhere," Manolo said.

"I didn't do anything."

"An industrial dispute." He chuckled. "They were probably fighting over *you*. They have rules in these places, you know."

"Like what?"

He shrugged.

"Sometimes you don't find out about the rules until you break them," he said. "And sometimes you can change the rules."

"Thanks for the advice."

"Come on," he said, clinking his glass against mine. "It could have been worse."

Esperanza never returned, but we were assured that she was fine. At closing time the boss lady called the girls over to the cash register to count their chits and record them in a big ledger that looked like the ones they used in Dickens novels. Then the bartender turned up the lights and the Roxi went dead.

I said goodnight to Manolo and walked the three blocks to my apartment. It was a neighborhood thick with thieves and the drunks they rolled and the tiny pink and pistachio row houses on 17th Street—the whores sitting on their beds or leaning bare-assed over the half-doors of their stalls. There was something for everyone on 17th Street. Dark, perfumed dens and immaculate shrines with holy art on the wall and dollhouses with stuffed animals on the chairs; and for those who had achieved the sublime state of living without illusion, just a roll of toilet paper on the bed and a handy Coke bottle for a douche.

I had trouble sleeping and climbed the six flights to the roof of my building to get some air. The valley lay silent in the hazy dawn. I thought about Camus' notebooks, his intense feeling for the Algerian countryside, the rooms of his house, the way it was all fused with his childhood and emotional growth. Why didn't I have a connection like that? Maybe I did and didn't know it, but when I thought about home it was wherever I happened to be living at the time—the Upper West Side of Manhattan during my four years at

Columbia and for most of my childhood the deadening quiet of a tree-lined Boston suburb.

The clouds sailed past at eye level. I had never seen clouds like this before I'd arrived here, their lush interiors glowing in the sunrise. Mountains like wild gashes in the earth as I flew into the country and then these improbable clouds, almost close enough to touch, and the flat, elevated valley with its scrim of roads and houses and planted fields and then those same savage mountains reduced now to a soft, gray silhouette on the horizon.

The two volcanoes, Agua and Fuego, were much closer. I could count the scorched trees on their lower slopes and follow the paths that snaked to the rims. Then the stunted skyline of the city caught my eye, the bronze dome of the cathedral set like a semi-precious stone in the bland concrete.

Maybe home was something you could invent or might uncover in the course of an interesting life. Work. Ideas. A great love. God.

I babbled and even worse enjoyed listening to these garbled soliloquies, but this was ridiculous. I wanted answers and just kept turning up more questions. Perhaps only in moments of serene loneliness like this did I feel truly at home, but I couldn't accept that either. It doesn't fix any of the things I broke in this time, but I can see now I was still a very confused young man.

On the other side of the roof I looked down at the old railroad station with its concrete plaza and statue of a great 19th century general who became president, rearing on his horse.

The old railroad station was right across the street from my apartment. The railroad had thrived once, linking United Fruit Company plantations on both coasts with the capital in the mountains, but after the Arbenz trouble in the '50s the company had moved much of its operation to friendlier Central American countries farther south. The train arrived once a week now, the only hour of the week the bare concrete plaza came to life as taxis hunted their fares, crews went to work on the loading docks in back of the station, and families rushed into one another's arms.

At this hour women were stoking their charcoal fires and stirring their pots as the beggars slept like fallen soldiers around the statue of the great general who became president. The men dozing in their carts were there too, the same grim men you saw during the day, trotting through the streets harnessed to these same carts, and I thought of Orwell in Marrakech and that hard, sardonic vision of empire rotting on the strangeness and invisibility of people like this.

Are they really the same flesh as yourself? Do they even have names?

Questions that—I realize now—had already begun to give way to old and powerful needs. It happened to most of the Americans I knew there, the country reduced to mere backdrop for the drama of our very private and imported psyches. Sometimes it seemed that I had come with a mind so perversely wide open that all experience would flow through it without leaving a trace of meaning.   Remember that in these days the corpse in the ditch had landed there for the typical misfortunes—a jealous husband, a gang of thieves—and did not yet have a note with the assassin's proud signature pinned to an eyeball.

FOUR

The next day I ran into a new problem at the Ministry of Education. Colonel Ramirez, the boss who came in once a week from his beach house in San José, had left orders to keep me out of the very files he'd finally granted me permission to see. The secretary was polite but had her orders. I was disgusted. The guy had jerked me around from the start, complaining to Thornby, then one phony excuse after another, and now this.

I went to the embassy to see Thornby and also to pick up my monthly check. In those days the embassy was still located in the downtown business district and had not yet moved to its fortress-like setting in the suburbs.

Waiting for visas was a line of people that stretched out to the street and down the block. The Marine guard in the lobby waved me through and I took the elevator to Thornby's office on the fourth floor. His secretary had the check and also a letter from my father. I put the check and letter into my small briefcase.

Thornby was in his usual bureaucratic mode behind the clunky manual typewriter on his desk, mumbling about all the paperwork for Washington. But there was always about Thornby the air of a man out of place. The large, powerful hands belonged to heavier machinery. The crew cut and weathered face, the muscled body beyond its prime but not yet flabby with corruption, even the big lumberjack pipe—suggested another life, outside of offices, far from typewriters.

"How are things going at the *IGA*?" he asked me.

Thornby ran the *Instituto Guatemalteco Americano* and had arranged for me to teach an English class there to pick up a little extra money.

"Pretty good."

"So what brings you in today?"

I told him what had happened with Colonel Ramirez. He lit the pipe and watched the smoke, liquid-thick, rise toward a vent in the ceiling. Sometimes it seemed that was the only thing we had in common. We both smoked a pipe.

"You disappoint me, kid. You're supposed to be smart. That's why we gave you this grant, right? You've got Colonel Ramirez upset, very upset, all those questions about the cost of the literacy centers."

Thornby could go weeks without mentioning my project, then something would happen and he knew more about it than I did. I was often surprised by what Thornby knew.

"It's just one of many questions for the study," I said. "It's all in the Scope of Work for my proposal. It was approved in Washington."

"Well, I just *un*-approved it."

I was stunned but tried to stay focused.

"We've got a right to know how the money's being spent, don't we? Most of it's ours."

He shook his head slowly as he tamped his pipe.

"Look, I like you, kid, I really do. Which is why I'm not going to let you get your fucking brains blown out on my watch. What do you want to prove? That the guy's robbing us blind?"

"That wasn't my intention at all. I just wanted to make an estimate of the average cost of running one of these centers and extrapolate per-student cost from there."

"*Extrapolate*," he said. "I like those twenty-dollar words. Look, it's the price of doing business in this place. Don't go stepping on people's toes. Listen to me carefully." His knuckles on the pipe had turned yellow-white. "I was in Chile before landing in this shit heap and we had *hundreds* of very smart guys like you running around doing their big studies. They wrote them up and we filed them away and maybe one day someone will come along who needs one of them for a study *he's* doing. That's how it works. You just go ahead and do your study — without those cost figures—and give it to us. Then *we* decide what to do with it. Ok? By the way, how'd you make out with that Peace Corps volunteer last night? A very nice young lady."

I barely heard the question. I was trying to process what he had just told me. This friendly guy I had liked was a rigid bureaucrat who couldn't have cared less about the substance of my work. At the time I just chalked it up to the moral hazard with which junior cultural affairs officers in U.S. embassies operated around the world, but twenty years later Thornby's name would surface as the CIA station chief in Honduras during some pretty nasty business there.

"We're having dinner tonight," I said blankly.

"Congratulations. I didn't think you'd get anywhere with that one." He waited for me to bite, but I wasn't interested in his opinion on the subject—which just prompted him to continue. "She fell for this guy when they were in training. They tried to get sent to the same country together but that's a no-no. Now he doesn't answer her letters. I'm told she cries herself to sleep every night up there in Santa Cruz."

"How do you *know* all this?"

"It's my *job* to know." He puffed on his pipe. "Good luck with your dinner tonight." I got up to leave; he raised his hand. "Something I forgot to mention," he said. "Your monthly reports are sort of skimpy."

"Skimpy?"

"Yeah, no details. Who you talk to, what they say, where you been. You've spent some time at the university, right? You never say anything about the university. We're very interested in what goes on there."

"I went to a couple of lectures."

"We'd just appreciate it, you know, if your reports had a little more *substance*."

Fernando Garcia was sitting outside the office. Fernando did odd jobs for Thornby and loved Americans. He had a face like a fox and a potbelly and was always on the make.

"*Gringo desgraciado!* Where you been? I haven't seen you in weeks!"

"Been busy, Fernando."

"You work too hard," he said, then lowered his voice. "This weekend we pay a little visit to Locha's, eh? Remember Locha's?"

"I remember Locha's."

"Heard the definition of eloquence?" I shook my head. "Describe Jayne Mansfield without using your hands!"

I smiled, which seemed to be enough.

"See you later, Fernando."

I walked through the open work area. Violeta stood by a file cabinet, pretending not to see me. I waited at the elevator. She looked great in her spiked heels and the cream-colored dress clinging to the hollows of her ass, and for a moment the sight of her took the edge off Thornby's sting. Then I remembered the night she had told anyone who would listen what a bastard I was, how I was supposed to marry her, had deceived her. A serious failure to communicate there. It was the religious stuff that finally drove me nuts, like the afternoon she announced it *had* to rain because it was San Lucas Day, standing there with her hand on her hip daring me to say something blasphemous, which I did of course. Then a little later she was asking wide-eyed if it were true that Negroes had things *that* big because she'd heard that once a girl got it that way she could never be satisfied by a white guy again.

Her own mestizo skin was a smooth rich walnut, but Violeta was not the type to make those connections. Suffice it to say that Violeta confirmed my belief that there is no better way to learn the customs of another country than to sleep with a native. I could fall in love or something like it with such ridiculous ease in those days that I had very little idea who the object of my desire actually was.

I walked along Sixth Avenue, weaving my way through the kids selling Chiclets and their parents and grandparents who had graduated to portable stands of razor blades and batteries and sheets of lottery tickets, though the border between selling and begging would often completely dissolve. One of the kids trailed me for a block before finally saying "Well, why don't you just give me a little nickel anyway?" The kid was selling shoelaces, one for a nickel, two for 15 cents, three for 25—market information that I figured Jacob Stein could add to his indictment of economic backwardness.

It was a carnival of a street with sound trucks blasting music and breathless spiels on the stupendous deals to be had at this grand opening or that going-out-of-business sale. I walked past the Pan American Hotel, Rosenberg's Department Store, the Shoe Store of Nueva York, Fu Lu Sho Chinese Restaurant, past the Indians slumped in the doorways along the avenue, doorways with displays of more stereos and shoes and jewelry and home appliances than could ever be consumed by the inhabitants of this city.

I still had some time to kill before going to Laura Jenson's *pensión*. I bought the afternoon papers and went to the *pastelería* in the Bank of America building, a subdued place that allowed you to forget for a little while what was just outside the door.

The big story of the day was the death of a Paris fashion model known for her almond eyes and undulant walk, an intimate of Coco Chanel. The Minister of Tourism would soon prohibit the sale of postcards showing bare-breasted Indian women, deemed inconsistent with the national standard of femininity. A columnist for *El Imparcial* claimed the Judicial Police now had incontrovertible proof the recent wave of bombings was the work of Bulgarians who had infiltrated the student movement.

I opened the letter from my father. It contained the usual money troubles and a sad note about a cousin who had killed herself. A tragedy, my father said, he had always liked her. What a crock. Had he forgotten how he and the others had treated her? Once I heard an uncle say she was a communist, but in my apolitical family that only meant she read too many books and wore no make-up and believed in free love, whatever that was. I didn't know her well, but now my cold-blooded streak kicked in. She must have been in her early 30s, old enough I figured to know what she was doing. What did we have here but the calculated demise of an outcast? The tragedy my father had in mind was the impact on the family, the shame and stigma, the sense of failure. Yes, that would have been what he had in mind.

My mother was about the same age when they found her at the foot of the stairs, the house stinking with gas. He never talked about her, but from time to time as I grew up I would attempt a kind of sentimental calculus of my own personality. The tendency to rationalize defeat I recognized as my old man's. The book-learned sensibilities were harder to detect but usually gave themselves away by their lack of staying power. What remained was an aching emptiness of the spirit through which I deduced my mother's mysterious sorrow.

I put the letter back in my pocket and walked the five blocks to Laura Jenson's *pensión*.

We went to dinner that night at a smoky little *churrasco* place on the Reforma. The steaks were thick and came with garlic bread and salad. We ordered a strong Spanish wine and proceeded to get slightly blotto. At least I did. Laura was drinking too but mostly she listened. That was one of the things about her. She listened in a way that made you feel you were saying something very important. I would soon learn that she did it with everyone, which sometimes made me jealous, but that night she had me babbling away — about Orwell and the men with their carts in the plaza and the kids in the fried chicken joint and Thornby and Colonel Ramirez and my idea for a teacher's guide and the general hollowness of the Alliance for Progress.

It came out like a confession, a desperate release. I had not met anyone in Guatemala I'd felt comfortable talking to like this; but when I paused long enough to catch my own echo, I stopped, embarrassed by my self-absorption.

"What are you thinking?" I asked her. "You haven't said a word."

She tilted her head and smiled.

"Your food's getting cold."

"I talk too much."

"I like listening to you." She sipped her wine. "Do you think you'd be interested in me if we met in the States?"

The truth was I tended toward the flashier babes, not too flashy, but the kind like Violeta who dressed up a bit and carried themselves with a certain discreet sexiness. This was not Laura Jenson. And what about my weakness for the pure carnality of the Roxis and Esperanzas of this world?

"I don't know," I said.

"An honest man."

"One of the few I know."

"What are you going to do when you go back to the States?"

"I was thinking of law school, or maybe journalism."

"You'd make a good lawyer," she said.

"What makes you so sure?"

"You like to argue."

"No I don't." We laughed. "What do you do in Santa Cruz besides literacy classes?"

"The big deal when I got there was a water project, but the chief engineer ran off with the funds and the whole thing is on hold. It's so frustrating. I do whatever I can. I get powdered milk from the embassy for the one school in town and we've started a weaving cooperative. But it's mostly the literacy classes."

"It's an uphill battle," I said.

She began folding her paper napkin into smaller and smaller squares.

"The second week I was here someone said that before anything good could happen in this country you had to line the first twenty families up against the wall."

She kept looking at me, as if I might be able to resolve the enormity of that thought with everything else we had been told about the place. I was tempted to ask who had said this, but at the moment the remark still sounded more theatrical than menacing and of course Manolo Ortiz was not the only person in the country capable of making such a statement.

"And?" I prodded.

"I was shocked. That wasn't the way I'd learned it at Smith."

"Are you still shocked?"

She ran her hand slowly through her hair and tucked a strand behind her ear.

"I'm not sure what to believe anymore."

"Literacy helps."

"You know what they did in Cuba," she said.

Everyone knew. They had mobilized the entire country and in one year increased the national literacy rate from 60 to 96 percent. Along with its sweeping land reform, massive public health programs and nationalization of the big American monopolies, the Cuban Revolution had set in motion a popular revolt throughout most of the Western Hemisphere.

"I'd like to come see one of your literacy classes in Santa Cruz," I said. "I haven't been to Quiché yet. It's on my list."

She sipped at her wine, her eyes never leaving mine, and then very slowly placed the glass on the table.

"You don't have to go that far to see one of my literacy classes," she said. "I've got one in the *Penitenciaría Central*."

"In the *prison?*"

"I can take you tomorrow. It's an assignment I got while I was still living in the city before they shipped me out to Santa Cruz. I come back to check in on them about twice a month."

"A captive audience."

I thought this was clever, but she seemed offended.

"The classes are voluntary. They're good students."

She tilted her head at a quizzical angle, as if to say surely this is not something you would question. It was the first hint I had of a stubbornness so gentle you could not easily detect its obsessive roots. If I had recognized then how vulnerable it made her to the almost metaphysical appeal of revolutionary politics you could not avoid in those days, would I have done anything differently? I still don't know. But given the choices she finally made and the way I abetted them, I would like to think so.

FIVE

The Central Penitentiary was just up the street from the old railroad station, its walls the same pale green and not much higher. It seemed an odd location for a prison, in the heart of the city, separated from adjacent rooftops by streets not much wider than alleys. There was a line of women at the big iron door, waiting to visit with their parcels of food wrapped in newspaper.

I sat on a bench and watched the traffic. A mixed patrol went by, the soldiers in front and the sailors in back looking snazzy in white puttees and blue shirts. You would forget there was a navy until the junta got nervous and sent out these mixed patrols to advertise the unity of the armed forces. The jets would come out too, roaring so low they rattled plates on the table.

Laura came trundling down the street, her big knit bag slung over her shoulder with that plowing-ahead walk. She saw me and came over.

"Something's going on," she said, glancing toward the street.

"Do you think we'll have a problem getting in?"

"Getting in is easy," she said. "The problem is getting out."

"For *us*?"

"I was just kidding."

The muzzle of a black Tommy gun showed through the barred window of the big door. Inside a squad of young soldiers stood at ragged attention as the duty officer examined our papers. He took us up a flight of stairs to the *comandante*, a heavy-set man in a wrinkled uniform. His Spanish was inflected with the self-confident authority of *La Escuela Politécnica*, Guatemala's West Point.

"Ah, the blonde angel of illiteracy has returned — and with reinforcements! I can report that we are making great progress. The embassy should be pleased. We will soon have the most literate population of criminals in the Western Hemisphere. But we've missed you, my dear."

The duty officer stood crisply by the door.

"I've been meaning to come, Colonel. I've just been so busy."

"You Americans," he said fondly. "You know how to work. For people who know how to work this is a virgin country. I ran into one of your compatriots the other day. He's staying here. He'll make a fortune. Fantastic, you Americans. Put *shit* in a package you can sell it," he concluded, his tone one of genuine admiration.

He looked over my passport and then the duty officer took us back down the stairs to the edge of the main compound where 2,000 men swarmed in the glaring sunlight of the concrete yard. If once they had worn prison uniforms, there were now only remnants, clothing, like food, brought in and sold according to the ubiquitous laws of supply and demand. It could have been a town square on market day, the packed crowd, the smoky food stands and cluttered stalls of merchandise baking in the white dusty heat. Only here the men at the huge round *pila*, the communal stone tub of every village, were washing their own clothes, and the man with his wrists taped, jogging in tight circles off in a corner, had a killer's face with eyes that followed us as we went past. Laura seemed oblivious to the stir and buzz rippling in our wake.

"They keep the *politicos* over there," she said, with a surreptitious glance toward a black gate across the yard.

"Is that where we're going?"

"They won't let anyone near them. But there's an incredible communications system in this place."

We walked through a low archway where a man was waiting.

"*Señorita*, so good to see you again."

"How goes it, Don Igdalecio?"

"Very well. Come see."

The guy was about five feet tall, hunchbacked, dragging one foot in a heavy black boot. His eyes bulged behind small thick glasses. Teeth-twisted lips bent his mouth out of shape and fixed to his face a foolish and perpetual grin. I kept thinking about the soft cheerfulness of Laura's greeting, as if nothing were wrong with the man, the way she was with all of them, working her way through each class with the chairs lined up in a long narrow space behind a row of cells and against the outer prison wall.

You could see how she loved it, the questions, the gentle reprimand, the word of encouragement—the small but palpable victories of the teacher. Yet I could not get out of my head how these guys got here. The tabloids ate this stuff up. The kid eyeing her now, with the spiked Indian hair and the cracked orange cheeks of the high mountains, for all I knew was the crazed Julian Juárez Vincente doing 40 years for beating to death the old witch doctor who put the whammy on poor Julian's cornfield. Or maybe he was Carlos Sanchez who had smashed his sister over the head one night for no reason at all and hurled her lifeless body into a well. And Don Igdalecio, the hunchback, always at Laura's side, supervising the flow of worksheets, books, student papers. What was he in for? He noticed me looking at a book on his desk and came over to show it to me —*The Memoirs of Madame de Stahl*. He asked if I had read it.

"No."

He winked. "Very close to Napoleon."

Larceny, I figured.

"I didn't know."

"Oh, yes. Very influential." The twisted, grotesque mouth pointed toward Laura. "A strong one, like her."

"A strong one," I agreed.

Before we left, he gave Laura a folder with what appeared to be test results that she dropped into her bag.

We retraced our steps across the main compound, which was now empty and still, as if the inhabitants had been suddenly evacuated. And now I noticed the guards on top of the wall and how much higher the wall looked from the inside. Stalks of corn grew along its base, springing from cracks in the concrete.

The duty officer wasn't at the front gate and someone went to find him. The sergeant apologized for making us wait. Laura said we understood perfectly and were not at all inconvenienced. Her Spanish was fluent when it came to all the polite phrases she needed in Santa Cruz. I remembered her remark about getting in and out of this place.

"Do you think there's a problem?" I asked her.

Her reply was not encouraging.

"I hope not."

I began to think about who we would call, but the duty officer finally came, annoyed, with a napkin in his hand. He opened the metal door built into the high wooden gate and we walked through it into air that was clear and a sky that was blue and where the ordinary din of traffic was like a symphony.

"The place is so self-contained," she said. "Did you see the corn? They just reproduce their outside lives."

"It's depressing."

"I guess I've gotten used to it." She thought about that for a moment. "But it's not something anyone should get used to."

A gang of prisoners came straggling up the street, tied together, cops herding them along. One of the prisoners kept banging into the cop who had him handcuffed. Every time the prisoner stumbled the chain jerked and the whole crew almost went down. This lone resister kept snarling obscenities at his guard, who would soon have to call on the cop with the bullwhip.

We got a bus that left us about a block from Laura's *pensión*. I walked her down the stone path to the front door.

"I hope you'll let me know the next time you're in the city," I said.

"I'll try."

"When will you be back?"

"In a couple of weeks."

"It would be nice to get together," I said. "And maybe I could even get to see one of your non-captive literacy classes."

She smiled and kissed me on the cheek, then turned away quickly and went inside.

Two weeks went by and then a month and another two weeks and I began to think I'd seen the last of Laura Jenson. In some ways I wish that had been true.

SIX

All I had to worry about now was my work.

In Chiquimula, The Pearl of the East, in a hut along a broken trail where mules picked their way, hooves clattering and kicking up mud, four men sat copying articles from old newspapers into their notebooks, "just for practice," one explained apologetically, suggesting the activity lacked a certain seriousness.

A few miles north of the El Salvador border in the parched Quezada Valley I found a man reading in the dark corner of his cousin's house. The book rested on a high wooden crate and he was standing. It was an old textbook on human biology, falling apart, without a binding. He came whenever he could, he said, about once a week, to read the book and on that day was reading about the digestive system.

"What's so interesting about the book?" I asked.

"Oh, everything," he said. "But I'm looking for the part about bleeding."

Two years ago his brother had accidentally cut his wrist and bled to death. Nobody knew how to stop the bleeding. "All they did was hold a pan under his wrist so the blood wouldn't get all over the place," he said. I showed him how to use the index and table of contents, but there wasn't anything that explained what he wanted to know.

I made a note to include a booklet on first aid for the complementary reading material I'd been thinking about.

On a swing through Chimaltenango I visited a farm that 50 workers had somehow managed to turn into a cooperative. One of the first things they did was set up literacy classes. "Even for the women," a man said proudly.

In a settlement on the thick green Usumacinta River with monkeys flying through the trees I talked to a man who had just sold a cow and was thrilled that he did not have to pay someone 25 cents to read the deed for him since he could do it himself. His neighbor, also a recent graduate of the literacy course, had started a business transporting bananas to markets in the highlands. I got as far west as Retalhuleu, just above the steamy coastal plain, where some of the *campesinos* attending the class had gotten the idea to use fertilizers for their orange crop but still tied the traditional strips of petticoats to the orange trees, just in case this new-fangled method didn't work.

Something else happened on these trips. At some point in the visit, I would be asked to say a few words. The students seemed to have such high expectations of the visiting foreigner that I sensed they were usually disappointed by what I had to say.

What it has taken me many years to understand is that I have a low center of emotional gravity that can make me sound technical and dispassionate but that center is excitable and when it is ignited by something honest and good I am moved by great feelings of love, as I was one night at the end of this trip.

In the barn of a *finca* outside of Acatenango I heard myself talking about the millions of people around the world, poor *campesinos* just like themselves, who were also learning to read and write and what a tremendous thing that was, how powerful that made them, and I saw the smiles and their eyes come alive as they murmured their agreement and pushed me deeper into this surge of collective energy that felt invincible and could keep us all going forever. I remember it was one of those rare moments that I felt grateful to my government for having sent me to this heartbreaking country.

It's an extremely seductive feeling with an intoxicating power that would take me many years to recognize—tapping into that primitive core of our humanity that enables religious life and shapes our politics and if not properly managed can erupt with awful and tragic force. But I saw now more clearly than ever that denying people the ability to use the written language was a form of slavery.

That's when I began to realize what had changed with Thornby. I had as much of an obligation to these people as I did to him. I had no idea the world of trouble that meant.

On my return late in the evening from this last trip I found a note under my door. Laura was in town and wanted to take me to another literacy center an hour outside the city.

SEVEN

The bus to Amatitlán banged violently along a mountain road. Below, the cold ultramarine lake was cupped in the volcano, as pretty as all the postcards.

It was a long walk down the path littered with yellow and red petals and the air sprinkled with butterflies. Then the path ended suddenly and there were clouds below us and below the clouds a trail to the village with lanes of green grass and crimson bougainvillea springing over fences. We just stood there for a while, taking in the view.

"Did you ever wonder why people never see anything ugly in nature?" Laura said.

"I'm probably guilty of that myself," I said.

"Nature makes people think of God."

"I don't believe in God," I said.

"Really?"

"Most of the time."

"I hope you're not making fun of me."

"Do you?"

"I believe in something," she said. Ever since I was a little kid, I've felt there was something out there bigger than anything we can ever comprehend, and that hasn't changed. Not just out there but inside too. Everyone has it, this big beautiful incomprehensible thing inside them that connects them to everyone and everything else. Some people call it God. I guess others call it love. It has nothing to do with religion."

"It sounds like you believe we have souls."

"Don't you?"

"I refuse to answer on the grounds it will indict me."

She smiled.

"You know you do."

We spent an hour working our way down the steep slope of the valley to the village and then to the one-room house that also served as the literacy center. It had a dirt floor and the rafters were black with soot. There were a man and woman sitting at a long wooden table and two boys standing behind them. Laura introduced me.

"Don Julio is an excellent teacher," she said.

"*Mucho gusto,*" the man said.

He had bird-like bones under his loose skin and the whole family had the same consumptive cough.

His wife served us coffee boiled in a tin can. She moved very slowly and the sockets of her eyes were dark and flabby. I wondered how old she was. These country women seemed to pass directly from puberty to weary old age like a year without summer. Laura was looking into the dim musty room at a bulge in the hammock. The woman went over to the hammock and turned back the flap and a child let out a weak scream.

He was the size of a newborn, his legs shriveled and bent like a frog's and his face white and wrinkled. The woman lifted him gently and took him outside, but the light made him cry harder and she lowered him back into the hammock.

She had purged him several times, she said, but couldn't get rid of the worms. Laura asked why she hadn't taken him to the clinic.

"Clinic's the same as the pharmacy," she said. "No good."

"The clinic's different, *Señora*."

"I had a little girl that died," the woman explained. "Medicine didn't help. Four *quetzales* worth of medicine and it didn't help at all."

"What did she die from?"

"Food that offended her." The mother's eyes were sad and red, but whether from remembering her little girl or from the smoky hut or just the routine burden of the years, I couldn't tell. "The beans hadn't come up yet and there was no money to buy anything. I picked corn that was still green and made a mush. She ate a lot because she liked it."

"Was she a strong child?" Laura asked.

"Plenty strong."

"She didn't have worms?"

"She had worms, but not so many. When she was little I was afraid to see her eat so much and never get fat. The people showed me remedies to give her. I made her tea, a batter of laxative, and she passed quantities of worms, *quantities* of little worms, and she started getting better. The people say she died of worms but I think she died of that green corn I gave her. It attacked her head. That's the way she ended up, like somebody who doesn't know where they are, like stupid. That was the beginning of the night. At dawn she began calling *mama mama mama mama, pick me up, it's time, mama.* When I went to her, she said, *mama, open the door, I want to go out.* I opened the door and she went out and when she came in her head sagged and her eyes were gray. That's when she lost her senses. My husband took her to the pharmacist but the pharmacist said he couldn't figure out what she had. He sold us this medicine that didn't work at all. Four *pesotes* for medicine that didn't work at all. When she woke up the next morning she shouted and shouted. But not like someone with pain. It was more like she was tired, like she didn't know where she was. It was like she was tired in the body and the head, and that's when she died."

A breeze had come up as she talked, cool and damp, clearing the smoke from the hut, and then the sky went dark and moisture settled thickly on everything like a layer of dust. A cloud was passing through the valley.

"You've got to take him to the doctor," Laura said.

"It's too late, Señorita."

"The doctor has many *different* medicines." Laura was struggling to stay composed. "Some might work, even now."

"It's too late," the woman said firmly.

Laura gave me a look, formulating a question that wouldn't come. She looked at the bulge in the hammock and then at some literacy materials on a table against the wall.

"I think you should find out what's happening with the class," she said to me. "It's getting dark."

I went outside to talk with Don Julio, who said there was a problem with the class. The students couldn't afford the extra fuel for their lanterns, fifteen cents a week. The Ministry of Education was supposed to pay for it, but somebody at the ministry was pocketing the money. Hardly anyone had shown up for several weeks.

"But I think maybe some of the boys will come tonight," he said.

"Why do you say this?"

"They knew *La Laura* was coming."

I went back inside the house and explained the problem to Laura and asked her how long she thought we should wait for them. It was already an hour after the scheduled time for the class.

"It wouldn't be right to leave now," she said.

"We'll miss the bus."

"We already missed it."

She was studying an attendance chart, as if being stranded for the night in this remote village was no more than a minor inconvenience. Where would we sleep? What would we do for food? There wasn't even an outhouse in sight. I didn't need four-star accommodations, but this seemed a little nuts.

"Isn't that a problem?" I asked.

"What's the matter, *vos*? Got a heavy date tonight?"

The *vos* caught me off guard. That odd archaic pronoun used by the local aristocracy to address their servants but which, in an act of grammatical insurrection, had been appropriated by the lower classes as a term of familiarity and endearment.

"They'll come," she said. "You'll see."

And they did, about a dozen of them, young ones with sunbaked faces and grizzled old coots without teeth, a few pure Indians, all of them with the dust of the field still on their sandaled feet. We sat at the table against the wall inside the house. Don Julio had lit a candle. I didn't ask the questions I usually asked on my field trips. It was late and this was not a usual field trip.

Everyone went to class, they said. Wonderful classes. *La Laura* this, *La Laura* that. They thought I was there checking up on her. They told me the kinds of stories I had heard on other trips, how they could read the street signs now and the notices in the window of the *municipio* and on the bus and how nobody could ever cheat them like before, and I was drawn into this wonderful conversation, telling them about all the books they could read now and someone asked how many books there were in the world and I found myself actually trying to make that calculation. I did not succeed and saw they were disappointed.

"But they don't want us to learn," somebody said. He was an older man, looking hard at me, his watery eyes daring me to ask the obvious question.

"Who are *they*?"

"The big landowners, the rich, the government." He said it with an idle wave of his hand, as if commenting on the weather. "But we want to learn. Not just literacy. We want to learn how to pronounce the difficult words and what the—" he hooked a comma in the air—"means and all the other signs." He opened a book he had brought with him and touched his split-dry fingernail to a random word. "Like this one," he said. "How do you pronounce it?" I read the word aloud and he repeated it, smiling and nodding as the others murmured their approval while I stood there sweating that somebody might ask me what the damn word *meant* because I did not have the slightest idea.

After the class, three of the men walked us out to the Amatitlán road by a much shorter route than the one we had taken in and where they said we could find a truck driver who made regular trips into the city. We did find him, napping in his truck on the side of the road. The problem was he had "a little errand" to run first, but in the meantime there was a fine tavern down the road where he would take us to wait.

He motioned for Laura and me to sit in the front. The men from the class climbed into the open back of the truck and immediately pulled out a bottle and began singing.

The driver talked about the difficulty he had making payments on the truck, the village in Huehuetenango where he had a wife and five kids, and about his little errand which turned out to be a visit with a girlfriend in a nearby town. Then he pulled a flask out of the glove compartment and offered us a drink.

"To get in the mood," he said, jerking his head toward the men singing in the back.

"Maybe later," Laura said politely.

"Later we are all dead!" he shouted, taking a swig and gunning the engine around a treacherous turn.

"If he keeps driving like this," I said in English, "we're all going to be dead sooner rather than later."

"It would just make matters worse if we said anything about it to him," she said. She asked him about his family and his work, which seemed to slow him down. I relaxed a little and listened to the men singing in back, a strange song in their own language. There are 17 Indian languages spoken in the country and I didn't understand a word of any of them. They sang and swayed with a tuneless cadence that became hypnotic in the chilled night air as the road dipped and rose and dropped again like an erratic current through the mountains. Lights of a town would pass below and looming always above was the massive hulk of the mountains, black and solid against the bright clouds.

I was seized by an inexplicable aching happiness in the sheer quality of the night, asking myself all the eternal questions about what the hell I was doing in this country in this truck with this woman and coming up with all the eternal answers, genius that I was.

The tavern was a modest little inn with a real dining room where we met a couple from Connecticut, a banker with a silky white moustache and matching hair and his wife who had not aged as elegantly. They wore identical khaki outfits and had come to hunt tigers.

"Tigers?" asked Laura. "That sounds dangerous."

"Oh, they're not real tigers," the man said. "More like our mountain lion. But fighters. Splendid country. Deer, turkey, you name it."

He demonstrated his *tigrero*, a gourd with waxed horse-hairs stretched its length like a miniature violin. The instrument's moaning vibrato set a dog howling just beyond the window.

Laura and I adjourned to the bar in the next room, which was empty, except for the bartender, who it turned out had been a nightclub bouncer in the capital. He was an ugly man with a cauliflower face but gentle eyes that gazed on Laura as if she were the Virgin Mary herself. She tended to have that effect on men. After a while he said the bar was closing, but we could stay and left us with a bottle of rum on the house and a bucket of ice.

"He's being so discreet," she said.

"Good man."

"What did you think of Mr. and Mrs. Connecticut?" she asked.

"They're alright."

"He reminds me of my stepfather."

"Your parents divorced?"

"My father was killed in the Korean War."

I refreshed our drinks and took a long, slow swallow from mine.

"My mother died when I was nine," I said.

"Then you understand."

I thought I did, but it was many years before I understood there was this terrible aching place inside me, an insatiable craving for love so alien to what we are told is normal that you must either kill it or learn to live as an outsider. So I couldn't explain then what I didn't yet understand, couldn't talk about what I really would have wanted to talk about, not directly anyway.

"I remember very little about her," I said.

"It must have been very painful," she said.

She turned on the stool and looked across the room. There was a clean stone fireplace on one side and on the other a picture window with a view of the mountain dark and very close and the sky incredibly clear, tingling with stars.

"What's your mother like?" I asked.

"A total wreck." She studied the glass in her hand. "Drinks too much for one thing." She sipped at her drink. "Runs in the family."

"You don't seem to drink that much," I said.

"I don't?"

"I don't think so."

She smiled.

"You're a nice person," she said. "You really are."

"An angel."

"I wouldn't go that far."

We were still looking through the window with its view of the mountain and the stars. A truck rose slowly in the darkness along the steep grade of the mountain. The red-lighted outline of the truck seemed to move on air, rising on some invisible tram.

"It's a beautiful night," she said. "It's the whole reason we're here, isn't it? Those people back there. Sometimes you forget. I'm learning so much here. I feel like people have given me so much more than I can ever give them."

"Like what?"

"We put so much emphasis on material things. When you get rid of all that—which is very easy to do here, right?—you see life is just about relationships with the people who mean the most to you. I don't know, maybe it's just a sense of humility I never had. Sometimes I feel like I don't want to leave here at all." She smiled and shrugged her shoulders. "Let's make a fire."

We brought our drinks over to the fireplace and sat on the carpeted floor. The wood was damp, but I was glad for something to make me busy because with her sitting there, legs tucked under her and dress falling loosely over her thighs, I didn't know if I could keep my hands off her. I got a smoky little fire going and we sat there talking about what would happen with the sick kid and the literacy class and whether what we were doing counted for anything when you came right down to it.

"Maybe every little bit really doesn't help," she said.

But I was very happy, just being there with her. The booze helped, but I was thinking how much I liked her. Liked the way she wouldn't leave until the class came and the way she handled the truck driver and how she always seemed to know what she wanted or at least knew what questions to ask. I was thinking too about her father and felt a sudden kinship in this early, intimate loss.

"The fire's going out," she said.

I threw another log on and we started talking about something else, words drifting weightlessly in the warm shadows, long pauses, the firelight picking up the gold flecks in her green eyes, then the kind of kiss that felt like each of us had a hundred changing faces. She drew back and put her fingers over my lips.

"I was afraid this would happen," she said.

"Let it happen."

"It's not that simple, *vos*."

I decided to leap.

"Is it that guy you met in training?"

"Who told you about him?"

"Thornby."

I told her what Thornby had also said about my grant and not making trouble.

"Troublemakers," she said. She made a face. "People like him don't understand people like us."

"But that's why it's not that simple? Because of that guy?"

"That's part of it. I don't know what's going to happen when I see Paul," she said. "I don't know what to expect." There was a pause, and then more quietly, "I don't know what to expect."

"Where is he?"

"India. He said there was no point in writing each other long letters like lovesick teenagers for two years. I wrote him a couple of times but he never answered."

What's he like?"

"Very intelligent. A potential genius." She made a face because she didn't know what to say next. "He has a receding hairline." She shook her head. "I'm glad I'm not a writer and have to describe people. Anything I can think of sounds so incomplete."

Λ potential genius, I thought. I've never been up against a potential genius before.

"Look, you get back to the States and you discover one of two things. Either he's a bastard, you have to at least consider that possibility" — "I have," she said — "in which case you wouldn't want to have anything to do with him anyway, or it's the real thing and you live happily ever after. In the meantime he's 15,000 miles away and I'm here."

"You're so logical."

"Most of the time."

"And tough." She gave me that sensational smile. "Come on, toughie. Throw another log on the fire."

The thick length of pine smoldered for a few minutes and then burst into flames. I poked at the fire and felt her drifting away, making other connections.

"Do you think that truck driver is coming back?" I asked her.

"Eventually," she said.

He came back about an hour later. The three men from the literacy class were still in the back of the truck. When we let them off, they almost could not believe that there was no charge for the ride. They thanked Laura, the driver and myself separately, clasping each of us by the shoulders, using both hands to shake our hand, saying *Dios se lo pague, Dios se lo pague,* over and over, with a reverence to this common phrase that I had never heard before. It was a promise and a prediction: God *will* repay you for this good deed. They turned to wave one last time as their small draped figures disappeared down the mountainside and into the night.

Back in the truck Laura watched the headlights graze the ledge along the road.

"There's always a screen there," she said.

I knew what she meant.

"I thought it might be different for you. The way you live out there in Santa Cruz, so, I don't know, so *integrated.*"

"Sometimes I think it's not there," she said. "But then something happens and I realize it's still there."

By midnight we were back in the city, where the driver dropped us off at Laura's *pensión.* I walked her to the door and she put her hand on the knob.

"When will I see you again?"

"I don't know," she said.

I kissed her lightly on the lips. I thought she was about to say something, but she just opened the door and went inside.

EIGHT

"You're a good detective," she said.

"And I have information you'd like a nice dinner."

"You're impossible," she laughed.

I had found out she was in the city only when Manolo mentioned he was going to be at some meeting with her. He said it was about the rural medical clinics the student association was setting up. I took a chance and went to her *pensión* and waited for her to get back after the meeting. She was not pleased to see me sitting in the lobby but began to relax when we got to the *churrasco* place.

"You should write an article for *The New York Times* about all this," she said. We had been talking about Amatitlán and also my last few trips to other centers.

I laughed.

"And next a Nobel Prize," I said.

"You're making fun of me."

"It's just not very realistic."

"What have you got to lose? If they don't take it, you try somewhere else. I'll bet you're a good writer."

"Let me think about it," I said. "You weren't planning to get in touch with me. Why not?"

"It just seemed like a complication that neither of us needs right now. But I'm glad we're here. I've been thinking about a teacher's guide. Remember what you said about that?"

She dug into her bag and pulled out a notebook to show me what she had written. It was a list of the little booklets about a *campesino* named Juan, used in the literacy centers, with notations beside each for discussion topics, quizzes, and other reading materials a teacher could use to make sure the student was learning.

"This is an excellent start," I said.

"I'm stuck," she said. "You're the one who really knows this stuff."

"This is very good," I said. "What do you want me to do?"

"You should write this guide."

I laughed.

"You want me to write this guide *and* an article for *The New York Times*. What else did you have in mind?"

"You're very smart."

"You wrote papers and things for school," I said.

"You would do this much better than I could."

"Let me go over your notes and see where we are," I said. "How long are you in the city?"

"Just until tomorrow."

"Why don't you test some of this stuff out on your classes in Santa Cruz and the *penitenciaría*? It will give us some data. I could come up for a few days and help out. You know I'm very curious about Santa Cruz."

She folded her napkin into a little square.

"It's probably not that different from a lot of other places you've been."

"Except you're there."

She smiled.

"I'd like you to come."

"When?"

"I don't know. Let me think about it some more."

This isn't going to work out, I thought.

Outside the night was damp with the remnant of the afternoon rain. From one of the great walled estates a dog burst into frenzied yelps and others took up the alarm.

"Let's go to your place for a while," she said. "But just a little while."

The road veered around the pint-sized Eiffel Tower with its frame outlined in blue neon and we entered the tight regular streets of the old city. We walked the three blocks down 18th Street to my building and then up the one flight of stairs to my apartment. I opened the door and turned on the light.

"It looks like the jungle," she said.

There were a lot of plants and not much space. Two good-sized *manos de león* did quite well in the dismal light of this interior unit at the bottom of an airshaft. I had a desk, chair and bookcase, all of the same raw lumber, and an old steamer trunk for a coffee table. A straw mattress covered with a bright Indian *tela* served as a sofa. There was a bedroom and bathroom and a tiny kitchen. The only thing I missed was a telephone, for which there was a three-year waiting list. But the place was functional and all I could afford. I was quite happy there.

I got two beers out of the refrigerator while Laura poked at some papers on the desk. Then she sat down on the sofa, pried off her sandals and pulled her legs up under her.

"I didn't know you were a poet, *vos*," she said.

"I'm not."

She glanced toward the desk.

"Who wrote that poem?"

I went over to the desk. I did write poems, not very good ones, but I was beginning to think of myself as some kind of writer. I'd been an editor on the *Columbia*

Spectator and really liked it. I thought of these literary endeavors as just having a little fun. She asked me to read something, which I did, and then stopped to await her verdict.

"It's a little romantic," she offered cautiously.

"You didn't like it?"

"I didn't say that. Read some more."

As I read now, I would glance at those heavy brooding lips ready to pounce on one of my clever aphorisms ("The sentimental illusion looks backward, the intellectual illusion forward," I intoned. "Or vice versa," she said, making me laugh at my incorrigible self-importance).

I lit my pipe. I had taken up a pipe in college to break the cigarette habit, which I had almost done, but now of course I was overly attached to the pipe. I liked the feel of the wood and the tang of the tobacco and mastering the technique of keeping a steady low burn, in addition to all the other good reasons people get hooked on nicotine.

"Why do you like to write?"

I gave her some dumb answer I can't remember now, but looking back all these years when it's much too late to tell her anything, I know why I felt that way. The beauty of the language. Its capacity for truth telling. The flow of pen on paper. The manual labor of the typewriter. Most of these mechanics of course now lost in the computer age, but the emotions as alive as they were that night 50 years ago.

"You like the way it feels," she said.

"That's what I mean."

We talked about writers, tossing out names, probing for connections. She had been reading Henry Miller and seemed to approve of the old goat. I was surprised.

"I like his naughtiness," she said. "But he's probably an awful man, don't you think?"

"I don't think of writers as people."

"What are they?"

"Books."

She made a face.

"That's very detached."

I kissed her lightly on the lips, as if to say, no, I don't mean to be detached, and she stayed very still. I tried her cheek, her neck, the edge of her mouth, and she began moving, moving with me, into me, her body yielding until we were lost in each other's mouths. I unbuttoned the top of her dress, touched her stiff nipples, and then my hand was between her legs, priming the pump, all the juices beginning to flow and stink up the little room with that wonderful aroma. She was biting her lip, her eyes closed.

Then she stopped, cold, went dead.

"What's wrong?" I asked.

"Can't you tell?"

"No."

She sat up.

"It's not right," she said. "I'm not all here. It wouldn't be very good."

"You seemed to be enjoying yourself," I said.

"That's the problem."

Then I had a disturbing thought.

"Are you a virgin?"

"Would that make it easier?"

"It might."

"No."

After that we just went round and round, thrust and parry in a hopeless verbal duel.

It was close to dawn when we left the apartment. I loved the musty feeling of that early morning hour, the carts rattling over the concrete plaza, the women prodding their breakfast fires and the air cindery with the scent of burning charcoal. We passed a drunk mummified in a doorway, taxis parked along the curb waiting for the buses from the provinces. Around the corner on 17th Street some of the girls would still be open for business.

Laura was smiling.

"Don't you like the way people look at us," she said. "They think we're evil."

"We are," I said. "Unspeakable sins of omission."

"You'll get over it, *vos*."

But I don't *want* to get over it, I thought, as I listened to the noisy birds hidden in the stunted trees along 18th Street, excited birds, squeaking like an old baby carriage.

NINE

Sometimes she would still come to see me when she was in the city, but it was different now. Mostly we talked about work. She had brought me a book by Frank Laubach, an American missionary in the Philippines in the 1930s where he first developed a simple and effective method for teaching literacy and then spent the rest of his life refining the technique in a dozen countries. I had incorporated her notations for the teacher's guide plus some material from Laubach into a draft that I was ready to deliver to Thornby and Colonel Ramirez.

I had also decided to take a shot on a *New York Times Magazine* article and was almost done with it.

One day toward the end of October I came across a short item in *Prensa Libre* with some statistics about the literacy program. I showed it to Laura. We were sitting in the bar of the Pan American Hotel with its stately clutter of ragged palms and the muffled tinkling of a marimba somewhere out of sight.

"These are the numbers Ramirez wouldn't give me," I said. "You could make the whole country literate with what we give the military here in a month."

"The whole thing is crazy," she said.

This reminded me of a question I had been meaning to ask her about the Christian missionary Laubach and the little argument we had the night we met about the Marxist Freire.

"How can you reconcile them?" I asked.

She started folding and refolding her napkin until it was a tiny square.

"Do I have to reconcile them?"

"They come at the problem with two very different worldviews."

"But come out at the same place."

We had stopped at the bar on our way back to her *pensión* from the *churrasco* place. She was not exactly starving herself, but she had gotten this notion about not eating more than her neighbors in Santa Cruz, which would have been about 1500 calories a day. She was losing weight and had become lean and angular, bordering on gaunt. So when she was in town I insisted we go somewhere like the *churrasco* place or the *pastelería* in the Bank of America building and watched her savor every last morsel of meat or chocolate cake or anything else I could lure her into eating.

I also had the sense that she saw this time with me as a respite from the harshness of village life, a taste of civilization that she missed more than she wanted to admit. Sometimes we went to a movie or the National Symphony, which to my tin ear sounded pretty good. She knew a lot more than I did about the music and would sometimes suggest that a performance left something to be desired. Walking back to her *pensión* one night, it came out that she played the cello.

"You never told me about that," I said.

"There's a lot I haven't told you."

"Why not?"

"I don't want to bore you."

"You never bore me."

"That's hard to believe," she said.

We were walking along Sixth Avenue toward her *pension* on that cool October night after we left the Pan American Hotel. The steel shutters were down over all the stores and the street had the feel of a ghost town with halos of fine mist around the streetlights.

I picked up the faint scent of the night-blooming jasmine from the manicured grounds of the National Police building on the next block. The scent grew stronger as we got closer. This thin straggly bush with its pale, cream-colored flowers was odorless during the day but released a fragrance at night so sweet and powerful you almost could not breathe when you were next to it. The National Police building loomed like a dark castle with its ramps and turrets. General Ubico, a president who had a fondness for dungeons but got along famously with the fruit company, had built it in the 1930s.

In the driveway were the new Ford patrol cars recently presented with much fanfare by the embassy. Guards in overcoats with submachine guns over their shoulders leaned on the cars. One guard shifted his weapon and started our way, coming slowly, a bandana across the lower half of his face to ward off the chilly dampness. Laura took my arm. You read about these guys scared out of their wits shooting at strangers in the night.

"Don't stop," she said. We kept going and the guard went on by. "Why did you take us past this place?"

The question threw me; it was almost an accusation.

"It's the shortest way to your *pensión*."

"Don't you know what goes on in there?"

"I've heard stories."

"They're not *stories*."

Then I felt her slipping away, changing inside, that wonderful calm softness not gone from her face but driven now by a great reserve of will that was her secret and her pride.

TEN

It took longer than I thought to finish the draft of the teacher's guide. For one thing, I still didn't have the questionnaires Laura had taken for her classes in Santa Cruz. I had cabled her about this and maybe my coming there but got nothing back. I was again beginning to think that I had seen the last of her.

A couple of weeks after I sent the cable, a thin man in his late 30s showed up at my apartment with an envelope full of completed questionnaires from Santa Cruz. He also had a note from Laura.

It was a short note saying sorry she hadn't been in touch, she'd been very busy, but the bearer of the envelope, Jose Sierra Chocó, was a friend *de confianza*.

"*La Laura* asked that I place this directly in your own hand," he said.

He somewhat reluctantly accepted my offer of a beer and sat down on the sofa with a nervous smile. He kept turning a floppy straw hat in his hands. I thanked him for bringing the envelope.

"It's for a literacy project we're working on," I explained.

"I know. I'm a teacher and an agronomist. This is very important work."

"Are you from Santa Cruz?" I asked.

"No. From Cobán, but unfortunately I can't go back there now."

He had recently been fired. He showed me the official discharge paper from the Ministry of Education. No cause was stated, but everyone knew. It happened all over the country after the 1954 CIA coup. Many books and PhD theses have examined this period, but this was the first person I met who had paid such a personal price.

He had been in prison twice since 1954, the first time for three years. He had worked in the Land Reform Institute in Cobán during Arbenz and was responsible for the redistribution of all uncultivated parcels over 20 acres to peasants without land. That was the law, but then Castillo Armas was in power, courtesy of the CIA, and Jose Sierra Chocó was in the Central Penitentiary. When he got out he picked up some work here and there and then made the foolish mistake of shouting

Viva Arbenz! in a bar one night, which got him put away for another couple of years. On the street this time he had been more careful and finally landed the teacher's job in Cobán, which lasted 22 days. He asked if I knew of any kind of work available, perhaps as a gardener or even a janitor.

"I'm sorry," I said. "I really wish there were something I could do. I'll keep my eyes open."

"That's kind of you. I would appreciate that."

"Are you in any danger?"

He smiled. "Not as long as I keep my big mouth shut." He finished the beer and got up to leave, still turning the hat in his hands. "You'll let me know if you hear about a job."

"Of course. How will I get in touch with you?"

"Well, at the moment I don't have a fixed residence, but that shouldn't be a problem."

"All I have is your name," I said.

He was standing at the door.

"*La Laura* knows where to find me."

"Did she say anything about my coming to Santa Cruz?"

"She didn't say anything about that," he said, and I felt a familiar melancholy at the prospect of never seeing her again.

When I think back to this visit, I realize now this was the first time she trusted me enough to share one of her political contacts. But it also made me apprehensive, not only for her but also about my own sudden responsibility for the secrets of these strangers. Only the anchor of my work, as it would for so much of my life, kept me focused during those days.

With the questionnaires from Santa Cruz I filled in the missing pieces and finally finished the 23-page *Guía de Maestros para los Folletos Juan y la Lectura Complementaria de Alfabetización*. I was rather pleased. I thought about putting my byline on it then decided on a note in back citing both Laura and myself as the *responsables*. I wondered about doing that. We had not hidden our collaboration, but it was still something I wanted to check with her.

I had tried one last time to reach her and was unhappy that she didn't get back to me, but I wasn't going to worry about that any more. I loved seeing our names together on this little masterpiece. I prevailed on an artist friend to do a tasteful pen and ink drawing for the cover of some *campesinos* reading by candlelight and personally delivered copies to Thornby and Colonel Ramirez, neither of whom seemed terribly impressed but said they would reply promptly.

On my way home I stopped as I often did to look in the window of a big shoe store on the corner of my block.

Baby shoes in bright colors, plastic shoes, canvas shoes, golden sandals, high-heeled spikes with thin elegant straps fit over chipped alabaster forms and men's shoes of perforated black and brown leather, imitation alligator, blue velvet loafers and tasseled

shoes and handsome boots. This display had acquired
a special meaning for me. One afternoon a man passed
me on the sidewalk near the store, a shaggy-headed
guy in an old pinstriped double-breasted suit, an
umbrella hooked jauntily over his arm—and barefoot. I
realized then that I had stopped seeing the hundreds of
bare feet that I had seen at first and now did not see.

ELEVEN

"Women like you would not believe," Fernando Garcia
said, weighing the imaginary fruit in his hand. "Have
you heard the definition of Hollywood? Where you lay
on the sand and look at the stars"—he raised his
eyebrows for the punch line—"or the opposite!"

I didn't know quite what I was doing in the car with
this guy, or why I had agreed to take this trip. He had
lately been on a campaign to cheer me up, and so on
this Saturday morning we took off for a weekend on
the coast that he said I would not soon forget.

I smiled and resigned myself to whatever silly little
adventure he had planned. It could not be any worse, I
thought, than the sadness that came over me whenever
I thought about Laura.

Coming down out of the mountains you begin to see
the corn, patches cut into the slopes, clinging to the
land at impossible angles, sprouting among the onions
and tomatoes and the stumpy banana plants with their
lurid purple bulbs, corn pressing against huts, not an
inch of earth spared from *Madre Milpa*, old Mother

Corn. Then a short distance after Palín—suspended above the coastal plain and the soupy light of the Pacific—the tropics.

Closer to the coast white lilies bob on flooded fields, compliments of the rainy season and the air is laced with vanilla. Then the road flies straight to the sea, past the barbed wire of the San José military base and over a narrow canal built by the fruit company many years ago. Naked boys play on an abandoned railroad bridge, diving from its rusty columns into the opaque water of the canal.

The Land of Eternal Spring, according to the tourist brochures.

Fernando turned off the highway and drove another mile to a small rotary with a gate and two armed guards. He showed the guards his identity card and said Colonel Ramirez was expecting us.

"*My* Colonel Ramirez?" I asked.

"He's really a good guy," Fernando said.

"Why didn't you tell me?"

"I have a standing invitation," he said.

I was pissed. It wasn't what I had in mind. You never knew with Fernando.

The dirt road meandered along a dry streambed, broke into the open and there suddenly was the sea and a beach of dark volcanic sand. There was a stretch of new A-frames along the beach and then only green wilderness.

Fernando stopped the car. He leaned on the steering wheel and looked at me sadly.

"Don't you want to be friends with me, Peter?"

Something was really off about this guy.

"Look, Fernando, how do people become friends? It's not that easy. I think you have to go through a lot together and share important things and then one day you just sort of realize you've become friends. You don't just pick someone out like a pair of socks and decide you'll be friends. Right now you've taken me somewhere I wasn't planning to go. So I don't feel particularly friendly."

He looked terribly hurt.

"I understand," he said contritely.

Colonel Ramirez and two other men sat in sturdy wooden chairs around a swimming pool with the glare from the beach rising above a high wall. They wore bathing suits, their smooth legs crossed, drinks in hand, dipping saltines in onion mix. Behind them two women lay in the grass, deep in conversation, but close enough to the men to hear what they were saying.

Colonel Ramirez looked scrawny out of uniform, gray hairs bristling from his knobby shoulders. I wondered if he might have arranged this trip to discuss the teacher's guide in a more relaxed setting.

"Ah, the American scholar," he said by way of greeting.

"Colonel Ramirez."

"Please. I am Enrique."

"*Don* Enrique," said Fernando.

Ramirez waved him off.

"Today we dispense with formalities." He smiled. "Gringo style."

His complaints to Thornby, the months of evasion and bureaucratic obstacles; it was as if they never existed.

The men returned to their talk about the sorry state of the country. Colonel Ramirez had caught a thief breaking into his car. His eyes opened deliciously. "Right in front of the Palace of Justice! Caught him red-handed. I grabbed a riding crop I keep under the front seat and beat the shit out of him. He didn't even fight back. That's the strange part. Ducked his head and walked away, didn't even run, just walked down the street with me whacking away for half a block."

He laughed, shaking his head, and snapped a cracker into his mouth.

Then they started joking about the next government. Colonel Ramirez appointed himself President. Beginning with the man on his right, he went around the group. "You will be Minister of Exterior Relations. You, Hacienda. Fernando, Culture, of course. And our quiet American friend over there, why, you will have to be Minister of *Silence!*"

Everyone laughed; I felt myself blushing.

"What about me?" asked one of the women on the grass, pouting with mock neglect.

"You, my dear? How could I have forgotten? You will be my Minister of *Love*."

She smothered a giggle and turned back to her companion. I asked Fernando who they were.

"The pretty one is Argelia," he whispered. "The other I forget." His eyes brightened. "You like her?"

"She *is* pretty."

"I will arrange it."

"Please, Fernando." I was whispering now too. "Don't make trouble."

"No trouble," he said. "Trust me."

She sat on the wall facing the ocean. Her hair was thick and long and that deep black that was almost blue in sunlight. She had a transistor radio to her ear and was singing along with the song. She didn't see me until my shadow crossed the book in her lap.

She was startled, her hand pressed to her chest.

"Such a fright you gave me!"

"Sorry." The book was *Basic English One*. "You're studying English."

"Yes, but she doesn't know anything," she said in Spanish.

I noted the peculiar reference to herself in the third person, as if she thought it advisable to maintain a discrete distance from this person who was speaking. Her face was like a painted doll's with heavy eyeliner and fiery red lips and powder that robbed all texture from her light skin. Her eyes were large and a brown so dark they looked black like her hair.

"Why are you studying English?"

"I'm going to the United States."

"Anywhere in particular?"

"New Orleans, Miami, New York, Boston, Baltimore."

"Baltimore?"

"I want to go *everywhere!*"

She must have her reasons, I thought.

We went for a walk on the hot volcanic sand. The beach was deserted in the early afternoon heat, the air thick. She was wearing a white blouse and tight blue slacks. A wave caught her by surprise and she tied the bottom of the blouse above her waist and went splashing through the warm surf. I could not take my eyes off her perfect ass. I mean, not just the solid plumpness of the buns packed into the wet slacks, but the ensemble, the delicious curve of the line joining torso, buttocks and thigh, a shape like those female fertility figures they find in ancient ruins. Here it was, life-size and in living color, the myth of the holy ass that men have worshipped since the dawn of consciousness.

It was necessary from time to time, I thought, to apply a little historical perspective to my obsessions.

That night Fernando and I took Argelia and her friend to a club in town. The friend's name was Margo.

She was older and dumpy and a little worn, her dry hair bleached the same shade of apricot as her cheeks. Fernando seemed taken with her. The three of them giggled a lot and told jokes with double entendres I didn't always catch, which made them laugh even harder, as we downed our beers and snacked on avocado *bocadillos*. Then Fernando and Margo disappeared. Argelia drank rapidly and I had trouble keeping up. We danced once.

"You don't dance bad for a gringo," she said back at the table.

"You'd be surprised what gringos can do."

"I know. People say gringos are potatoes without salt, but it's like anything else, right? There's good and bad wherever you go. I had a gringo boyfriend once." She nodded heavily, a sexy half-drunk drowsiness around her eyes. "The gringos are ok. *A toda madre los gringos.*"

"What does that mean?"

"Later, my love. I'll tell you everything you want to know." She grinned; one of her big front teeth was tinted green. In the morning we would have black beans at breakfast and I would notice the funny tooth again—stained the precise hue of the beans.

"Do you have to go back to Don Enrique's tonight?" I asked.

"Why do you ask?"

I didn't need any more trouble with Colonel Ramirez, but we were pretty far gone by now.

"I'd like to spend the night with you."

"Please!"

"I'm sorry."

"I understand. Here we are drinking and partying it up. What else can you think?"

"Exactly."

"You're a very attractive guy."

We went for a quick swim and then warmed up fooling around in the shower stall. We ran upstairs to a tiny room with a low wooden bunk. There was no bedding on the bunk, just a thin straw mat. The room was dark and a hallway light spilled over the partition like a cheap floorshow.

At first she wouldn't let me kiss her. We were naked on the hard straw mat and still plenty drunk—and she wouldn't let me kiss her. Turning her head away, fighting me off and after a while I realized she wanted to be taken. The way I think of it now is that she brought out the worst in me, right from the beginning, that night in an alcoholic haze; her teasing resistance, the hidden rhythm to her tossing and twisting, this uncontrollable coupling of savagery and tenderness.

In the morning we swam in a calm sea and washed down an enormous breakfast with Tecate beer, which Argelia insisted could only be consumed with fresh lime and salt.

Who was she and where did she come from, this little *Chapina* with the body of a grape, in the keen phrase of an admirer she cited; and judging by the way it rolled off her lips--*Chapina con cuerpo de uva*--a description that delighted her. We drove back to the city the next morning and she stayed in my apartment for two days and two nights.

The first thing I noticed was the difference now that we were alone. With Margo and Fernando she was always cracking jokes and fast-talking and seemed very tough. Now I sensed something else.

She loved to tell stories, adventures with boyfriends and girlfriends with dialogue and turns of plot worthy of great soap opera. Lying in bed at night, she told me about her baby.

"I kept getting sick in school and didn't figure it out until six months when my belly started to swell. But she is not stupid. She sewed an extra piece of cloth into her school uniform to hide the big belly. I told the father the only thing I wanted from him was to let the kid have his name. He said all right and signed the papers. I haven't seen him in a year—and good riddance!"

After the baby there were more stories: about a terrible beating at the hands of her brother; about a flight to the coast on an airplane belonging to the richest man in the country and parties with the names of very important people I was supposed to recognize, but most of whom I did not.

It sounded like an exciting life. The very next day she was on her way to Puerto Barrios to meet a Greek named Demetrious who worked on a freighter out of New Orleans. The ship came in once a month and there'd be a blast on board with Greek songs and dances and all kinds of presents.

I remember kissing her goodbye at the door, vaguely amused at the notion of playing second fiddle to a Greek sailor. I figured that was it, one of those rare little flings that end with no regrets. The idea that she might have any connection to the work of Robert Thornby or that I might ever see her again did not cross my mind, but a couple of weeks later Thornby invited me to a gathering at his house that I look back at now as the beginning of the premature end of my stay in *The Land of Eternal Spring*.

TWELVE

To this day I'm still not sure if Thornby set me up that night, or, to be a little less paranoid about it, if he was testing me and I flunked. Of course, it's just as likely that this was just one of those utterly common instances of youthful naiveté smashed by a system that could not have cared less about the slightly tainted romantic illusions of young men like myself.

Thornby lived in a ranch house with a dramatic view of the valley from the back lawn, where I lingered as long as I could. Heat lightning spurted red behind the clouds and then the sky took on a glow of ghostly mauve. I tried not to think about Laura, but that never worked when I was alone at these gatherings of my fellow compatriots and those who loved us, so I went in to face the music.

The place was jammed. I recognized a number of Thornby's embassy colleagues, some of whom I liked, and the usual hangers-on. Fernando Garcia with a new joke. I got a drink and tried to keep moving. Jacob Stein, the guy with the grant to study setting up a stock market, was dancing with a woman I didn't know and waved to me without missing a beat.

I was introduced to the new Fulbright Scholar, a young woman in a well-filled striped jersey and a blazer, who was doing her thesis on Castillo Armas. She had met a man in Quetzaltenango the other day who made a good point, she said. "You shouldn't give people something for nothing." What exactly did she mean by that, I asked. Land reform, she said. It was a short discussion. I didn't have any patience left for that stuff.

I had just refreshed my drink when Thornby brought me over to meet Professor Seth Wright, who was talking with Fred Dubrow, the embassy's economic officer. Fred was one of the guys I liked.

"This is the young man I told you about," Thornby said to Professor Wright, who was gray haired and bespectacled but looked like he had once been a tough bantamweight and was still in fighting trim.

"Ah, yes," he said, shaking my hand. "The chap doing that brilliant study on the literacy program here."

By then I was getting used to my illustrious reputation preceding me.

He whipped out a notebook and asked what I had found. I was flattered of course. This was *the* Professor Seth Wright, PhD in International Education and Foreign Relations, advisor to UNESCO, consultant to USAID, who was conducting a series of seminars for high officials throughout Central America. He agreed with everything I said about the literacy program.

I forgot how comfortable I could feel with men like this, who, unlike Thornby, seemed to grapple and engage with the substance of these ideas about development. In such moments I even toyed with the notion of a Foreign Service career myself instead of law school or journalism, but I wasn't ready to make any decisions just yet.

From time to time Fred Dubrow would offer an encouraging thought, subtle and sympathetic, always seeing my point of view even if he could not completely agree. Some of these State Department types could be so *reasonable* it drove me nuts. Thornby listened, bored with the intricacies but taking it all in. Fred and Professor Wright didn't think much of Laubach, though they did agree on the importance of literacy. It was the "Newtonian watershed" of the 20th century, the difference between a man who lives alone, afraid and submissive, and one who is capable of adapting to modern society.

The problem was the cost, Fred said.

"It would take hundreds of millions of dollars to make this country literate."

"That's not true," I said.

"Several million then," he said. "It's still prohibitive. We don't have the manpower or material to do the job for them. We have to give them the capability to do the job themselves."

"They do it now for 62 cents a student," I said.

"That sounds low," Professor Wright said.

"Where did you get that number?" Thornby asked suspiciously.

"An article in *Prensa Libre*."

"You can't believe anything you read in that rag," he said.

"We could ask Colonel Ramirez," I said innocently.

Now Professor Wright had something to say. It wasn't easy to follow his reasoning. He agreed with Fred and he agreed with me. But there was a way to cut through the dilemma.

"Television," he said.

Mass instruction by television was the only cost-effective way of organizing literacy centers in the remote rural regions where they were most needed. You would begin by calling together a meeting of all the doctors, lawyers and professional men in the town....

I stopped listening and waited for him to pause.

"Eighty percent of the population doesn't have electricity," I said. "That's for the whole country. In rural areas it must be at least 95 percent."

"It *will* take time," the professor said.

I wanted to get out of there, but Fred was so eager to convince me, so earnest, so patient, explaining once again how industrialization and foreign capital would eventually lift the Guatemalan people out of their all-too-obvious misery.

"Eventually," I said.

"Yes, eventually," Fred said. "Development takes time. Look at our own country. We had our trusts and robber barons and sweatshops. It takes time."

"But why do they have to go through all that?"

"There's no other way."

"You could start by teaching people how to read and write," I said. "How do you expect this country to improve itself without doing *at least* that?"

I don't know how long we went on like this. There was some kind of disconnect. I'd ask a question, he'd answer, mostly with the nostrums that had not changed since I first heard them in a sophomore international relations course, and I would come back at him. I had just finished reading another William Appleman Williams book Manolo had given me, this one on the U.S. and Cuba, and it made a lot of sense; though something told me not to cite this source for Fred Dubrow. I felt a little like Laura now, playing devil's advocate, half hoping my arguments would be shot down, but Fred was getting frustrated.

He looked around the room and lowered his voice.

"Look, I wouldn't tell this to a Guatemalan or any foreigner for that matter, but I couldn't care less if this country *improves itself* as long as we maintain the power and influence we have here today. When the Russians build a dam in Egypt, I'm not interested in how many more Egyptians have water. I'm interested in what the Russians are doing to displace us there. If Arbenz had been allowed to continue here, do you have any idea what this would have done to us?"

"Maybe I don't."

"Arbenz was a dupe. Have you ever read the Schneider book?"

Communism in Guatemala, 1944-1954 was the embassy's bible, a carefully researched study meant to demonstrate how the Guatemalan Communist Party had seized control of the Arbenz government. It was impressively detailed, but its conclusions did not support the embassy's point about Arbenz being a dupe. Sometimes people just see what they need to see.

"Does that mean that anything the Communists support we should oppose?"

"Of course not," he said. "It's a question of stability."

"Fred, as long as half the people in this country are walking around in rags, I think you're going to have some instability."

"That's why we stay on good terms with the army." His eyes narrowed. "Have you ever met a Communist?"

As far as I knew, I had never met one of these mythical creatures.

"No."

"In troubled waters," he said ominously, "the Communists fish with success."

I'd had a few drinks. I was thinking about those people in the troubled waters of Chiquimula and the Quezada Valley and Chimaltenango and that settlement on the Usumacinta River and then thinking about that idiot professor with his mass instruction by television assisted by all those doctors and lawyers who didn't exist. I was thinking about Laura. And I was thinking about this decent, intelligent man in front of me with an obsession that I did not happen to share.

"Fred," I said, looking him in the eye, "I like you, I really do, but someday I might have to shoot you."

He seemed to think this was funny. I did too, at the time.

Thornby was shaking his head slowly. Before I left, he took me aside and told me to come by his office the following day.

THIRTEEN

Thornby leaned back in the chair behind his desk, tamping his pipe.

"I can't believe you said that last night to Fred Dubrow."

"It was a joke."

"It wasn't funny."

"He didn't seem to mind."

"He's a diplomat. I can tell you for a fact he was very upset."

What the hell, I thought.

"I'll apologize."

Thornby lit his pipe and watched the smoke stream toward a ceiling vent. He opened a folder on the desk. The teacher's guide was on top of what looked to be several other documents.

"I've got some bad news for you. There's nothing in the fiscal '64 budget to keep funding the literacy campaign. As of next October, any assistance for this stuff will be going through the military's Civic Action program. The army here is a lot more efficient than the Ministry of Education, believe me."

"The army will just use it as another counter-insurgency tool."

"And what's wrong with that?"

The question felt like a trap.

"Nothing," I said.

He gave me a look somewhere between annoyed and angry. He knew I was lying. Through the window I saw the green trees in the park and the vendors around the dry fountain—the remoteness of the sunny afternoon magnified by the cool stillness of the office.

"This place isn't safe for you," he said. "There's a war going on here and you're a civilian who doesn't know how to stay out of trouble."

"What kind of trouble?"

He held up the teacher's guide.

"You sent a copy of this to Colonel Ramirez."

"I thought that was appropriate."

"Your co-author is on a list. Not the kind of list you want to have your name on in this country."

"What list?"

"*Judiciales.*"

The National Police, like the FBI.

"That doesn't make any sense," I said.

"Nothing makes any sense in this country."

"Does she know about this?" I asked him.

"She should. I told her boss."

"When?"

"As soon as I found out." He got up and went over to the window and kept his back to me. "You went into the Central Penitentiary with her. What were the two of you doing there?"

"If you know we were there, you must also know we were visiting the literacy class she has there."

He turned around.

"Which she uses as a cover to pass messages to and from the political prisoners," he said.

"She has no contact with them."

"Is that what she told you?"

I remembered what she said about there being a communication system inside. And my visitor, her friend *de confianza* from Cobán and former resident of the Central Penitentiary.

"It's what I saw," I said. "Or rather what I didn't see.

"You took a trip with her to Amatitlán. What were the two of you doing *there?*"

"Visiting a literacy class."

"Why there?"

"She knew people there."

"But she's based in Santa Cruz."

"She knew them from before. When she first came and was still living here in the capital."

"That's what she said?" I nodded and realized that I better stop talking. There were too many ways to say something I shouldn't. Thornby was still standing by the window, his face dark against the harsh backlight. "Do you have any idea what's going on in Santa Cruz?"

"Very little. I've never been there."

"It's a sty, my friend. A festering, stinking sty. Arbenz gave out some of the big farms there to the workers and after we got rid of Arbenz they gave the farms back to the big guys. Nasty business. Outside agitators all over the place. Last month an army patrol took a nine-millimeter combat pistol off a character claiming to be a traveling salesman. Now there are these so-called work camps, hundreds of men sitting around all day with nothing to do. Land occupations. A classic insurrectionary situation. That's what your girlfriend is involved with."

"She's hardly my girlfriend."

"Your collaborator then. Worse. Can I give you a piece of advice?"

"Be my guest."

"We can arrange to have the checks for the last three months of your grant—March, April, May—sent to the embassy in Mexico City. You finish up your business here by the end of February, give me a final report to take care of the grant requirement and then find something to keep yourself busy in Mexico City."

"That sounds a bit drastic."

"Look. We have a problem. You've done some good work, don't get me wrong, but we've got a fucking *war* going on here."

"That's very different from what you used to say."

"Circumstances change."

"You're telling me I have to leave? What about the Fulbright people?"

"We'll talk to them."

"What if I want to stay here until the end of the grant?"

He tamped and relit his pipe and studied the big open appointment book on the desk.

"Come see me tomorrow at one," he said. "I've got to talk with some other people about this."

On the way home, I wondered why Laura hadn't said anything to me about the list. Maybe she *didn't* know about it. Maybe Thornby didn't tell the Peace Corps Country Director, or maybe the Country Director thought it would be better not to tell her. No, the most likely explanation was she just didn't trust me enough to say something about it.

I'm ready to get out of this place, I thought. I hadn't heard anything back from the *Times* yet and there was obviously nothing more to do on the teacher's guide. If she were on that list — and Thornby's information about those things had usually been accurate — that would be another reason for her avoiding me.

I felt a little like Jacob Stein, with a project that went nowhere and now six months on my hands with nothing to do but write up a final report. So maybe a three-month free vacation in Mexico City wasn't such a bad idea. Now I also had to start thinking seriously about what I was going to do when I got back to the States and the rest of my life.

That night I dreamed Laura's lover in India wrote he was coming to Guatemala very soon on a ship called the *Latinamericana*.

FOURTEEN

The next day the big story in all the papers was the military takeover in neighboring Honduras, just a week after the reformer Juan Bosch got kicked out of the Dominican Republic and 10 days after Central

American heads of state met to condemn military takeovers. Guatemala did not attend, of course, its own military junta having removed the civilian government just five months earlier. In the next few months we would see Ecuador, Bolivia and Brazil join the military junta club, with barely a peep from Washington.

Farther back in one of the papers was a local story about a girl from a good family who had "inexplicably" been caught with communists in a raid in Zone 12. Another girl, 19, burned badly in the same raid lay in a hospital bed, refusing to give any information, name, address, nothing. They were both suspected members of a communist cell responsible for the recent seizure of farms in Sololá by *campesinos.* Little books were found among these illiterate Indian *campesinos* claiming that they were the rightful owners of the land, that it had belonged to their ancestors, had been stolen by the Spanish conquistadors who passed it down to generation after generation of their own families to the current great landholders.

Not helpful for the Great National Literacy Campaign, I thought, and of course not meant to be, even leaving aside the question of how these illiterate Indians were able to read these subversive little books.

Shortly after noon I put my draft of the teacher's guide, a copy of the Fulbright grant agreement and carbon copies of all my monthly reports to Thornby into a briefcase and headed for the embassy. I had no idea what he would have to tell me but wanted to make sure I had the relevant documents at hand to back up whatever I might want to say. I wasn't ready to leave yet.

It was a short walk, late November, the air cooler and drier, but there was a commotion just up the street from my apartment.

A mule pulling one of the little yellow municipal garbage carts couldn't get up the slight incline of one of the narrow north-south side streets. The mule kept slipping, stumbling, regaining its feet. The driver had jumped off the seat and was now pulling hard on the reins, leaning into it with all his weight, shouting *eeeeahh! macho! macho!* straining with all his might to move the beast and cart to the side of the street to let the angry traffic pass.

Saliva foamed from the mule's mouth as he clattered unsteadily forward, a clickety clack as the hooves slid across the pavement and the animal nearly fell as car horns blasted away. Finally a man got out of his car and pushed the cart, just enough so the mule got going, head bobbing, all the way to the top of the slight incline, picking up momentum, and then nearly crashed into a passing bus at the next intersection.

It was quite a show, spectators packed along the sidewalks with everyone rooting for the mule.

I walked into the large work area outside of Thornby's office and gave a cheerful hello to one of the secretaries. She looked at me in disbelief.

"You don't know?" I shook my head. "The President's been shot." The President of Guatemala was a general, not a president. I could not recall anyone referring to him as President. She sensed my confusion. "President Kennedy is dead," she said.

I sat down. The secretaries were typing away, though with no special urgency. Phones were not ringing off the hook. Voices were not hushed. Everyone in shock, I thought. I don't know how long I sat there. I finally got up and went in to see Thornby. He was at his desk, working on some papers.

"We'll have to reschedule," he said abruptly, but I was paralyzed and needed any kind of human contact.

"When did it happen?"

"Twelve thirty. Dallas. A sniper."

I slumped into a chair.

"It's unreal," I said.

He looked up now and massaged the back of his neck. Maybe he was thinking about whether or not he should say what he said next, but for all his calculation and hardheaded realism, Robert Thornby was not, finally, a careful man.

"I just hope they bury him before he starts to stink."

Then he began going through a file as if I weren't even there, as if he didn't care what I had heard or what I thought about it. Could it be his perverse idea of a joke? Was he testing me in some obscure way? The man could be so strange. I got up and left, but I kept thinking about him on my way home. I picked up the papers that had just hit the street and then listened to the radio bulletins in my apartment.

Were there others like Thornby in the government? Merely to ask the question, even in the privacy of one's own thoughts, was to enter a bewildering new world. I opened a bottle of beer and thought about that possibility for a while and decided it was crazy. Thornby was a frustrated, warped man. He was an idiot. Period.

There was only one person I felt like seeing now and she was not available. I would have liked to talk to Manolo too, but I hadn't heard from him in a couple of months.

A neighbor came by to offer his condolences and a theory about the Masons being at the center of the plot. We had a beer together and he left. I went back to the papers. There was the AP shot of Jackie holding her husband's head in the back of the car and a lot of wire service copy from Dallas. I had another beer and waited for something to hit me but nothing did. Shortly after dark there was a knock on the door and I thought it was the neighbor again.

It was Laura.

"I had to come see you," she said. "It's unbelievable."

The women in Santa Cruz had come to her house with flowers and talked of the widow with her husband's blood still on her skirt. The men came later. They asked if Johnson had done it. They wanted to know if Laura would have to leave the country now. But there was something else. "I could almost hear them saying, 'See what it's like? You thought these things only happened *here*, didn't you?' They're right. That's what I did think. What does it mean, *vos?*"

I shook my head; there was too much rushing through it.

"Do you think anything is going to change?" she asked.

"Not much," I said.

"I know, but he had a way about him, something hopeful."

"He was a good politician."

"It's the system," she said. "You see it here so clearly. Do you think Johnson had anything to do with it?"

"I doubt it. We haven't sunk that low yet."

I knew I had to tell her about Thornby, what he had said about Kennedy and the day before about herself. I wanted to wait until she settled down a bit but decided there would be no good time to do it.

I told her about burying him before he started to stink.

"That's sick," she said.

Then I told her about the business from the day before, about him wanting me to leave early and her name being on the *Judiciales'* list.

She shook her head slowly with her lovely smile, at once thoughtful and sad.

"You don't have to do much to get on that list," she said.

"What did *you* do?"

"Talk to the wrong people."

"Like who?"

"Your friend Manolo, for one."

"That's ridiculous. I talk to him all the time."

"When was the last time you talked to him?"

"It's been awhile. Maybe a couple of months."

She nodded slowly.

"The situation has changed."

"That's what Thornby said."

"They want to kick me out of the country," she said.

"Maybe we can leave together."

"It's not funny, *vos*."

"I've got something to maybe cheer you up a little," I said and gave her a copy of the teacher's guide. "Our subversive document."

She held it out at arm's length, admiring the cover.

"It *looks* nice." Then she started leafing through it, nodding her approval, lingering on a page, commenting now and then, "It's good, *vos*, it really is."

"Look at the inside back cover," I said. "That's where I got us in trouble, putting our names on it—"

"It's *ok*," she said softly. "It's fine."

"I gave a copy to Thornby and Ramirez. A lot of good that'll do."

"There are people who will use it."

"Do you think so?"

"I'm sure."

We talked some more, resolving nothing, but it felt good just being able to talk with her now. She was gnawing on a stick of raw sugarcane she had pulled out of her bag. She used it to help her quit smoking and as a cheap source of energy, satisfying her sweet tooth while she was at it. We nursed our beers as the conversation wandered through Washington politics and Guatemalan reality. We heard music from another apartment. Sometimes nothing sounds farther away than music in another room.

Then I realized I was looking at her differently. *What was wrong with me?* She was slouched on the straw mattress against the wall, chewing on the sugarcane, struggling with the meaning of this catastrophic event, and here I was trying not to notice the firm bare thigh peeking out from the shade of her dress.

"When are you going back to Santa Cruz?"

She looked at her watch and stood up abruptly.

"In the morning. The Country Director called a meeting at the *pensión* tonight. Then everyone goes back to their villages."

I kissed her cheek and she leaned back and looked at me. I kissed her again, on her sugarcane lips.

"This isn't why I came," she said softly.

"I know. But I still don't understand how such a smart girl like you can be so foolish about some things."

"You mean why haven't I taken advantage of such a marvelous opportunity."

"Something like that."

She took my face in both her hands.

"I have to go," she said. "It's not fair to you. It's selfish. I shouldn't have come."

"I'm glad you did."

She pulled a comb out of her bag and raked it slowly through her hair, catching at invisible tangles. I wondered if she ever used a mirror.

I walked her to the *pensión*. We passed a row of beggars with their weary eyes and patriarchal beards sitting against a store window and then the *Hotel Mundial,* its Christ-like statue over the entrance holding a small glass globe engraved *sea bien venido.*

Laura glanced at me.

"Americans walk with their hands in their pockets," she said.

"And their hearts on their sleeves," I said.

She took my arm.

"Things will work out," she said. "You worry too much."

We were walking past the National Police building. I remembered the night it had spooked her. Troops in combat gear and an armored vehicle in the driveway had reinforced the regular guards. In the adjacent lot the renovation of the San Francisco church had been completed. They had torn down the old chipped wall surrounding the church and dug up the stone terrace to build two ugly little reflecting pools that glowed like radioactive green puddles in the spotlights. It was described as a routine public works project, but police stations had become targets and that wall so close to the biggest and baddest police station in the country must have been a concern.

In the darkness ahead came a faint ringing of bells. Then we saw the vendors in their white coats, waiting for the movies to let out, and suddenly the street was swarming with the headlights of parked cars coming alive and the vendors hollering *poporropo papaleeena maneeeeeya,* wailing and rhythmic, a lovely song in these brutal streets—so typical of the goddamn country, I thought, ready to kick you in the teeth one minute and the next these guys hustling popcorn and potato chips and peanuts and sounding for all the world like the Vienna Boys' Choir. Laura asked me what I was thinking and I told her.

"I always know what you're thinking," she said.

We moved through the crowd in front of the theaters. She took my arm.

"When can you come to Santa Cruz?"

"Whenever you want."

"Next week. But don't tell Thornby where you're going."

Other than the embassy suspending regular business for a few days after Dallas, not much seemed

to change. We were so far away from it, severed from
the ritual of national mourning, the stream of television
images, the connection with community and family
and friends, that we could only dimly imagine this
terrible thing that had happened. It was almost
abstract. Maybe I was just in shock. I had my doubts
about the guy, but it would be many years before I
realized that day was the first time I was conscious of a
political event penetrating my interior life.

The following week I cabled Laura to say I'd be
catching an early bus the next day. I made sure to
avoid Thornby before I left. There would be plenty of
time when I got back to reschedule the meeting with
him.

I was finally on my way to Santa Cruz.

II

Santa Cruz del Quiché

FIFTEEN

The bus sped along the straightaways leaving the
capital. It was an ancient but practical vehicle with its
outside ladder leading to the roof and jump seats that
folded into the aisle to accommodate the human cargo.
But the shocks were gone, the windows were cracked
and broken, and the metal sheeting was so rusted and
flimsy you could have pried it off with a can opener.

Inscribed on a brass plate above the driver was the parentage of this mechanical marvel.

Blue Bird Body Co.
Fort Valley, Georgia

I sat back to enjoy the ride, the thrilling countryside and the odd sense of security I often felt in the company of strangers. The bus was full and there was a lot of chatter. The old man sitting across the aisle next to me was plucking whiskers from his chin with tweezers. The jump seat between us was empty.

Sometimes looking out the window I saw the jagged faults of the *barrancos* and sometimes I saw the mountains, but I could not see them together. The geological origin of the terrain was puzzling. I would see the top of the peaks at what appeared to be the same height and think that once there had been a higher plane and the plunging space of the *barrancos* had been carved out of it; but then I would look and see only the sharp upward thrust of the mountains dominating the land and think *that* was how they had been formed, erupting from below. The two elements would not stay fixed, one always overpowering the other, and after a while I gave up and pulled out my book, *The Rise and Fall of The Third Reich*, and began reading.

A finger pointed to some bold type on the page.

"*Esto es inglés, no?*" the old man sitting across the aisle asked. He had a slack gray face and watery eyes—and by now a clean chin.

"Yes," I said in Spanish. "It's English."

"You understand that?" he asked.

"Yes."

"Speak it?"

"Yes, I can."

"You understand any others?"

"Just Spanish," I said.

"You understand Spanish too?"

The question seemed foolish, since we were speaking Spanish, but I was curious about where he was heading.

"Yes, Spanish too. Can you understand English?"

"Oh, no."

He was nearly toothless and his watermelon gums looked painfully soft.

"It's not hard to learn," I said.

"I like English better."

I was surprised.

"Better than Spanish?"

"Oh, no. I just like it better."

"But better than *what?* What do you like English better *than?*"

"I don't know. Just like it better. I wonder why that is."

He scratched his chin and seemed confused. I wondered if he was putting me on, but I gave it another shot.

"Better than *what* do you like English? What do you like English better *than*?"

"I don't know." Then a light went on. "Better than the *others*," he said happily.

I figured I had him now, one way or the other, that he had played his hand about as far as he could go.

"*What* others?"

"I don't know," he said, "French. Greek. The others. I wonder why."

He leaned back in his seat, somewhat satisfied but still in a mild muddle, and I returned to the book. Churchill was giving one of his grand speeches. I was fascinated by the war—the drama, the horror, the heroic resistance. There was also a feeling I couldn't shake. It came from the moral comfort of knowing you were on the right side, a feeling I took so much for granted back in those days that I couldn't name it or imagine living without it. I finished the chapter and closed the book.

The window was cold. We were well into the mountains now, the rocky cliffs covered with fuzzy earth and green vines and clumps of wildflowers. We would grind upward and then cut loose coming down with cargo pounding on the roof and pebbles flying in our wake.

"Where you headed?" asked the old man.

"Santa Cruz."

"Santa Cruz. You don't say."

"I'm going to visit a friend."

"You don't say."

"How much farther is it?"

He looked out the window, rubbing his smooth jaw.

"Not far now."

"This bus is hard on the kidneys," I said.

"Very hard. Not like the kind where you come from, right?"

"We've got all kinds there."

"Not like this one." He flicked the seat with disgust. "All we get in Guatemala is the junk."

"They've got some new buses in the capital," I said.

"For the rich." He laughed. "I'm an old man and say whatever I like." He looked out the window. "We're making good time. This driver is serious."

"You live in Santa Cruz?"

"All my life. A *Santacruzeño* through and through." He looked down and pursed his lips toward my feet. "Nice boots. How much they cost you?"

They were calf-high Herman's of reddish leather that I kept in good shape.

"About 40 dollars."

"Expensive."

"Yes."

"Where'd you buy 'em?"

"New York."

This seemed to explain the price, the quality, and other matters he'd been contemplating. He nodded slowly and ran his fingers delicately around his mouth.

"You are a friend of *La Laura*?"

"Yes. You know her?"

"Oh, yes. A good worker. Not like the others they sent."

"What others?"

I immediately regretted the question, but this time there was no problem.

"From the capital. They stayed in their houses all day and taught the women how to sew." He made a face. "No good for anything."

"Do you know where she lives?"

She had given me such vague directions to her house that I half imagined arriving in town and not finding her.

"Of course."

"Perhaps you can show me."

"I'll take you."

We looped and twisted through the mountains for another hour and then we hit a rise where houses hugged the road. In the distance I saw the tiled roofs of Santa Cruz, stepping away from some approximate center like a huge amphitheater. I felt the bus leave the dusty gravel and click onto the brick street as low adobe houses skimmed past, a final lurching turn, and we stopped.

The old man's nephew met our bus. He was tall with blue eyes. Five hundred years ago one of those Andalusian blonds in Alvarado's army had taken an Indian girl not far from where we stood and these blue eyes had been turning up ever since. The young man climbed the ladder and hauled down a big sack.

The bus pulled out of the plaza, a patch of rocky dark earth with a lopsided kiosk in the middle and ragged palms at the edges. The stores around the plaza had hitching posts. On the surrounding hills a few bright houses stood out among the dun adobes.

"Where is everyone?" I asked.

"Oh, around," the old man said.

"It looks deserted."

"This time of year is very sad," he agreed. "Many leave for the coast."

The two-ton trucks came from the cotton and sugar estates on the coast to transport their seasonal labor. The men often took their families with them, dreading the muggy heat of the lowlands and the diseases it would breed in their susceptible bodies, but at the end of the line were two dollars a day that kept them and their children alive.

We went over to where his nephew was roping the big sack onto a mule. I asked him what he had in the sack.

"Goodyears," the old man said.

"What?"

"Tires. I make sandals." He showed off his own footwear. "Not like yours, huh? Look at those boots, Diego," he said to his nephew. "How much do you think they cost?"

Diego scratched his head.

"More than yours, I'd say."

The young man had a peculiar voice, an anxious tenor that seemed oddly appropriate for his atypical, almost Nordic looks.

Just then the stillness of the town was broken by music, its source hidden but growing closer.

"Only a funeral," the old man explained.

The procession came straggling out a side street and headed across the plaza, a man in front with hat in hand, head bowed, behind him the musicians—two violins, two guitars, drum and concertina—the music restrained but gay, like a slow square dance. Behind the musicians came the women dressed in black and in their midst was a small white coffin covered with pink carnations. A church bell began ringing wildly.

"It's the custom here to carry the little ones away with music," Diego said. "Very primitive."

"How old was this one?"

"Oh, this was a tender one."

"Tender?"

"Six or seven."

The old man caught my eye and nodded toward the funeral party.

"Your *compatriota*," he said. The black shawl hid her face but she was at least a head taller than the others and I recognized the walk, that stiff shambling gait like a kid who had shot up too fast.

He crossed the plaza to where they had stopped by the church and took Laura aside. Then they both came walking back. The shawl was over her shoulders now.

"Hello, *vos*," she said. "I see you've met Don Guillermo."

"On the bus."

Don Guillermo nodded.

"He asks a lot of questions," he said.

"I guess I came at a bad time," I said.

She shrugged.

"It's alright. I got your telegram."

"With permission," the old man said. "We have to be going."

"You don't have to leave," Laura said.

"You know my woman. She'll think I was bending the elbow at the *cantina*."

"Tell her the truth."

"You *don't* know my woman." He jerked his head for Diego to follow. "The truth," he mused, shaking his head as they walked away.

Laura and I followed the funeral party up the road to the cemetery. I asked her how the kid had died.

"Worms. The third one the family's lost. It's a miracle they keep finding godfathers." She saw I didn't understand. "The godfather has to pay for the funeral."

The red dirt road led up a long hill to the cemetery. The land all around was brown and scrubby, cut away by a deep *barranco*, but the cemetery on the hill was a lush green with a smooth red path curving past white tombstones in a grove of pines. The hilltop was so perfect it could have been a mirage.

And a question came to mind that I had never dared ask anyone but myself.

"Maybe when you lose so many like that..." I hesitated at the enormity of the question. "Maybe they don't feel it the way we would."

"I thought that at first," she said.

"But not now."

"No."

Where we stood, at the bottom of the hill, the road dipped through a shallow stream before rising into the cemetery. She walked along the bank of the stream for a few feet and then motioned me over. "I want you to meet some real troublemakers," she said. Tiny white worms swam in the sluggish current, leaving their diminutive wakes in the slime. "Do you know what it would cost to get rid of them?" she said. "About one tenth of the money your government wastes in this country every year. Without even counting what goes to the army."

"*Our* government," I said. "Since when were you disowned?"

"My country right or wrong, is that what you believe?"

"No."

We walked up the hill and into the cemetery. Here by the brick gate at the entrance were huge engraved tombs, some the size of the smaller houses around the plaza, monuments with glass casements and slabs of marble inside covered with fresh flowers. Then the path leveled off, passing plain mounds of earth that commemorated the equally but less fortunate dead, some marked with a stone and others bare. Through the pines we saw the funeral party standing around the open grave. A priest had one hand on the small coffin and held a Bible in the other. His lips were moving.

"I tried so hard to get the water project back on track." She shook her head slowly. "You'd think they'd learn," she said, her voice low and curiously flat. "You tell them once, you tell them a hundred times. You've got to boil the water, *Señora*. No, you cannot use that filthy water for your *tortillas*. It only *looks* ok you tell them. Why is that so hard to understand? You'd think…"

She had begun to cry. The words had dissolved so fluidly into gentle sobs that I didn't realize until her voice cracked and the words stopped. I didn't know what to say. The idea of her being someone who might need comforting was still so clotted by my longing for her, I didn't know where to begin.

We circled back along the path. Two vultures drifted above the *barranco* like weightless flat rocks. The sky had a twilight glow, a faint coppery patina over the first stars and the crescent of a new moon. It was a cold and very foreign sky.

SIXTEEN

She lived in a one-room cement house halfway up one of the hills that surrounded the plaza. There was a table, four chairs and a bookcase, all of raw lumber like my furniture in the city.

The bookcase had what you'd expect: a report on cooperatives, Laubach and Freire, a bilingual dictionary. Then it got a little more interesting. I noted some Camus, a volume of Chekhov stories, *The Mentor Book of Major American Poets*. I didn't see our old friend Henry Miller, but there was *The Alexandria Quartet* and a volume of E.E. Cummings. There were also titles I didn't recognize—*The Deputy* by Rolf Hochhuth, *The Notebooks of Simone Weil*. I recall those two because I subsequently read them, hoping to find some answers about what was going on inside her. They helped a little, but as happens so often when I think about her, they left me with new questions and very few answers to old ones.

Near the window with its view of the town and the countryside beyond was a reading chair with a

Coleman lamp on a wooden crate. *The Grapes of Wrath* was next to the lamp. The small bed in a corner of the room was unmade.

She got a fire going in the wood-burning stove and put a pot of water on to boil. She brought the water in from a well out back. Then she began slicing up tomatoes and lettuce. I sat in the chair by the window and watched her at these domestic chores, a moment of living together. I looked at the unmade bed. Did she really cry herself to sleep every night? I tried to stop thinking about that. It wasn't right to want her like this, I thought, not here, not now. Nobody had a right to such personal happiness in the midst of such squalor.

We sat down to a meal of spaghetti, salad and a bottle of wine that had gone bad a long time ago. Everything else tasted faintly of the Halazone tablets she used to purify the water. We talked about the literacy materials for a while. We talked about a kid in town who needed an eye operation. I began to relax a little. We were nearly done eating when she hit me with it.

"I heard from Paul," she said.

I waited for her to go on, but she didn't.

"What'd he say?"

"He got married." Her eyes were steady on mine. "Someone he met there," she added softly.

I couldn't think. It felt like my world had been turned upside down.

"Is he going to stay there?" I asked, almost like a reflex, knowing there were other questions I wanted to ask but couldn't.

"It wasn't a long letter," she said.

I wanted to touch her, hold her, but I was frozen in this reflection of my own pain.

"I never understood it," I said.

She lit a cigarette and fixed me with a brittle look.

"We had a lovely time, we really did. I don't regret it. We could talk for hours, for days, all these ideas he had. I had never met anyone like him. We went away together at the end of the training session. Most people went home for the week, but we just got on a bus and went wherever it took us. We rode horses on the beach in Kitty Hawk—" Her voice cracked and I thought she was going to break like she did in the cemetery, but she was beyond that now. "I knew what he was like, I did, but it was so good, so right, just the right time. Oh, *vos*! Why should it have to be like that? To have something like that and then not have it?"

A dog barked, its puny howl sinking into the depths of rural night.

It was wonderful to be rid of this absentee tyrant but I also feared the damage he'd done. Simply removing him from the picture did not necessarily bring her any closer to me. And maybe even made it harder.

"It can happen again," I said.

A lone cricket chirped in the backyard, over and over again, like some discarded electronic device.

"Would you like to listen to some music?" she asked.

"Sure."

She went over to the bookcase and pulled out a record from a set of Beethoven symphonies.

"Mister B," she said.

The *Pastoral* filled the room. I listened from a distance at first, trying to understand with my rudimentary musical knowledge how this masterpiece was constructed, the hints and teasing of themes that circled each other and then fused so naturally and with so much power. Laura seemed to know the music by heart, stretched out on the floor, propped on her elbow, anticipating the shifts in mood with a little smile or tightening her eyes as if to brace herself for the next surge. And then we were into the third movement, the melody gathering everything together and washing over us in waves of astonishing sweetness—it was all mixed up, Laura and the music, something beautiful and untouchable, locked inside.

"What's the matter, *vos?*"

"Nothing."

The music had stopped.

There was a small photo on the bookcase of a young man in uniform, his fair handsome face enhanced by the old portrait photography. I saw the resemblance immediately.

"Your father?"

She nodded.

"My mother said he was the spitting image of Ronald Colman." She smiled. "Without the moustache."

"How old was he?"

"Twenty-six."

"They married young."

"They were very much in love," she said.

I got up and walked over to the window and thought about leaving. Overhead the lone light bulb in the room dimmed, flickered back to life, and died.

"They turn off the town generator at nine o'clock," she said.

I stood there in the dark, looking out the window. There were candles in a few windows along the street but everything else was shapeless and black. Something caught my eye, high on the horizon. Spots of orange light drifted down the dark mountain like a lava flow.

"What's going on?" I asked her.

She came over to the window beside me.

"Something's happened," she said. "They're meeting again."

"Who?"

"*Campesinos*. The army's setting up *cercos*. They question anyone they catch in the net and arrest people. Sometimes you don't see them again."

We watched the lights coming down the mountain. A solitary torch would bob into view, zig-zag down for a short distance then link up with one or two or three others and soon a river of glowing orange was pouring out of the darkness. We watched it streaming downward until it was swallowed by the mountain and everything went dark again.

"I love those lights," she said.

I thought she was going to elaborate but she didn't.

"Why do you love those lights?"

"Remember I told you about this feeling when I was a kid, something so much bigger than myself or any one person or thing and never being able to understand what it was? Now I know. Everyone is connected to every one else in the deepest way. Most of the time we don't see it. Otherwise people wouldn't treat each other the way they do. But it's true, at the most basic level it's true, we are made of the same stuff as everyone else and every other particle in the universe, dust to dust and all that stuff. Isn't that true, Mister Rationality?"

"And ashes to ashes. I can't argue with that."

"Those lights make that connection visible. Those lights," she said, giving me a look of no uncertain authority, "make me feel closer to God."

There was a knock at the door.

We looked at each other with mock surprise and laughed. She opened the door.

It was Diego, working his hat nervously in his hands. He glanced around the room and then spoke in that high anxious voice.

"He needs to see you," he said to Laura.

"Where?"

"The clinic."

She started putting things into her bag—a flashlight, a pack of *Payasos*—a vile local brand of cigarettes with black tobacco that you could buy loose for a penny apiece in the market.

"What's up?" I asked her in English.

"I have to go, *vos*." She finished with the bag. "Where are you staying tonight?"

I caught myself looking at the bed in the corner and hoped she hadn't noticed.

"Good question," I said.

"There's a *pensión* in town. You shouldn't have a problem getting a room."

"Ok."

"Can you take the *compañero* to the *pensión*?" she said to Diego.

"There are many soldiers," Diego said.

"Do you have your passport, *vos*?"

"Yes."

"Take him to the *pensión*," she instructed Diego. "But not through the plaza. Go around."

Laura lowered the wick in the lamp and the flame sputtered out.

"Who's at the clinic?" I asked.

She had her hand on the knob of the door. It was very dark, but I could see she was looking at me.

"You have to promise not to tell anyone, even if you decide you don't agree with what we're doing." She knew I didn't have to think about that. "Manolo," she said.

Diego and I left her by the house and when I looked back she was gone. We walked up the road and then veered into a dry field, cut across another field, through thickets and barbed wire that tore my shirt, moving rapidly in the dark. It was cold but I was sweating, breathing hard, stumbling after Diego. Finally he stopped and lowered himself against a big rock.

"We'll wait here a bit," he said. "They're right by the *pensión*."

He pointed through the trees to the plaza below. There were soldiers in two jeeps parked in front of a low wooden building.

"How long is a little bit?"

"It's only a patrol. Not long."

I slumped against the rock and thought about Manolo and wondered how much time he spent here and exactly what he was doing. At least it explained why I hadn't seen him for a while. I thought about Laura and wondered exactly what *she* was doing. I thought about that jerk Paul and how he could have done what he did to her. I thought about myself and wondered what the hell I was doing here. Diego was staring at me.

"Are you a revolutionary?" he asked.

I almost laughed at the question

"I work on the literacy campaign," I said cautiously.

"But are you a revolutionary?" he insisted,

Two possibilities came to mind as we waited there in the dark. The gaunt features and curious soft voice suggested some vague anomaly, a touch of rural idiocy perhaps—or someone had gotten their wires crossed. Both, I supposed, were possible.

"I came here to study the literacy program. I write down what I see and try to improve it. I wrote a guide for teachers, with the *compañera* Laura."

"Oh yes. *La Guía*. Very helpful."

I was surprised.

"You know it?"

"Very helpful," he said. I thought that would end it, but disappointment flickered across Diego's long face.

"You're not with us then?"

I couldn't decide which was more frustrating, his not understanding that for and against were not the only categories in this matter—or my trying to explain why I believed that. His face went blank and he lapsed into a distracted silence.

It would take some time before I could fully appreciate what had happened that night. I had stumbled into the activities of the early organizational stage of the *Fuerzas Armadas Rebeldes* (*FAR*). The first armed units had already established base areas deep in the mountains and cadre like Diego helped set up supply routes, recruit local supporters and provide information on the movement of army troops. This was a war zone. Thornby had been right about that.

Diego motioned me to follow him. The jeeps in front of the *pensión* had left. We stopped at the edge of the plaza and shook hands.

"*Hasta pronto*," he said.

I couldn't sleep. I tried to read but couldn't concentrate. I kept thinking how ridiculous my explanation to Diego must have sounded — why I could not answer yes, I was with them. But what did I know about these people? Well, Laura and Manolo. I knew a good deal about them. I loved them both and understood why they were doing this, but I didn't think it would work. Not that I had a better idea.

Everything kept coming back to Laura. How long it would take, if ever, for Laura Jenson to love a man again? Now she and Manolo. I felt jealous. I thought about Diego, his disappointment with me. Thornby waiting to spring a question or two about this trip when I got back to the city. I wished someone had shown me this lousy script before I applied for the grant that, to tell you the truth, I really didn't think I would get. I still wonder if I would have signed on if I had known what was coming.

I forced myself back into my book. The Nazis had just launched their Operation Barbarossa offensive into Russia, Hitler's armies smashing through everything on a thousand-mile front. The usually cautious General

Halder noted in his diary that it would all be over in a matter of weeks. I marvel at the hubris of the powerful and sleep like a baby.

SEVENTEEN

I woke drenched in rich vanilla light pouring through the window with Laura sitting at the foot of my bed.

"You're a sound sleeper."

Through the window behind her, green leaves glowed with the morning sunlight. I was not surprised to see her sitting there. It seemed perfectly natural; the morning, Laura on my bed.

"How long have you been there?"

"Not long," she said. "I knocked. You were in dreamland."

"I don't know where I was, but I'm glad you're here. What's on the agenda for today?"

"Manolo says he'd like to see you."

"There are some things I hope you'll explain."

She crossed her lips with a forefinger.

"Get dressed," she said. "I'll wait in the dining room."

She was sitting at a table looking through the window at two jeeps and soldiers in battle gear parked in front of the *pensión*.

"They were there last night for a while," I said.

"I know."

"Problem?"

"We don't think so."

I had a glass of orange juice and a roll and we left, heading across the plaza toward the clinic, when another jeep came around the corner. There was an officer and driver in front and two soldiers behind a mounted machine gun in back. This one meant business. The officer stood up and the jeep stopped. He waved us over.

"Good morning," he said in Spanish. "Americans?"

"Yes," Laura said.

"Peace Corps?"

"Yes."

"And you, sir?"

"I work with the Ministry of Education."

"You have identification, of course," he said, looking at us both.

We handed him our passports. He studied them, pulling at his chin, then gave them back.

"This is not a safe place for foreigners," he said.

"I've lived here for six months, Lieutenant."

She said it with that phenomenal smile, but the young officer was not moved.

"Then you must know what I'm talking about, *Señorita.* Frankly, I'm a little surprised they let you stay here. I would advise you both to be very careful."

"Thank you, Lieutenant," she said. "We certainly will."

"Just a word of friendly advice," he said to me, man-to-man, as if Laura could not fully appreciate his meaning.

He sat down and they drove off, taking the road to the highway. We crossed the plaza toward the clinic, a dirt-caked adobe house like all the others on the plaza. A woman was watching from the window. She opened the door as we approached and then latched it quickly behind us. She was very short and wore a dark nylon parka and dark slacks.

"*Compañera*," she said, greeting Laura, and then extended her hand to me. "I am Yolanda." I took her hand. It wasn't a hearty American handshake. You didn't do that with Guatemalan women. Her hand was offered for me to touch, which I did, lingering perhaps a moment too long. She nodded almost imperceptibly and did not smile. She had high Indian cheeks and brown eyes. It was a round and smooth face and pretty in a plain way. "You're the literacy scholar we've heard so much about," she said, her tone clearly sarcastic.

Ok, I thought, but hardly what I expected.

I sat down beside Laura on a long wooden bench. The clinic was a single large room with a curtain across the middle and a shelf with a few paperback books, glass jars with handwritten labels and a box of Johnson & Johnson absorbent cotton. Under the shelf was a cabinet with several drawers. It was cold and damp and there was not a sound until Manolo pulled the curtain back. He stood there with his hands on his hips and his pensive smile.

"You picked a hell of a time for a visit," he said to me.

His eyes were an almost solid red from a filarial infection he had picked up years ago and had not treated properly. When he got tired or run down the redness came back and made him look very sick. He walked over to the window with its view of the plaza.

"What did our friend out there have to say?"

"He told us to be careful."

"Excellent advice." He tapped his forefinger to his lips with that pensive air he took on from time to time. "This is not a good time for your research."

"Laura said it could be difficult."

"Your famous literacy campaign," he said, shaking his head. "Your *compatriota* has organized half the province. I'm not kidding. A veritable literacy *empire!*"

"Come on, Manolo," Laura said.

"Modest to a fault. You know, we had to finally stop her from going out at night. 'What's wrong with going out at night?' she says. 'I've got a flashlight.' A little flashlight like this." He held his hands a few inches apart—and cracked up. "I've got a flashlight!" He was gasping in a fit of uncontrollable laughter and I found myself drawn into the sheer energy and hysteria of his private uproar; then Laura too, the three of us swept away in convulsions of laughter long after we could remember why we were laughing so hard.

Even stern little Yolanda, sitting on the floor with her arms wrapped tightly around her knees, was smiling. We finally pulled ourselves together.

"Do you have any idea what goes on out there at night?" Manolo said.

"But the classes are at night," Laura protested.

"But the classes are at night," he mimicked gleefully. "As are most of the rapes, murders, robberies, little machete chops to the back of the neck. Not to mention our trigger-happy soldiers." He shook his head slowly, that soft chuckle caught in his throat. "She's a fanatic."

"*Compañero*," Yolanda said to Manolo, her Spanish low and hurried. "Someone needs help back there."

A low moaning came from behind the curtain. Yolanda got up and pulled it back. A man lay on a canvas cot, his head hanging stiffly over the edge. A basin on the floor was splattered with deep red blood. Manolo went inside and drew the curtain behind him.

"Another casualty of our glorious army," Yolanda said.

"What happened?"

"They've thrown up another *cerco*," she said. "They surround an area and slowly close the noose. They usually miss the people they want and take it out on everyone else."

"Sometimes they send them to a work camp," Laura said.

"Sometimes they'll send their whole families with them," Yolanda said. "They don't understand what they're doing. I still hold that."

"I think a lot of people would agree with you," I said.

Yolanda looked at me curiously.

"You know about the work camps, Mister Franklin?"

"Just the little I've read in the papers."

"Just what you've read in the papers."

"Yes. Is that so strange?"

Manolo came out and slumped into a chair.

"I find it somewhat strange," Yolanda said to me. "A man in your position might be more familiar with the problem."

I was beginning not to like Yolanda.

"My position is to study the literacy campaign."

"I see."

She stared at me for a long time: then came her question, soft, low and menacing.

"How did you understand that verb so well?"

"What verb?"

"Sostener. When I said *todavía la sostenga."*

Manolo and Laura looked as puzzled as I was.

"To hold is a very common verb," I said. "What's so unusual about that?"

"Only a person very well studied would understand the sense in which I just used it."

"I happen to be very well studied."

Manolo was shaking his head slowly.

"Very," Yolanda said. "It seems you are someone with specialized training."

"What are you implying?"

Yolanda sat very straight on the bench, her dark eyes burning.

"If the glove fits, wear it."

"Please, *compañera*," Manolo said sternly. "This isn't right."

"Perhaps there are things you don't see."

"I see you're upset."

"I'm not upset. I'm telling you there are too many coincidences. The *cerco*, the arrival of this gentleman."

"Coincidences do occur, *compañera*."

"True," she said. "And the enemy does not rest."

The man behind the curtain began moaning again. Manolo took a deep breath. He pulled a little notebook out of his shirt pocket, flicked through it and then looked at Laura.

"Someone needs to take that Sanchez kid into the city for his cataract procedure," he said. "Could you do it?"

"When's his appointment?"

"Tomorrow morning."

"I can go on the evening bus," Laura said.

So much for our literacy centers, I thought.

"But not alone," Manolo said. "Peter goes with you." He smiled. "You make an attractive couple." Laura and I looked at each other awkwardly. "Good. It's settled." He rubbed his hands together. "Give me a few minutes to clean this guy up. Have you seen the ruins?" he asked me.

"No."

"I'm going to take you to see the ruins," he said and
went back behind the curtain. Yolanda went in behind
him.

Laura said the bus came through at about five
o'clock and we should meet in the plaza at four thirty. I
offered to take the kid by myself.

"I wouldn't feel right about that," she said.

"Or I could stay here and look at the literacy centers
myself."

"You'd never find them."

"What about Yolanda? Couldn't she take the kid
in?"

Laura shook her head firmly.

"She has to stay here."

Manolo came out of the back room and checked his
watch.

"Go find the Sanchez boy," he said to Laura. "Get
him back here by 4: 30."

Yolanda came through the curtain and went over to
the only window in the room.

"It's clear," she said.

Laura slung her bag over her shoulder.

"See you later, *vos*."

Manolo and Yolanda watched her from the window
for a few minutes. I sat on the bench. Manolo was
saying something to Yolanda I couldn't hear. Then she
looked at her watch.

"You will be here at 4:30," she said to me.

"Yes."

"Four thirty sharp," she said. "It was a pleasure to have met you, Mister Franklin."

"Equally."

She closed the door carefully behind her and Manolo watched through the window. Then he went over to the cabinet and unlocked a drawer. He pulled out a pistol and tucked it into his waist so it was concealed under his loose woolen shirt. He took me by the arm.

"Come on," he said. "We should get out of here ourselves for a little while. I'll take you to see the famous ruins of Santa Cruz."

EIGHTEEN

The ruins were a 20-minute walk from the plaza and you could have easily missed the faded wooden sign marking the path. Even then the clearing with rocky mounds around its edges could have been mistaken for just an old pasture with goats feeding on its stubby grass. Manolo gave me the standard tour: the ball court that had occupied the clearing; the royal pavilion now rubble at the far end; evidence of a causeway in the line of boulders that disappeared into the woods.

We climbed one of the mounds. It was flat on top with a small cave that sheltered the stray goats feeding below. We sat there for a while, Manolo with his arms clasped around his knees, relaxed but unhappy.

"Look at it," he said. "Look at what's left. Do you know they could measure time as accurately as we do today?"

"They should fix the place up. It's a shame."

"It's calculated neglect, this contempt for what was once a magnificent civilization. This is what happens to those foolish enough to resist conquering white armies. That's the message. Very useful for maintaining an inferiority complex in people you have reason to fear. Have you ever read any Jung? The collective unconscious? It has political applications nobody talks about."

"I'm sure somebody does."

He stared at me with those ravaged eyes that were so beautiful when he was healthy.

"You understand," he said. "We can't let you get too close."

"You mean *Compañera* Yolanda."

He chuckled.

"She's tough. But I told you what a lot of people think you're really doing here. You can't blame them, given our history. You've already learned things, simply by being here, that could be of value to the enemy."

"Can I stop you there?"

"By all means."

"If we're so evil, what is this connection you have to the embassy?"

"Connection I *had*. Mutual interest. Thornby thought he was getting useful information from me." He shrugged. "It was nothing but gave him something to include in his reporting. I was getting all kinds of medical supplies that we used to save lives. But we both know that's over now."

"And what have I learned of value to the enemy?"

"For one thing, you know where I am, at least right now."

"This trip is not something I'm going to talk about."

A few clouds drifted on the horizon; we could hear the goats ripping the grass as they grazed.

"Even if they tortured you?"

It was like Diego's question. It seemed to come from a parallel universe of myth and terror and martyrdom.

"I don't think that's likely," I said.

"Why? Because you're an American? Or because you think they don't do things like that?"

"A little of both."

"About the first you might be correct, though I am beginning to doubt even that. About the second there is no question. I speak from personal experience."

Once, on the Upper West Side of Manhattan, I sat at a dinner table next to a Polish Jew with a number tattooed on his arm. We chatted amiably about his furniture store downtown and his two kids in college, but all I could think about was that number and the camps. After dinner we kept talking. This subject from his past never came up, the way you would avoid an obscenity in polite company. With Manolo it was like that now but not exactly the same. What had happened to Manolo, whatever it was, was happening now and nobody could say when it would end.

"Can you tell me anything about it?"

"It would be better for you not to know."

"I'd like to."

He gave me a puzzled look

"Why?"

"Because you're my friend."

"I hope that's true."

He was struggling with questions that I only half understood, but I saw that he had made a decision.

"There are certain things I can't tell you, certain errors I made. These I have discussed with my *compañeros*."

"I understand."

"I got very active in the student movement here when I came back from Madison. There were huge demonstrations. This was about a year before you got here. They grabbed me coming out of a meeting. They had me blindfolded at first but later I figured out they had taken me to the National Police building. They asked questions. Contacts. Organizational structure. Methods of communication. During this time an American was present."

He paused, anticipating my incredulity. In some ways he knew me better than I knew myself.

"Are you sure?"

"Remember, I lived in Madison for two years. He didn't talk much but he had a heavy accent. Pure gringo. After he left, they threw me into a windowless room with cement walls and a cement floor. There was a table, a black box with batteries and long wires. They'd taken the blindfold off. They didn't care if I saw them." He stroked his chin and thought about this with that faint, inward smile. "That's when I thought I was going to die." It took him a while to resume, but when he did it was in a flat mechanical voice that was almost casual. "They began easy, slapping me around a bit, asking the same questions. Then they mixed in electric shocks with the beatings. Once in a while they'd stop to ask questions and think up new insults to shout in my face. With the shocks they began here, the nipple. Like a pinprick, that's all. I said to myself this isn't going to be so bad, then I saw my fingers twitching and the jolt went through me and my arm went crazy." He flapped his arms like the wings of a bird struggling to take flight. "That's what scares you, the loss of motor control. That's what they're trying to do all the time, get it into your head that you're powerless, totally at their mercy. Sometimes they will make a *compañera* parade naked in front of them, just to make her feel ashamed, humiliated. It's a science. They learned a lot from the French in Algeria, something else your friend Camus seems to have missed. Techniques that have been updated and improved by someone the American Embassy calls its Public Safety

Advisor. But it's only the body you can't control. What goes on here," he tapped the side of his head, "that's still your decision."

I looked out at the goats grazing in the lost geometry of the clearing as Manolo continued in the same even tone.

"They applied the shocks everywhere: anus, penis, eyes, fillings in teeth. Ingenious bastards. The worst exploded in the head, a wire plugged into each ear. But they had a problem with me. I passed out too quickly. They kept looking for places that would keep me conscious longer. Every time I passed out they got angry. But I was getting weaker. They'd throw me in a cell and give me some rotten soup I couldn't hold down and then bring me back whenever they felt like it; a few hours, a day, I lost track. Everything hurt. I was pissing blood. The tip of my penis was infected from the contact with the wires. But every time they'd get me in there I'd pass out before they could get anything. They couldn't stand it. They kept trying new tricks. One of them took one of those long razors and shaved a strip down the middle of my head. Big joke, everyone laughing, but the razor peeled into my scalp. Blood pouring over my face. It made me crazy. I spit at the guy and he smashed me in the face and I spit again, blood and chips of teeth right in his face."

He stopped abruptly.

"Now here's the interesting part," he said, shifting into the amused off-key tone he reserved for his more didactic points. "At a certain point I felt happy. The first time I lost consciousness. It's true. I felt that I had reached the border between life and death and when I realized I could resist to that point I was no longer afraid. I was ready to die. I welcomed the release of death. But this too is weakness, is it not? When they threw me back into the cell that time, I realized that I must not die, that I had to stay alive, that my life was not *my* life but belonged to something larger and that I had to resist, survive, return to the struggle."

He stroked his chin, his eyes hard, as if forcing himself back to the mere facts of the story.

"There was one last session. After it I woke up in a small dark space. I had no idea where I was. I could see the shapes of other people tossed around. I whispered, 'Does anyone know where we are?' There was no answer. I thought I heard groaning and tugged at the man next to me. The arm felt abnormally loose and I realized it was not attached to anything. I crawled over to the next person, and the next, working my way around until I was quite sure that everyone was dead. I have no idea how long I was there."

"But how did you get out?"

He smiled.

"I assume courtesy of army transport. I woke up in the river." He smiled. "Not far from your apartment."

The wind had picked up and bloated gray clouds skimmed above the hills. It was getting late and looked like rain. We had to think about leaving.

"Does Laura know about this?"

"Not in such detail."

"Thornby said her name was on a list."

"Yes. I know."

"Is she in danger?"

"More than she realizes. We are all in danger," he said. "That's why I carry this." He touched his hip where the pistol was. "I couldn't go through that again."

"But the way you travel around. They must know where you are."

"I keep moving." He studied the clouds coming over the hills. "We'd better head back."

"Can I ask you a stupid question?"

"It wouldn't be the first time."

"How could you get back into the university after all that happened? How could you work with Thornby and live so openly?"

That got a chuckle out of him.

"Army Intelligence isn't that intelligent. They never got my real name after they grabbed me. I just happened to be in the wrong place at the wrong time. They didn't know who they had. They won't make that mistake again."

There was one last stop on Manolo's tour, an old church on the plaza. Actually, all that remained of the colonial structure was an encrusted stonewall and behind it a small and rather ugly new church with wooden rafters and the usual icons. We stood by the front door for a while as I feigned a respectful silence. Two perfect columns of sunlight entered the darkened space from pinhole openings above the rafters and broke up against a near section of pews.

But the main source of light emanated from the floor in front of the marble altar. Flickering candles, some freshly lit, others nearly dead and guttering onto the cement floor, gave off an eerie golden glow that seemed to touch everything and yet illuminated nothing in the cool darkness. Barefoot Indians scuffed down the aisle, fixed new candles to the floor as they knelt to whisper a prayer, and then walked out slowly into the brutal sun. The church charged them 25 cents per candle.

A priest walked past us down the center aisle toward the door, his black shoes clicking smartly. Then he stopped in the doorway, hands on his hips, squinting into the grimy yard between the church and the wall.

A beggar—a clump of long filthy hair, ragged skin draped over bones— slumped against the base of a statue. The priest stood there glaring and then strode over to this apparition.

"You have to move," he said. The beggar's eyes never left the ground, but he mumbled a protest, his arms out, palms up, as if feeling for rain or perhaps beseeching the mercy of God. "You shut your mouth or

I'll shut it for you," the priest said. "You're not allowed in here. It's against the law. Now move!"

The man did as he was told, and the priest went back into the church.

"That's another reason we need a revolution in this country," Manolo said.

I went over to take a closer look at the statue. A woman with a Madonna's face, her body fluid in classical Greek finery, held two boys, one suckling and the other peering nobly into the distance. The inscription on the pedestal was very clear.

> *To Man and Woman*
> *Bless your Mother alive or dead because*
> *she is the branch of the tree from which*
> *you descend and the lamp of the country to*
> *which you go — A. Velasquez.*

I asked Manolo who A. Velasquez was. "Never heard of him," he said. He looked at his watch. "Come on. You've got a bus to catch."

NINETEEN

Laura sat next to the window with the little Sanchez boy in her lap. He wore a blue Superman T-shirt with the red S in a yellow triangle, his face covered with a long black kerchief to protect his sensitive eyes. He asked a lot of questions about where we were going. She did not have that patronizing tone that so many adults take with children. They were having a conversation.

We drove for a long time in the dark and after a while the boy fell asleep. Laura leaned her head on my shoulder and looked out at the night sky, crisp with stars, over the mountain wilderness.

"My mother has this expression," she said. "The sun, the moon, the stars. Whenever I asked for something I couldn't have. The sun and the moon are tough, she'd say, but I'll see what I can do about the stars. If I was lucky, I'd end up with a *little* piece of star."

"Were you disappointed?"

"I always felt guilty for expecting so much." She stroked the boy's head, soothing him into a deeper sleep. "My mother never got over my father getting killed. She remarried, got divorced, and of course the drinking doesn't help. I know she loves me, worries about me, but she doesn't understand what I'm doing here. At all."

"She should meet my father," I said. "Sounds like they'd be perfect for each other."

"Maybe we could arrange it."

"That would make us sister and brother," I said.

"You wouldn't like that."

"I wouldn't mind so much. We're practically that now anyway."

The boy began to stir, his tiny hand poking out from under the long veil and then roaming over Laura's face. "And Pedro," he called out for me, "where is Pedro?" and then with an edge of royal displeasure, "Where *are* you, Pedro?"

"Here I am."

The answer made him laugh, an old man's snorting laugh that, hidden behind the kerchief, sounded happy and absurd. "Your whiskers tickle," he said, touching my jaw, his other hand on Laura's cheek. "How come she hasn't any?"

The bus rattled violently.

"I'm a woman," she said.

And as I looked out at the dark mountain and bright stars I saw us in a quiet playground together pushing a kid on a swing. We were very happy and had known each other for a long time.

"What are you going to do when you go back to the States?" I asked her.

"You mean *if* I go back."

"How can you not go back? Actually, you might *have* to go back, right? If they kick you out."

"I don't think they will. My Country Director said he wanted me to stay."

"But eventually you'll leave," I said.

"I don't think I can do that."

"Of course you can."

"No." She shook her head slowly, her eyes steady on mine. "There are things we can do here that really would make a difference, *vos*."

"Like what? The Revolution?"

"Don't say it that way. *We* had a revolution, didn't we? And they had a revolution here in '44 that we strangled 10 years later. There are a lot of other people in this country like Manolo. We *need* you, *vos.*"

We. Not *I*. Not the two of us. At least I got that right. I was learning to read the signs now without having to get hit over the head.

"Ok," I said. "*If* you went back to the States, what would you do?"

"I don't know. Work in the South maybe."

It wasn't what I had in mind, but you never knew.

"Maybe we'll see each other sometime," I said.

The boy was getting restless again and she ran her hand in soft slow circles over his back. Then she stopped and looked at me.

"What do you want to do," she said, "pick up the pieces?"

I went dead inside. I wanted to tell her yes, I would even be willing to pick up the pieces, but I knew that wouldn't do any good either.

We were coming into the city now. The mixed patrols were out again, prowling the streets with their radios squawking. We pulled into the bus station on *Plaza Libertad* across the park from the National Palace. There were lights on in the Palace and sandbags piled on the steps.

We got off the bus and walked along the arcade until we found the local bus to Zone 12 that Laura and the kid needed to take. She helped him up the first step and turned around.

"Be careful," she said.

"You too."

She kissed me on the cheek and got on the bus behind the kid. In the arcade's shabby light I could barely make out her face in the window. The bus backed out and I watched from the corner until it was gone. Across the street some children were playing a game. Three girls had lined up in the spotlight against the mustard wall of the cathedral and now two boys pretended to execute them. I watched the girls fall forward, one by one.

After that night, I would hear from somebody that she'd been in town and when this happened two or three times and I didn't hear from her, I realized. It made sense. We'd finished the teacher's guide and didn't have that business to kick around anymore. What she was doing in Santa Cruz beyond her literacy centers was not something that included me. We both understood that. What remained was strictly personal and evidently not enough to interest her.

I left notes at her *pensión*, sent messages with people who might see her. Nothing came back. I was hurt that she'd done it that way, but I figured those were the breaks and did a pretty good job of convincing myself that it was now necessary to get on with whatever was left of my last couple of months in *The Land of Eternal Spring* without Laura Jenson.

One afternoon I went by the embassy to see Thornby and pick up my monthly check. He wasn't in but there was the check and a letter from some State Department official in Washington confirming the Mexico City arrangement for the last three months of my grant. I was ready to go. The sooner I forgot about Thornby and Laura and Manolo and all of these people, the better I would sleep at night.

I felt bad not being able to tell Laura that the *Times* had accepted the article. I was pleased to see the galleys: they had kept in just about all my critique of the literacy program. I made a few edits and sent them back. They hadn't given me a publication date, but I figured it would be just about the time I was on my way to Mexico.

III

Argelia

TWENTY

Late one afternoon about a week after I had heard from the *Times* there was a knock on my door. It was little Argelia with the body of a grape decked out in a new dress, three-inch heels and a fake leopard skin hat.

"See? I told you I'd be back, and here I am!"

The truth was that I did not recall her saying she'd be back. I didn't even remember about the Greek until later that night when she pulled out a set of panties, seven pairs in seven different colors, the latest booty from New Orleans.

"What do they say in your house when you go away on trips like this?"

"Oh, I tell them I'm going with a bunch of girlfriends to the country or the *puerto*. The trouble starts like now, when I stay away too long. Then my brother really wallops me. With a strap. I still have bruises from the last time." She displayed a large, dark area on the back of her arm. "This time he'll really let me have it. But it's worth it to see my baby. They don't even tell him that I'm his *mama*. When my friends call, they say I don't live there anymore. The last time my brother hit me so hard I had to stay in bed for three days. But she got even; she sold all the suits in his closet to some old bum who came around the house. For one quetzal! He was *furious*."

"And beat you again."

"He was too busy looking for the bum." Her eyes opened wide and locked on mine. "Nobody but nobody gets the best of *this* little girl."

She leaned back on the bed to unroll her stocking. There was a small mark on the inside of her thigh; I touched it.

"What happened here?"

"A dog bit me."

"Come on."

"That's the truth." I almost knew what was coming next. "A dog named Demetrious."

It was a joke that we both enjoyed.

"When's he coming back?"

"We had a fight. I could care less." She looked away shyly. "You must have someone, a guy like you."

I wondered how much Fernando had told her.

"I did," I said. "It didn't work out."

"I'm sorry to hear that."

What in the world went through my head in that moment? I was saving her from her wicked brother; I was living in sin; I was getting it for free. Even after Violeta and Laura and one or two other episodes that should have taught me something, I couldn't resist little Argelia with the body of a grape.

"Why don't you stay here for a while?"

She pressed her hand to her chest.

"You're going to give me a heart attack!"

"That means no?"

She let her head sink into the pillow and stared up dreamily at the ceiling.

"Well, I am more or less between residences at the moment."

She would go out two or three afternoons a week, occasionally at night, and I welcomed the blocks of time to work on my final report for Thornby because she quickly got bored when she stayed around the apartment. She had tired of solitaire, especially after I explained about cheating. We spent hours over the checkerboard. She was very careless, except when we had a bet, and then she would often win. She loved movies, the more epic and spectacular the better, and regularly reported on dreams of making it with Charlton Heston in the blazing desert or running naked through the marble halls of the palace in *Quo Vadis*.

She spent a week looking for a job, or so she said, assisted by an Uncle Gonzalo. There wasn't much that she could do and what there was paid miserably, but that wasn't the big problem. Argelia Mendizabal Cruz, who played at the beach houses of army colonels and once flew in the private plane of the richest man in the country, was not about to take a job as a waitress or sales clerk or—God forbid!—factory hand.

I didn't mind. She had her own spending money, borrowed from friends, she said, or drawn from a savings account she had prudently salted away for just such a contingency.

I was puzzled at first by small discrepancies. She was 21, then 19; she would leave the apartment on one errand and return chattering of another. Whenever I caught her in one of these inconsistencies, I would lecture her on mutual trust and the importance of telling the truth. She would bow her head and swear that she would never lie again, barely disguising her boredom with my high-minded ideas. I did believe them, however, believed that I could accept anything as long as it was the truth. It's still hard to admit, but this woman knew me better than I knew myself.

"You get more *Chapín* every day," Jacob Stein said. "You're never on time anymore."

He had invited me to lunch and was annoyed, but there was also a hint of peril in this unpatriotic fondness for the local customs. Jacob was getting ready to leave the country himself, never having been able to replace his stillborn national stock market study.

"I'm not *that* late," I said.

He smiled stiffly.

"That new broad keeps you busy."

"How'd you know about *her*?"

"Ran into Fernando García at the embassy. She sounds like a real doozy."

"She's interesting."

"You discuss Shakespeare and the great philosophers into the wee hours of the night."

I was not in the mood for this. Besides, when Jacob invited you to lunch he had an agenda. I was waiting for the ask.

"We have fun," I said.

Jacob squinted past me toward the street. We were in a little restaurant just off Sixth Avenue. It was cool and dark inside and the glare off the whitewashed walls outside was painful. Jacob leaned back in the chair, his fingers strumming the table.

"I'm going to Santa Cruz next week," he said, "and I'd really like you to come with me."

I tried not to think about the place.

"Why Santa Cruz?"

"It was Thornby's idea. He thought you'd like to go. They do it all over the country. Ambassadors of good will, people to people. I did it in Xela. You go to the school and answer a lot of dumb questions and then to some hacienda for a great meal. Come on, we'll have a ball. I don't want to go by myself."

"I've already been there."

"All the better!"

Across the street an Indian woman had stopped in front of a store window with a sign in English above her head—*MOST COMPLETE SELECTION OF AMERICAN PERIODICALS IN GUATEMALA*. It was unlikely that this woman could read or write *any* language, but she stood there gazing at the display of *Life, Good Housekeeping, Popular Mechanics*, standing there with hands clasped behind her back, feet apart, like a steady soldier in the point-blank sun. I tried to imagine what was going through her mind, and then I was thinking about Laura, wishing that she were here to see it too, this loaded, perishable image.

"I don't think so," I said.

"Come on. Do it for me."

"And help Thornby while we're at it."

"He's alright. Not an intellectual like us, but he means well. Deep down at heart he's just a grown-up farm boy. My only real complaint with the guy is that he doesn't appreciate the problems I had with my project."

I felt like needling him.

"What project?"

"You can joke about it. You're lucky. You've had something that really interests you. If it weren't for Cynthia, I don't know *what* I would have done."

Jacob had solved his woman problem—up to a point. Cynthia was a wealthy older American woman who took very good care of him, including in bed, about which I had gotten regular and embarrassingly detailed reports. The problem was they had agreed the relationship would end with his departure, which was imminent, and now she had changed her mind.

"It's like a Greek tragedy," he said. "You know what's going to happen but you're powerless to stop it. But it would never work. We have to end it." He leaned back and studied his fingernails. "I'm glad to leave this screwed up place, but I'm not looking forward to the rat race in New York. Are you still thinking about going to Mexico?"

"For a while. Maybe."

"When I think about it, what I could have done here, but how the hell did I know I was going to fall in love? As *Alber Camoo* says, when life appears absurd, one must admit defeat in the face of it." His mouth compressed thoughtfully, the point of his upper lip clamping down like a beak. "There's one last favor I'd like to ask of you. I need some letters of recommendation for my résumé. Would you mind doing one? You know, the regular crap, what a great guy I am. I got one from Thornby, a good letter, but that jerk Dubrow in the Economic Section gave me a very reluctant letter. Maybe he's still mad at me for dancing with his wife that night at Thornby's. She's a terrific dancer. He's a shit. I'm not going to use the letter. Of course you'll have to make yours sound like you're more important than you are."

"I'll give it a try."

"I knew I could count on you. I'll call you when I get back from Santa Cruz. Maybe I can pick up the letter then too."

I didn't think Jacob was such a bad guy, but it bothered me when he said how much alike we were. Maybe I just didn't want to see that. His style was more transparent and vulgar than mine, but he meant no harm. His mauling of Camus, on the other hand, seemed criminal at the time.

TWENTY-ONE

I got back to the apartment later in the afternoon and found Argelia sitting up in bed with a newspaper in her lap. She had taken a liking to my three-cent cigars, which I'd begun using as a cheap supplement to my pipe tobacco, and held one delicately between her fingers with a glass of beer in the other hand. I hesitated at the door and she laughed.

"*Mi mama* should see me now. Beer, cigar"—she slapped her belly with the cigar hand—"what sin!" I sat down on the bed and she found a page in the paper. She read only the horoscopes and society news. "Listen to Scorpio," she said. "A talk with someone in authority will give you a chance to air your views. Yet do not be too emphatic or seemingly abrupt. In the evening, friendly pleasure is favored."

"I like the last part."

I kissed her neck; she was naked under the sheet.

"It doesn't say anything about Mexico," she said.

She knew I was leaving and wanted to come. I'd been evasive for what seemed a perfectly good reason. I didn't know if I wanted her there. At least Jacob knew what he wanted and didn't want.

"That's because they only tell you what you already know," I said.

"You don't say."

She picked up a piece of paper and began studying it with sullen concentration.

"What's that?"

"Nothing."

"Let me see."

She threw it at me.

"You always have to know everything, don't you?" It was a list of song titles, beginning with "Love Is The Many Esplendor Ting." She wouldn't touch the paper when I put it down. "Are you satisfied now?" Her lips curled with lusty impudence. "All of a sudden you can't talk."

"I can talk."

"Talk then."

"I don't want to talk."

Her knee rose under the sheet as her hand reached out carelessly, her voice smooth and firm. "Come here, my love. She knows what you want." I sank into her, a good tight fit, and we did it quick and hard. When we fell away, she stared at the ceiling, a lone pinpoint of light in each eye.

"You were singing," I said.

In the dreary late afternoon light she looked young and vulnerable and almost beautiful.

That night we went to the *Llave*, a theoretically private club high on one of Argelia's lists where you had the privilege of paying way too much for a bottle of mediocre Scotch. We didn't have a key, but the doorman knew her and ushered us in like regulars. It was a dark room with a glowing red screen behind the bandstand and the tacky bareness of the silly imitation it was, the endeavor of a coffee *finquero* who had visited the new Playboy Club in New York and decided it was just what his country needed. The *Llave* would soon go broke and the *finquero* would find another venture for his pin money.

We ordered a bottle and greasy beef *tortas* and took a couple of turns on the dance floor. She was a great dancer, with all those whirls and dips and slow pointed kicks that I'd only seen in movies. But her real talent was in creating the illusion that I too could dance. She'd start to sway and pick up the beat and slowly bring me into it until I was moving along all on my own and right there with her. Back at the table I would watch the action and feel grateful for having been initiated into this wonderful society of dancers. We were not always successful, however, in disguising my clumsiness.

"You have to try this one," she said, taking my hand. "It's not hard."

The *Cumbia*, her latest passion, was my downfall that night. She showed me the steps while we waited for the music. Then the band started and I just couldn't follow her. We'd begin together, I'd lose the rhythm and she'd spin away until she was dancing alone, hands above her head and then curling down the contours of her body as though tracing an object of supreme sensuality. She was putting on quite a show. After a while it was just Argelia and the band. The music stopped to the applause of every man in the joint, a drunken shout, and we sat down. She stirred her watery drink, poking the ice cubes.

"I wouldn't mind being one of those go-go dancers. I've seen them in New Orleans. Either that or work in a record store."

"In New Orleans?"

"Anywhere. But New Orleans is a great place. Clubs like this everywhere, but not as expensive. And everyone knows all the neat songs."

"Not like me."

She laughed.

"You have other points to recommend you, my love."

"Like?"

"You know." She turned away with her little girl shyness. "Why do you always ask me questions you know the answers to? Just to hear me say stupidities?"

"They're not stupidities."

"They are. But what difference does it make. You're going to Mexico and you're leaving this little *Chapina* here. Tell me that's not true."

"I told you the problems. No job, not much money. We couldn't come to places like this."

"You think that's what interests me?" She shook her head. "You don't know me at all."

"Do we have to decide now?"

"It takes time to get my papers arranged."

"You could come after I found a job."

"Hah! I can see you don't know Mexican women. They're tigers and they're beautiful. You wouldn't last a minute—" She held up her hand. "You know the name of that song they're playing?"

"No."

"Time Erases All."

"It's only a song."

"But it means something. The man who wrote it had something in mind, didn't he?" I started to light a cigarette; she took the matches and struck one, cupping it expertly in her hand. "I never talk seriously," she said, "but that doesn't mean I don't love someone." I was feeling the booze, the room dimming into soft noisy fiber. "I'm going to be frank with you," she said. "I look over and see those women and wonder what will happen to me." There were two couples. The women laughed a lot and you could tell they were whores because they touched the men too often and too delicately. "I'm afraid. Especially after you leave."

"What are you talking about?"

She leaned forward and the words came rushing out.

"This. I am thinking that maybe each person is born with her destiny and some have the destiny of becoming a bad woman and others no. I'm telling you I'm afraid. I have friends like those girls. They come calling on *me*. Argelia, let's go here, let's go there, a big party, another tomorrow. They introduce you to a friend and then you go with the friend who introduces you to another." She jiggled the ice in her glass. "But I don't think I could ever do it for money. To go with some ugly old coot just because he can buy you nice things. I'd rather stay in my house where I have everything I need. I'd rather be a *servant*," though this last possibility did cause her to genuflect rapidly. "I don't know, maybe there's something wrong with me, but what does a man want with a woman like that? He's not interested in her face or what she's like or anything. He just wants to satisfy himself, right?" She finished her drink and cracked the ice in her mouth. "I'm afraid what will happen when you leave."

"Have you ever done that? Gone with a guy for money?"

"*Me!* Is *that* what you think of me? You think I would do something like that?" She stared into her empty glass, shaking her head. "If I had not heard this with my own ears, I would not have believed it. You have hurt me very much."

"I'm sorry."

"Not that I haven't had the chance."

"Tell me the truth, Argelia. Have you?"

"Never."

"Not even once?"

"Once," she said, without missing a beat.

"You did."

"Once I did." She laughed. "With that old fart Don Gonzalo."

"Your *uncle*?"

"He's not really my uncle. She just *told* you that. Now she's very embarrassed. You're not angry?"

I was not angry. She is who she is, I thought. At least now I understood the unpredictable hours, the confusing stories, the new friends who kept turning up and disappearing. I was also not a complete fool and did not believe it happened only once. What I missed entirely, so desperate to fill at least some of the emptiness left by Laura, was the timing of Argelia's reappearance so soon after my trip to Santa Cruz.

"You told me the truth," I said. "That's important."

"What about Mexico?"

Mexico, I thought, where the women were tigers and beautiful, like my ferocious little Argelia.

"You know the problems," I said.

She leaned back and threw her arms out grandly.

"My love, in these golden times, who has to worry about money?"

"Seriously, Argelia."

"Listen, in the few weeks we have left here do you know how much I can make? If I go out only five times with that old fart, that's five hundred bucks. Arithmetic I know, and they say she's stupid. In Mexico that's a small fortune, and in Mexico it will be different. Nobody to bother us, no stupid family, no more stupid work that pays you shit with that stupid Fernando and those stupid little booklets. We'll take trips to Acapulco, we'll go to the movies, and you should see the *bookstores* in Mexico. Hah! As if I didn't know, look at his eyes light up. And I have a friend there, Pinche, I could look him up. Any time you come to Mexico, he tells me, look up Pinche. He knows all the right people."

This did not sound good. "Let's not talk about it now," I said.

The band crashed into a furious merengue. Argelia
sat there, stone silent, smoking her cigarette between
rigid fingers.

TWENTY-TWO

Early the next morning there was an unusual amount
of activity in the apartment as her old crony Margo
showed up and was greeted by a dazzling Argelia—
new dress, swirling hairdo, blazing nail polish. I sat at
my desk reading the paper, half aware of the busy
noises from the bathroom, whispered conversation,
then the clatter of heels like an army on the march as
they came down the hallway from the bedroom.

"I'm walking Margo to the corner," she said.

"We need some coffee," I said.

She came over to get money for the coffee, turning
her face away. There was something awkward in the
gesture.

"See you in a little bit," she sang, closing the door
gently.

I went back to the paper. A Guatemala City
journalist, Julio Cesar de la Roca, 38, had been found
dead Thursday on the side of the road to
Quetzaltenango with a note pinned to his eye saying
"an eye for an eye—Anti-Communist Council of
Guatemala." Another note on his body said de la Roca
was a member of the Communist Party and the *Fuerzas
Armadas Rebeldes*, the leftist guerrilla group that had
"kidnapped and killed honored citizens." Two other

men had been killed in similar fashion earlier in the week. The bodies of Francisco Barreno, 35, and Elias Rojas, 33, were found Monday and Tuesday beside the highway between Guatemala City and El Salvador. The victims' families said they had been taken from their homes by gunmen.

I closed the paper and went back to work on the final report for Thornby. Time was getting short. He had asked me to fix up the draft I had given him. In the first place, he said, I had not followed the Project Exit Review Guidelines— eight dense pages of questions and prompts designed to suck every last morsel of conceivably useful information out of your brain. Secondly, the whole thing needed to be "toned down," he said. I didn't feel like fighting him any more-- though I refused to drop this wonderful quote from Laubach:

> *We now have the technical know-how to make illiterates literate on a large scale, and experience has demonstrated that mass literacy campaigns will work. What, then is missing? Can it be that the fires of enthusiasm and vision for literacy are still mere flickers in the hearts of too many of the world's leaders?*

"You're helping dig your own grave with that one, kid," was how Thornby terminated the discussion. He didn't know of course that I had put a version of it into the *Times* article.

At that moment I was laboring over the very last question in the official Project Exit Review Guidelines. *Please include any other information you think would be helpful for an American student in your host country.* It was the only time I laughed doing the report for Thornby.

I wasn't concerned when Argelia had still not returned by lunchtime. She would often leave with a breezy remark and not come back for hours. I went out for a walk and a bite to eat later in the afternoon. When I got back to the apartment, there was a note on the door from the janitor to call Margo with a phone number. I went up to his office to use the phone there.

"A terrible thing has happened," she began breathlessly. They had met up with Argelia's brother in the street. He had beaten her—with a strap, across the face—hurled her into his car and driven off. "It was horrible," she concluded.

I was dazed: that smooth bright face beaten to a bloody pulp.

"Have you called the police?" I asked.

"Oh no. It's her brother. I wouldn't worry. Well, I just wanted you to know," she said, and hung up.

I called Fernando.

"She's lying," he said.

"What happened then?"

"I don't know, but she does." There was a long pause. "Call her back and tell her if she doesn't tell you the truth, Fernando says she is going to be in big trouble."

I was now confused and very angry. I called her back and she repeated the story about running into the brother.

"Fernando says if you don't tell me the truth, you're going to be in big trouble."

It took her so long to respond I thought she might have hung up.

"You must promise never to tell her that I told you," she said finally.

"I promise."

"You know where she is."

"No, I don't."

"She's gone to the *puerto* to meet Demetrious."

It hit me like a physical blow. I could not believe how it hit me.

"Are you sure?"

"She's been planning it for weeks."

I went back to my apartment. The light scent of her perfume grew heavier toward the bedroom, a disturbing presence in the empty rooms. I would come home and find her in bed or sitting on the sofa with the radio pressed to her ear. A fast tune would send her dancing around the room and then something blue plunge her into deepest melancholy until she would have to sit down, eyes shut against the pain, awaiting the outcome of this or that version of love lost or love betrayed.

Her dirty clothes were piled in the closet next to her overnight case. I poked through the rubble of cosmetics, combs, scraps of paper with names and phone numbers—and two letters from Demetrious. How he missed her, wanted her, the presents he would bring from New Orleans, passionate declarations in broken Spanish and childish script. The language she needed to hear and that I denied her.

The man in the signed snapshot was older than I had imagined, hair thinning, a nice smile, leaning against the cabin of a ship. Perhaps he loved her, I thought, loved her more than I ever would. And this unfinished letter from Argelia—on *my* typewriter!— *Señor Demetrious Stanatopolous, my darling love, every day that passes are like years for me....*

I should have been relieved that her taking off like that had solved the Mexico problem, but nothing about my attraction to this woman was rational.

The bottoms of her pajamas were thrown over the back of a chair. Had she taken the tops? I saw her like that in the Greek's bed and felt a cold, murderous fury.

TWENTY-THREE

Fernando came by the next morning and immediately commenced drinking from his bottle of *indita*, a raw white alcohol with a rosy-cheeked maiden on the label.

He kept apologizing for introducing this miserable girl to me, his dear friend, and what I had to do was smack her around good when she came back because it was the only way they learned. I barely heard him. He was talking about two other people. He was talking about a world I didn't know. Besides, how could she come back now, after this?

He was angry and maudlin and manic in waves and after an hour or so I couldn't take it any more.

"I'd like to be alone, Fernando."

He looked at me like a child who had just been reprimanded.

"Sometimes you seem so distant, Peter. Like you don't care what happens with us." He took a swallow from his bottle of *indita*. "Or don't approve. That would be most sad." He shook his head. "Most sad."

He was giving me that lost-puppy-dog look again but then I saw the cunning that lurked behind it, something I liked but did not trust. He had his orderly political agenda but also the torment of an emotional life that neither he nor anyone he knew understood. He reached for the bottle again and then put his hand on my knee.

"You know," he said. "I like you a lot. I mean *a lot*."

His hand and intensity were disturbing.

"I know."

"I have always hoped we could become good friends, really good friends. Do you understand what I'm saying? When one man says that to another man?"

His eyes were pleading. "You don't understand, you don't understand," he said, and started to cry.

This I did not need. It didn't make any difference if he were making a pass or trying to tell me something else. He spoke in a code I couldn't decipher and didn't want to. But I also didn't want to make him feel any worse than he did.

"We *are* friends," I said. "I consider you a good friend."

"Do you mean that?"

"Of course."

But he could tell I was lying.

"The Saxon is cold," he said softly. "Your race is very distinct from the Latin."

The crisis had passed and his spirits revived. He insisted that I accompany him to a dinner that night at the Embassy Residence. I'd gotten the invitation myself and threw it away. There was some exhibit in town and they were also honoring Thornby, who had been reassigned somewhat abruptly to Washington. Everyone would be there, Fernando said. He was cheering himself up, talking about all the fun we would have. Fantastic food, important people, and then we go find two beautiful women at Locha's and lose ourselves in their succulent bodies. He was prancing around the room, putting the move on imaginary broads and guessing correctly that it would get me to smile at his antics. I felt sorry for him. It wouldn't help in the long run but at least made me feel a little less sorry for myself.

So I took a shower and got dressed. The occasion called for the Brooks Brothers suit my father had bought for my college graduation and I had worn maybe twice. I admired the handsome young man in the full-length mirror that Argelia had installed in the bedroom. My father would be proud, I thought, but it still felt like a disguise.

"A little detour," Fernando said on our way to the Embassy Residence. It was something I had to see. I would be pleased. There was one exhibit I would be *very* pleased with because—he paused for effect, the way he would with the punch line to one of his jokes— "They are using your literacy materials!"

"What are you *talking* about?"

"You'll see."

The Education for Progress Exhibit had been erected on a soccer field in one of the fancier suburbs, two corrugated huts the size of airplane hangars which would be dismantled when the show moved on to the next country. At the entrance was an enormous photo of Lyndon Johnson sporting his slightly constipated smile and, just above his head, *Education Creates A More Abundant Life For All.*

There were speedboats and swimming pools, model kitchens and model bathrooms and pyramids of TV sets and stereos blasting away. There was an alcove

with hair dryers, beauty creams and 14 varieties of
shampoo. There were huge tractors with shiny virgin
wheels surrounded by photos of happy American
farmers going to church and frolicking with their
children.

A live, blonde, blue-eyed Winchester cowgirl stood
on a platform, lifting rifles off a rack as men gawked at
her fish-netted legs and delicate behind.

Good job for Argelia, I thought, not knowing
whether to laugh or cry at what I was seeing. "Where's
the literacy stuff?" I asked Fernando.

The poor guy seemed almost as confused as I was
but also constantly distracted by the goods on display.
He suggested we try the next building. But the next
building was all cars, a great silky banner—IT'S 1964
AT WIDETRACK TOWN—floating above a shiny sea of
metal, a showroom to dwarf all showrooms and surely
for a lot of people that night a sight as dazzling as
those visions of gold that held the first Spaniards in
thrall.

"I think we missed it," I said.

So we doubled back and sure enough tucked behind
one of the model kitchens was the model literacy class.
The model teacher held a microphone, explaining a
movie you could barely see in the glare of the
fluorescent lights. The model students squirmed in
their plastic chairs. And there on a rear table was a
mock-up of the teacher's guide I had given Thornby
and the colonel, smartly placed between a set of

microscopes and two globes with translucent blue oceans and continents in jeweled relief. A sign thanked the Gotham Educational Equipment Company and Bell & Howell for their generous cooperation.

I couldn't believe it. I was glad Laura wasn't around to see this. I wondered if she even knew this circus was in town. Fernando put his arm around my shoulder.

"What did I tell you," he said.

"Fernando, there isn't a classroom like this in the whole goddamn country and never will be."

He had that hang-dog look again.

"You're not pleased?"

"Let's get out of here," I said.

He kept trying to explain as we drove to the Embassy Residence, how the exhibit was about the beautiful future and not the ugly present, but I wasn't listening now as we drove through the wide streets, past the big houses behind iron gates and walls with shards of broken glass cemented along the top.

Here and there soldiers stood guard at the home of one of the 400 colonels of an army reputed to have more colonels than lieutenants. It was a bad time for civilian governments throughout the hemisphere, but these soldiers in the shadows looked less like warriors than refugees, tense and weary, their stoic mountain faces and squat bodies too small under the surplus American helmets and fatigues.

There was a crowd at the Residence. Thornby had his wife in tow, an attractive, excessively cheerful woman with dangling gold earrings and rather hard eyes.

"This is *so* exciting," she said. "You must be very proud of the work you've done with Robert. He speaks so highly of you."

Thornby stood there, his huge hand wrapped around his drink, gazing absently into the noisy room.

"We just went to the exhibit," Fernando said. "They had one of Peter's booklets there."

"Oh, that *is* exciting," she said.

"It came in very handy," Thornby said to me now. "I wanted to thank you. Where you been? I assume you saw the letter approving the Mexico City arrangement. We still have some unfinished business." That would be Santa Cruz, I thought. "I want to get it resolved before I leave myself," he said.

"Have you ever been to Bolivia?" his wife asked me. "They're doing some *terribly* interesting things with literacy in Bolivia."

"I wasn't aware of that."

"Robert was there last month," she said. "In the middle of all that trouble with Estenssoro. But they got rid of that guy for good this time. The army's taken over, thank God. He was really a miserable president."

"Why do you say that?" I asked.

Mrs. Thornby was amazed.

"You don't *know?* Paz Estenssoro? Of course it's only a rumor, but they say he shot his wife so he could marry his mistress. They say she died of heart trouble." She broke into a charming smile. "A bullet in the heart."

"I love it!" Fernando said, then took her away by the arm. I caught his voice from across the room insisting with some people they had to hear this story. Thornby was watching them too. He glanced around, and then waved at someone.

"Well, look who's here," he said.

I had forgotten how beautiful she was. It was very strange. I had forgotten her face. For an instant I was startled to see the soft large mouth and high cheeks and the hair curled around her throat—then the old feelings snapped into place. Her voice came through the familiar screen of tension and a million unanswered questions.

"Hello, *vos.*"

"I didn't think you liked these affairs."

"No more than you," she said. "But I thought this one might be interesting."

It was bad enough having the knife stuck into this wound again, but with Argelia's treachery still so raw this was almost diabolical. I wanted this woman standing in front of me to explain herself, why she withdrew so completely from my life and why she was there now.

Thornby asked if she had been to the exhibition.

"Wouldn't have missed it," she said.

"How are things in Santa Cruz?" he asked.

Laura glanced at me and then smiled at Thornby.

"The usual," she said.

"I hope you're steering clear of these student demonstrations here," he said. "They're getting out of hand." The students had been in the streets for the past week, demanding that the military government of General Enrique Peralta Azurdia set a date for the long-delayed elections. Thornby was annoyed with the general. "Enrique's problem is he doesn't want to fight," he said. "He isn't a coward. But he isn't willing to spill Guatemalan blood."

"What do you think will happen?" Laura asked him.

"We'll find someone who is," he said. "One thing about these guys, they know which side their bread is buttered on."

Thornby sipped at his drink, his eyes scanning the room over the rim of his glass.

Laura and I looked at each other.

Everyone was summoned into the dining room and took our assigned seats. Thornby sat opposite me near the head of the table by the ambassador himself. Laura was a couple of chairs down from Thornby, just out of conversation range.

The ambassador was a California real estate developer who had put enough dough on a winning presidential candidate to land himself a third-rate embassy. A man of medium height, paunchy, his face flushed from booze or exertion or both: the daunting authority of the United States Ambassador to the Republic of Guatemala could be detected only in the confident gray eyes and deep voice.

A year later he would be killed by the *FAR* in a bungled kidnapping.

"So you decided on the soup after all," he said to his daughter, sitting next to me. As the conversation roamed through the culinary delights of the Western world, I became increasingly restless. Here was my chance to go right to the top with the problems in the literacy program—and it was being squandered in moronic small talk.

"And what do you do, Sandra?" I asked the young woman, who looked a lot like her father.

"Nothing," she said sweetly.

I sensed a trap and proceeded cautiously.

"Aren't you bored?"

"No." Her smile was fixed. "I used to take guitar lessons." Then, as if sensing my incomprehension, "I just love to be with my family. I guess that's old-fashioned these days."

"Not at all," I protested.

The ambassador chimed his knife against a glass to introduce the Assistant Director of the *Instituto Guatemalteco Americano*. A round little man rose at the far end of the table and held his glass out, his voice trembling.

"Tonight we honor a certain man, a great friend of Guatemala, a great friend of Latin America named Roberto Thornby. We cry for how much we will miss him. He does so much I cannot tell you, but *how* he has done all these things. We know the wonderful English classes he made at the Institute, but most important is how did Roberto teach, how did he teach his teachers to teach? I tell you. He showed us the English as a live thing. Adjective? What's that? Like something you eat? Every day more students are coming, little workers, big shot lawyers, doctors, police, you name it you got it." He lifted his head dramatically, his tone now hushed and solemn. "Roberto Thornby believes what Christ believed. He believes in making people happy. I am not going to make more speech but only to say what is in my heart. Roberto is very like another man who recently disappeared. I don't have to mention his name, a very great man who we all loved and who truly loved Latin America and wanted friendship and peace with all. That great man, John Fitzgerald Kennedy. And now"—he raised his glass—"*no tengo más que decir que* Long Live America!"

There was enthusiastic applause and the little round man took a couple of bows before sitting down.

Laura picked away at her ice cream, avoiding eye contact. The ambassador turned to me.

"You've done some work with Thornby, haven't you?"

"Yes, sir. With the literacy program. Studying the effectiveness of some of the materials they use."

"To tell you the truth," he said, "I think we've put too much emphasis on literacy. I don't see what good it does to teach people to read a lot of propaganda, frankly."

Laura was listening now. I was reminded of that night we met, when she had hovered at the edges of the argument I was having with those guys who thought the State Department was sowing the seeds of revolution.

"But if they can read propaganda," I said, "there's a lot of other things they can read."

The ambassador nodded diplomatically.

"Oh, I know. Health techniques, farming methods." He nodded again. "All very helpful stuff." Then he got up and went around the table shaking hands. I couldn't believe it. I thought about my article and regretted that I had not been a lot harder on these people.

"Daddy amazes me," Sandra said. "Whenever I try to argue with him he always knows so much about everything." Then she looked at me blankly. "Do you like it here?" she asked.

A moment later Laura came around the table and asked if I would like to get some fresh air. I got up and followed her toward the front hallway. A butler opened the door. On the steps outside she slowed down and took my arm but didn't look at me.

"I can't stand being in the same room with you," she
said

TWENTY-FOUR

Our footsteps crunched into the gravel driveway. The
Marine guard waved us through the gate and we
walked along the edge of the street, stepping over the
bony roots of trees that had cracked the pavement.
Laura stopped and leaned back against a tree and
looked me up and down.

"You look so dapper tonight," she said.

"Thank you."

She took my arm and leaned against me. "That's not
a *compliment*," she said sweetly. I'd forgotten that too,
the gentle way we could make fun of each other. I
wanted to kiss her, but I was remembering all the other
times when it only left me aching.

"Did you see the teacher's guide?" I asked.

She nodded. "I saw it."

"We worked so hard on that thing," I said.

"And it ends up a prop."

"Worse than a prop," I said. "A sales pitch for some
company in Chicago."

"We tried, *vos*."

"We tried and we failed." Then the question that
had been there from the moment I had seen her an
hour ago. "Why did you stop coming to see me?"

"It was just easier that way." Down the street people were coming out of the Residence and getting into cars. "It's also possible you're being watched."

"I haven't noticed anyone."

"You're not supposed to." A dog barked in the distance. "Someone told me you have a new girlfriend."

"I guess nobody has any secrets in this country."

"How's it going?"

"We have our good days and our bad days."

"Do you enjoy making love to her?"

That seemed like a very odd question.

"When she's around," I said. "At the moment she's gone, flown the coop, but I'm told she's coming back. It should be interesting."

"You always did like that word."

"It covers a lot of territory."

"I know." We started walking again. Some cars went past and then it was quiet, the air intense with night-blooming flowers, so sweet and moist, like entering another dimension. "What are you thinking, *vos?*"

"I wish you wouldn't ask me that."

"But I did."

"You know what I'm thinking. I'm hopelessly in love with you."

She gave me a troubled smile.

"You're in love with an *idea* you have of me, *vos*. I'm not even sure what it is. But it's not me."

"It *is* you."

"You'd get tired of me."

"Or vice versa."

"Don't you think it was a little insane," she said, "the way we were in the beginning?"

"Insane?"

"The way we laughed at everything. We were very silly."

"A little," I said. "We still are."

I could not believe how much I wanted her. We turned down the Reforma, walking along the path under the big heavy trees. There was a powder blue haze in the sky like a fine blizzard, a velvet darkness to the warm night. And then her hurried, almost furtive question.

"Can we go back to your place for a little while?"

It seemed like there was some justice in the world after all. I felt a balance restored, events and people settling into their assigned places in a moral universe: Argelia with the Greek and me with Laura. If you wanted something badly enough, it was still possible to believe that sooner or later the gods would deliver.

We made our way along the dark avenue, past the regular crew of hustlers and drunks on the corner by the railroad station, into my building and up the one flight of stairs. I hesitated at the door of the apartment, not knowing exactly why, and then, as I opened the door, realized that I never left the light on.

Argelia was sitting on the sofa in a white vest too small to fit over her bra, the effect both ludicrous and erotic. She tried to smile, but her head and eyes were too heavy and she couldn't bring it off. I noticed a jar of instant coffee on top of my typewriter. It took me a moment to recall that when she left the other morning I had asked her to bring back some coffee. Never missed a trick, my little *Chapina* with the body of a grape.

"Come in, my love. Don't be shy. And this must be your friend that I've heard so much about. How do you do? Pleased to meet you."

I closed the door.

"I didn't think you were coming back," I said.

"I'll *bet* you didn't." She gave Laura a big smile. "Can I get you a drink, sweetie?"

"No thank you."

"Something to eat?"

"I really can't stay," she said.

"Can't *stay?* I won't hear of it! I get you a little beer." She stood up, took a step, crashed into the bookcase and went sprawling on the floor. "How *clumsy* she is!" She raised a limp arm in my direction. "Help me up, dear."

I lifted her and she leaned into me, her arms tight around my waist; her heavy-lidded eyes struggling to focus on Laura.

"She's not so pretty. Look at that dress. I wouldn't let my *maid* wear a rag like that."

"Argelia."

"Yes, my love."

She snuggled into me, her breath pure alcohol.

"I'm putting you to bed," I said.

"Go ahead. Put her to bed. Give her the boot. Why do you need this piece of *shit*, right?"

I walked her down the hallway and she flopped onto the bed.

"I'll be back soon."

"Don't hurry, my love." She was crying. "I can take care of myself."

Laura was waiting at the door. We walked down the stairs to the street. The pool hall and the bars and one of the beauty parlors were still open. There were an astonishing number of beauty parlors in the city.

"Are you staying at the *pensión*?"

"No. In Zone 12. I can get a bus up the street here."

We started walking up 18th Street.

"When will I see you again?"

"I don't know," she said. "You're still going to Mexico next month?"

"That's the plan. I didn't tell you. The *Times* took the article."

"See? I told you."

"It was a long shot."

"A lot of good things in life are long shots."

We walked past the big shoe store with its window still lit up.

"I need a way to get in touch with you," I said.

"That's probably not a good idea now."

"In an emergency."

She took a matchbook out of her bag and wrote down an address in Zone 12.

"They usually know how to find me when I'm in the city," she said. "The house is right behind a big factory."

The buses were lined up across the street against the platform behind the Central Market. The bus for Zone 12 had its engine running and was boarding passengers.

We walked around a barefoot man sprawled under a lamppost, dirty spittle caked around his lips and chin, his eyes staring with terror into the streetlight.

"You never gave it a chance," I said. "With time, you don't know what might have happened with us."

"Not time," she said softly. "Timing."

The words had a terrible finality to them.

TWENTY-FIVE

In the bedroom Argelia lay very still under the covers. I went into the bathroom. The sink was smeared with blood. Then I noticed the clumps of stained Kleenex on the floor and my heart started racing. I went over to the bed and stood there. She had fresh lipstick and powder on her face, her eyes closed, like a corpse in an open casket. I pulled the blanket back and saw the scraped cuts on her wrists. Then her eyes opened.

"I loved you so much," she said.

I looked at her wrists and wondered if she had meant it. The cuts were superficial. I couldn't remember ever telling her about my mother. That only made it worse. She just knew how something like this would get to me.

"I didn't think you were coming back."

Her eyes flared.

"Why shouldn't I come back? Don't you know what happened?"

There was the evil brother, a chase through the streets, and a final harrowing escape to her auntie's house, where, trembling with fright, she had downed far too many little whiskies, to steady her nerves, you understand, this the cause of her "unfortunate state" at the moment.

"But that was almost two days ago," I said.

"Wait. There's more."

"Margo told me everything," I said.

"Fat mouth."

"Why did you go?"

"You won't believe me."

I felt a surge of anger.

"I want to know *why* you went, *why* you didn't tell me, *why* you came back. And I want the *truth*."

"So many *questions*. They make her poor little head spin," she said, twirling her finger in my face.

That's when I slapped her, hard, across the face. She ran her hand up and down her cheek.

"Nobody treats me this way," she said.

What was I doing? The murderous venom began to drain out of me.

"I'm sorry. I never did anything like that before."

"What an honor to be the first." She shook her head slowly. "I loved you so much. I only went to get my things so I could go to Mexico with you. Demetrious had my papers and passport because he was going to arrange a trip to New Orleans for me."

She could make anything sound plausible. Assume she's lying, I thought. Assume she is scheming right now about the next time the ship comes in. Assume that is just the way she is and nothing I can do will ever change her. Then what? I didn't know, except that there was something here I didn't want to lose. I was very tired and didn't have any answers and my stomach was growling. I patted her belly.

"You hungry?"

"Starved."

"Let's get something to eat."

"Okay. But first I have to get fixed up." She went into the bathroom and turned on the shower. "Aren't you going to say something about my hair?" We had a running argument about the beehives and bird nests and all the other constructions that ruined her thick black hair.

"I'm not saying a word."

She came out of the shower, wringing her hair, pretending to hunt for a towel so she wouldn't have to look me in the eye. It seemed impossible, this shyness, if that's what it was. I took her face in my hands but still could not get her to look at me. I dried her back with the towel. "You get me," she said, as I dabbed the wide soft shoulders that I did love and the pure black hair and the slow eyes stealing a look now, "you really get me."

There must be many ways to love a woman, I thought. Who could say that one kind of love was better than another? Standing there in the steamy room with Argelia and her moist nakedness, there was just more of it, more of her, and that overwhelmed the other that I wanted but did not believe I would ever have.

There was something else, about right and wrong, that eluded me at the moment.

Later that week the papers carried a blurred photo of a soldier pointing his rifle into a crowd. Three kids were killed. Now the high school students had taken to the streets, demanding that Peralta Azurdia and the junta resign. Evidently Thornby had found someone to give the order to shoot. There was also an item about an attack on a police station and the death of two terrorists during an operation conducted by the security forces in Zone Three.

"How long are you going to read that stupid paper?" Argelia said.

"You know what's happening?"

"I heard on the radio." She was doing her nails. "Do you like the color? Nacreous rose."

"Looks like bubble gum."

"You *would* say something like that." She shrugged. "What do I care? All my friends like it."

"It's a nice color."

There was something about this brief exchange that made me slightly ill. The stale smoke from my pipe that clung to just about everything in the room didn't help. I needed a break, from Argelia, the newspapers, the documents and the books that cluttered my desk. Thornby still wasn't happy with my report

"I'm going out for a walk," I said.

"It's late."

"I won't be long."

She went back to her nails without comment.

There was a fine mist in the night that felt good. I passed two girls huddled on the corner and saw Don Percy standing in the doorway of his *pensión*. He waved me over. He was a West Indian who had come to Guatemala after the 1937 hurricane and with all of his savings bought the *pensión*, which, as he often intimated, had once served a far better clientele than its current customers: whores and winos, dispossessed Indians, assorted hustlers and men on the run.

A tall, emaciated man staggered past in stocking feet.

"It's a hard little country," he said, the lilt of the islands still thick in his speech. "So many lost ones, spreading out all over the city." We are both foreigners, his heavy eyes said, we have a common perspective on this awful mess. "I just believe you should do good. A man should just try to do good and not bother his neighbor with his problems. He shouldn't go showing it on the streets like all these peoples. A man should bear his own sins and know his own pain."

His pudgy fingers probed under his dingy sweater, his brown face muted in the shadows of the doorway.

"What about women, Don Percy? Do the same rules apply?"

"Women are different. They are the weak creatures of God and the Devil knows it. He uses the woman to corrupt the man. That's in the Bible, you know." I asked him where in the Bible. "I doesn't recall at the moment," he said. "But you'll find it if you look."

He brought me a sliced apple and hot tea and would have kept me half the night serving up snacks and philosophy, but he nabbed a couple trying to sneak out on a two-quetzal tab and in the commotion I got away and went back to the apartment.

The light was on in the living room, the scent of her nail polish still strong. The bedroom was dark. I went over to the bed and she opened her eyes.

"You certainly took your time," she said.

She sat up and crossed her arms. She was wearing one of my turtlenecks. Then I saw the three suitcases lined up next to the door.

"What's with the suitcases?"

"I'm leaving."

It was pure soap opera. I felt like laughing.

"Where are you going?"

"I don't know. What do you care?"

She went into the bathroom. It was very quiet. I went over and listened at the door, thinking about the other night when she cut her wrists. I kept asking her what she was doing, but she didn't answer. In the silence I imagined the worst and then couldn't stand it. I slammed into the door, knocking her back against the toilet as bottles crashed to the floor. She stared at a broken bottle of aftershave lotion.

"That's how much you care about my present," she said.

The aftershave had been a recent peace offering.

"I'm sorry. It was an accident."

"Maybe I can't buy you nice things like your rich *gringa*. You should stay with her. You'd like that a lot better than the shit I give you."

"You've got it all wrong."

"Do I? Mister Innocent. Tell me you weren't just out seeing her."

"I wasn't just out seeing her. I went for a walk. I was talking with Don Percy."

"The queer that runs that fleabag? What were you doing *there*?" She was manufacturing another crisis with its opportunity to run through an astonishing but unpredictable and always exhausting emotional range. She was a genius at this, and I felt my life sliding out of control. This woman with her power over me and the other one I was still in love with and all the work that had added up to a big fat zero. This wasn't what I had in mind when I set out on my exemplary little mission to teach the masses how to read and write. Not what I had in mind at all. "Someone's at the door," she said.

I went into the living room and stood by the door. If there were someone on the other side, they were very quiet: then two hard raps, with authority.

"Who is it?"

"Your brother-in-law," Manolo said.

TWENTY-SIX

He came in with a tired smile, his eyes deep red from the filaria and he needed a shave. Under his arm was a small briefcase.

"Are you alone?"

"Argelia's in the bedroom."

"That woman you met in San José? I thought she left after a couple of days, which you didn't seem to mind."

"She came back."

I started to explain, but he stopped me, his hand raised like a traffic cop.

"You know what they say about thinking with your prick?" He laughed that low grumpy laugh and then turned serious. "There's something else we need to talk about. Have you seen Laura?"

"About a week ago."

"Do you know where she is now?"

"I thought she was staying in Zone 12."

"She's not there."

"She gave me an address in Zone 12 when I saw her a week ago."

"Can I see it?" I found the matchbook on my desk and showed him. He glanced toward the bedroom, where Argelia had turned on the radio. "How much does she know?"

"Very little."

"Are you sure?"

I thought about it.

"Yes."

"I've got something I'd like to leave with you for a little while." He unzipped the briefcase. There was a pistol and a large gray envelope. He pulled out the envelope and handed it to me. It was as heavy as a ream of paper and packed very tight, as if there were a thick piece of plywood inside. "When are you leaving?"

"Very soon," I said. "The end of the month. Maybe sooner, the way things are going."

He cocked his head toward the bedroom.

"What are you going to do about her?"

"She wants to come with me. I haven't decided yet."

It was an answer he had not anticipated. The idea that I might be contemplating some future life with Argelia was, judging by the baffled concern of his expression, both amusing and perilous.

"I find this hard to believe, you know. Hard to believe." He shook his head slowly. "Here you have a woman like Laura in love with you and you end up with" —his hand sputtered through the air—"this?"

I looked at him blankly. "She's not in love with me."

"I think she is," he said with that goddamn professorial air.

There was a clatter in the airshaft and he tensed, his hand edging into the briefcase.

"Garbage," I explained.

"Go look." There was a milk carton at the bottom of the airshaft; it had banged against the louvers coming down. Manolo was standing. "I have to go."

"What about this envelope?"

"Put it in a safe place. I'll send someone for it before you leave. I can't keep walking around with it."

"You have a place to stay?"

He checked his watch.

"I'll get a taxi up the street."

"I'll walk with you."

"It might be better if you didn't."

"I want to make sure you can get a taxi. They're more likely to take an American at this hour."

He shrugged, calculating whether or not to argue about this.

"Ok," he said. "Come on."

I went to the bedroom to get a jacket. Argelia was sitting on the bed smoking.

"I'm walking Manolo to the corner."

"We weren't finished talking."

"I'll be right back."

She stood up.

"I'm coming with you."

"I'll be right back."

"I'll bet."

She started for the door. I grabbed her arm, but she twisted free and hurried down the hallway ahead of me. Manolo stood by the door. Argelia was planted in the middle of the room, arms crossed, daring me to make a move.

"I can go by myself," he said.

"That's right," she said. "I'm sure the gentleman knows the way."

I felt the anger rising again. I didn't care what she did. I didn't care if she stayed or went or never came back again. But I wasn't going to let her make Manolo Ortiz walk out that door by himself. As it turned out, her coming with us on that brief walk did nobody any good.

"Let's go," I said.

There was a small van parked in front of the building with two guys tinkering under the hood. A fat man leaning against the vehicle smiled at Argelia and she smiled back. Manolo asked if she knew him.

"He looked familiar," she said.

"He seems to know you."

"I know a lot of men."

The street was dark and quiet, but we could see the taxis on the next block and beyond them an army jeep posted at the corner. Halfway up the block four or five men stood around a food stand. An electric bulb above the grill created a hard oasis of light in the milky darkness.

"I remember him now," Argelia said. "He's a friend of Fernando's."

Manolo and I turned around; the fat man was on our tail, the van creeping along beside him. We picked up the pace. As we came to the stand I wondered why the guy working the grill didn't look up to say hello the way he usually did. He wasn't going to see a thing.

Argelia stumbled against me. I turned to ask what happened. "Nothing happened," one of the men at the food stand said. Manolo went for his briefcase but they grabbed him from behind. They had me too, my arms pinned. A runt with a thick pompadour began jabbing methodically at my face. They were taking Manolo away. Three guys held him as he twisted and tugged and thrashed against them like a magnificent hooked fish. They drove him away in the van. The men inside had white bandanas across the lower half of their faces.

The two guys who had me pinned kept saying *don't fight, let's straighten this out,* while the runt kept punching. I felt the dull sour pressure at the back of my nose and the tang of blood and then the warm ooze over my lips. I tried to see if Argelia was alright. She was watching them ransack her pocketbook. There was blood dribbling out the corner of her mouth. The fat man handed her back the pocketbook and came over to me and stopped the runt; then he pressed his meaty finger into my chest.

"*Escúchame, mi amigo.* We're terribly sorry about all of this." I clamped my arm around Argelia and tried to push our way past him. He slapped me. "Please, I'm talking to you," he said.

"Where did you take Manolo?"

"Manolo?" He looked around. "Manolo? Anyone know a Manolo?" He shrugged apologetically. "Nobody knows Manolo."

"What do you want?"

"*Now* we're getting somewhere. *Quiero decirte algo, mi amigo.* You should go back where you came from. We don't like your type here. We have enough trouble with our own idiots. And you have such a pretty face, we wouldn't want anything worse to happen to it, now would we?" He looked at Argelia, as if wondering what he wanted to do about her; then he pinched her cheek and kept twisting until she winced. "You can stay, sweetheart. We can always use cunt like you." Then they just backed away and let us go. We got to the end of the block and I turned around. The street was empty except for the man working the grill and, on the far corner, the jeep that hadn't moved.

In the apartment we broke up some ice and made cold packs to bring down the swelling. My head was pounding. The main thing was not to panic, I thought.

He was still alive. Otherwise they would have shot him then and there. They wanted him alive, like the last time, at least for a while.

"We have to do something," I said.

"Forget it."

She lay on the bed with her arm over her eyes.

"They'll kill him," I said.

"He's already dead," she said.

"He's worth more to them alive."

"So what are you worried about?"

"Don't you care, damn it? Don't you care?"

She lifted her arm away from her eyes and stared at me.

"I care, but didn't you listen? You think I want to ride to Mexico next to a coffin?"

Her big front tooth that kept changing colors was gone. The gap in her mouth looked raw and painful and kind of goofy.

"You alright?"

"More or less," she said.

"What about the tooth?"

"It wasn't real. I was getting it replaced anyway."

I sat down at my desk and tried to think. Maybe Laura was still in Zone 12. I tried to remember what she had said about staying there.

It began to rain, a scratchy sound like pebbles on the tin louvers. There was a crack of thunder. I picked up the envelope Manolo had left and tucked it into the bottom of the big steamer trunk that served as a coffee table. He had to still be alive, I thought. In the morning I would go to Zone 12. I would maybe even make an appeal to Thornby on humanitarian grounds. He could do something if he wanted to. He wasn't a machine. He was a man and therefore unpredictable. It wasn't much of a plan but it was the best I could do. Argelia was standing behind me.

"I can't sleep," she said.

I held her for a long time. She was hurt and scared and it was my fault. It was pouring now. There was a boom of thunder and her fingers dug into my back. With her face smothered in my chest, she began laughing, low like a murmur and then louder and louder to an insane pitch. She stopped until the next crash set her off again, her hands running over my back, her eyes fixed on the ceiling, and always that wild laughter. With the thunder going away she still shuddered at the faintest rumble. At last she calmed down.

"Spring is coming," she said absently. "There will be earthquakes. The change of season."

TWENTY-SEVEN

In the morning I told her I was going out and under no circumstances should she leave the apartment.

"I don't like it," she said. "We should just go. You could get the bus for Mexico today. I'll get my papers in order and be there in a week."

"First I have to do this."

Her eyes narrowed.

"Stubborn."

"Just stay here," I said.

I did not really expect to find Laura in Zone 12. I looked for the address she had written on the matchbook and for the large factory she had mentioned. The streets were chaotic: a block almost upscale suburban except for a shack or two; then another block just the reverse, a solid slum with a solitary jewel of a house sitting, without rhyme or reason, in the midst of it. The stench of sewage rose from the fluid that oozed down the gutters in the silence of the hot afternoon.

A man directed me to the factory, which looked like a prison with barbed wire along the top of its high gray walls. Men trickled in and out through the front gate. Two kids begging scraps from the men's lunch pails were doing alright. One hit a ham sandwich, sat down and worked in the dirt, separating bits of ham from the mayonnaise and popping the meat into his mouth. The other was going through a pile of spoiled peaches, boring out the rotten spots with his grimy finger and then biting savagely into the soft dry fruit.

The house was behind the factory in an alley with wooden slats sinking into the mud. The man in front sat in a rocking chair, fanning himself with a piece of cardboard. Laura wasn't there.

"Do you know where she is?"

"Very hard to say, young man."

"Did she go back to Santa Cruz?"

"Could be." He offered a grudging nod. "You might try down the street. Lots of people there. At the funeral. One of them kids that got it yesterday." He got up and walked to the back end of the alley to point the way. "Can't miss it," he said.

There was a line of people about a quarter mile down the street. I got into the line but it was moving slowly and I couldn't see where it went. The heat was awful. Then I saw the head of the line entering a house. People were talking in quiet conversational tones, but as we shuffled toward the house the mood shifted into a low-keyed dread.

The casket and wreaths took up half the cool room. Laura wasn't there. A knot of teenagers stared impassively into the open end of the coffin. The bullet hole was barely visible, a slight puncture in the center of the boy's hairless chest. It could have been a birthmark or a bruise from the rough games of adolescent boys. I stood there for a moment, waiting in vain for some meaning to reveal itself, and then moved on past a woman sobbing at the edge of her chair and holding out a limp frail hand to be touched, which I did, and then I filed out and down a different path that spilled into the next street and knew I wouldn't find her now.

The scene was pandemonium. There were thousands of people packed into an intersection and overflowing down the avenue with banners swaying and bouncing to the rhythm of a bloodthirsty chant. *Pueblo si, junta no, Asesinos al paredón!* Over and over with a chorus-like clarity the words tore through the air until a new slogan would erupt in a section of the crowd and gather into an avalanche of intensity that seemed impossible to sustain. Then the coffin, draped in the national colors of blue and white, was bobbing over our heads, borne along the current of uplifted arms toward its destination at the front of the march.

The crowd surged, picking up speed as the street narrowed and onlookers braced themselves in doorways against this human torrent sweeping past them.

Suddenly the flow parted and people went diving to the ground. A lone soldier with an automatic rifle stood in the middle of the street. I landed on my belly, behind a fence, and looked around for a cue about what to do next. People were picking themselves up. They were working their way back to the march route, maneuvering in a wide arc through yards and alleyways around the soldier, and soon we had taken to the street again.

Then two shots rang out and everyone froze, heads buried in their arms as if the sky were falling, backs pressed against walls or hunkered down, dangerously exposed out in the open. I have to separate myself from this madness, I thought, but there was no place to go with people running everywhere, hitting the ground at the sound of shots or imaginary shots, waiting a few seconds, then picking themselves up and running again.

I reached a corner as three kids came racing toward me, frantically waving me back but momentum kept me going around the corner, and there, not a hundred feet away, was a sergeant in rumpled fatigues pumping the bolt of his rifle. The kids flew past me shouting "Run, man, run!"

I stopped dead, suddenly lucid, considering the options. I could turn and run and maybe get it in the back, or stay and maybe get it in the front, or try to explain to the guy that I was really not part of this rabble, just, you know, along for the ride. The sergeant clicked the bolt twice—fast menacing clicks—and crouched ready to shoot.

No sudden moves, I thought, taking big, slow, backward steps, hands open, away from my body. When I thought I was close enough to the corner, I turned and ran and didn't stop until I had a couple of walls between us in this desperate maze and realized I had caught up with the remnants of the march.

We entered the cemetery past a gauntlet of armored vehicles and a platoon of soldiers. The ceremony was over quickly, but as we started to leave some kids came running through the front gate with those frightened over-the-shoulder glances and we all took off, tombstones flying past while this time I expected with reasonable certainty a bullet in the back. I made the wall and leaped. Two guys reached down and helped me to the top, where I froze again. A jeep was crawling down the street, the three riflemen in the back seat with weapons pointed. The guys beside me dropped to the ground and sprinted off. I jumped but was slow getting up. One of the soldiers in the jeep kept his rifle sighted at my head. Look innocent, I told myself, and performed a ludicrous imitation of a man walking away without a care in the world.

The two guys were waiting for me at the corner. I was drenched with sweat. One of them patted my arm. He was a head shorter than me but through his torn shirt I could see the muscular chest and shoulders. His eyes were bright with excitement.

"You alright?" His hand lingered on my arm, a light, respectful touch.

"I think so."

"That bullet missed you by this much." His hand sliced through the air above his head; he was grinning.

"What bullet?" I asked.

He snapped off a couple of rounds with his finger.

"Back there on the wall. The soldier."

"I didn't see him shoot."

He and his buddy laughed.

"You're a foreigner."

"North American."

He stiffened.

"Gringo," he said, and spit emphatically.

Ok you little bastard, I felt like saying, next time tell that to your soldier boys. But I didn't say it. I didn't say anything. I only had enough strength to think it and once I did I realized there was nothing left inside me, not even gratitude at being alive, and I got myself onto the first bus that seemed to be going in the right direction.

Twice the bus was stopped at roadblocks, soldiers clearing everyone out, going through packages, bags, checking ID cards. They would see my passport and become very polite as I kept waiting for a question I couldn't answer. But the soldiers were distracted by the action in the streets, burning tires that sent up columns of swirling black smoke and gangs armed with rocks roaming in search of targets. I have to get out of this place, I thought, except there was Manolo and Laura and that woman waiting in the apartment. I had to believe this mess would somehow sort itself out before I got myself killed. In the meantime, I had one stop to make before going home.

There were extra Marines posted around the embassy. In the elevator, two men in civilian clothes got on carrying long narrow boxes I took to be weapons. They hurried out on the fourth floor and down the corridor toward the ambassador's suite.

Thornby was on the phone, his feet on the desk, his hand plowing through the thick crew cut. He hung up and waved me into the office.

"What happened, ole buddy? Run into a door?"

I felt my nose. It was still very sore. There had been a tug of affection in Thornby's question that I resisted.

"They grabbed Manolo Ortiz last night. Right on 18th Street. I was with him."

He nodded slowly, got up, closed the door and sat down again. He stared vacantly out the window, massaging those enormous hands.

"What the *hell* were you doing with *him*?"

"He's a friend."

"I'll just forget you said that, ok?"

"Don't we have some responsibility?"

He misunderstood my question.

"Who told you that?"

"I mean we *did* help him with those clinics."

"Very minimally."

"So we just let it happen."

His clasped hands, their knuckles white, rested on the desk.

"Maybe I don't like meddling," he said with a barely controlled rage.

"*Meddling*?"

"That's right. Meddling. Butting into other people's business. Interfering in the internal affairs of a sovereign country."

Did he expect me to believe this? Did he believe it himself? Was he so deluded about what he was doing that the statement struck him as entirely consistent with everything else he had said to me over the past eight months?

"Bob," I said. I hardly ever called him Bob. I was looking for a way to cut through the roles we had been assigned to play. "Aren't there some things more important than a man's politics?"

It took me years to realize that this question must have been incomprehensible to him. In every generation of every society there is a warrior class whose personal qualities run the gamut from noble to despicable but who share a too often blind loyalty to the state. Thornby was the first of this cohort I'd ever met, but far from the last.

He opened a folder on his desk and held up a copy of *The New York Times Magazine*, held it delicately as if it might soil his hands.

"You think I haven't seen this? You think the *ambassador* hasn't seen this? You think Colonel Ramirez hasn't seen it? You think nobody cares about what you said to Fred Dubrow that night at my house? What the hell do you think you're *doing*, my friend?"

My stomach tightened, my heart banging.

"I haven't seen the article myself yet."

"Don't give me that shit. You know what it says."

"What I wrote in the article is what I believe," I said. "And I think it's the truth."

"It's an attack on your *own* government, is what it is. I won't even bother to add the same government that has paid your way to go traipsing around this godforsaken country wherever you felt like and fucking every broad you could get your dick into."

The phone rang several times and stopped.

"I came here to talk to you about Manolo Ortiz," I said.

He looked at me with amused disbelief.

"You are in no position to talk to me about *anybody*. Don't you know what this is? One hundred percent, unadulterated, commie propaganda. With your goddamn name on it."

"*The New York Times* prints commie propaganda?"

He held up the magazine in both hands, shaking it in my face, and then read aloud with a dramatic mocking flourish.

"*The embassy has assigned a low priority to the program, preferring instead its traditional ties to the military which views popular literacy as just another threat to political stability.*" He sat back with an air of having conclusively proven his case, though if I had been asked to predict what in the article would have disturbed him most, it would not have been this mild observation of a fact obvious to everyone from the ambassador on down.

"It's true," I said.

He laughed, shaking his head again, leaning back in his chair, a forced laugh, more like a grunt. He gazed at the ceiling as if he could not bear to look at me, the subject of this disaster for which he was at least partially responsible. Then he leaned forward on his desk, his eyes tight on mine.

"You sabotaged me. You did this behind my back. Why did you do it? You had it made here. You had the credentials. You had a career. And you go out and do something like this. *You are one stupid son of a bitch, my friend.*"

I sat there frozen for a moment. Maybe it was the certainty, the tone of sad but indisputable fact that here we were dealing not with ordinary stupidity but something else, something far more ominous. I sat there wondering why I was so afraid, how he had slipped it to me, the doubt and the fear that he was right and I was wrong.

"Can I remind you of a very good piece of advice I gave you a little while ago? I've taken care of the Mexico City thing. If I were you, I'd get my ass out of this country as fast as I could."

The streets were crawling with jeep patrols. Near the railroad station the mob had left its calling card. The window of the big shoe store where I sometimes stopped at the display had a hole in the middle with spider-web cracks and the merchandise swept clean.

I bought a paper and walked down the street to the plaza and sat on a bench. A man on the bench next to me lay on his side gurgling like a baby. He had two seams sewn across the end of his arm where the hand had been amputated. Maybe lost the tongue and the hand together. They still did that.

A preacher was quoting scriptures and Rubén Darío in a rich baritone for a few stray Indians and the girls who worked the corner. I looked at the paper. Four more kids killed at the funeral that morning, another march scheduled for *their* funeral the next day.

I tried to think. Maybe I could get to the ambassador about Manolo. But why would he tell me anything different than Thornby? If the embassy wouldn't help, Manolo was a dead man. I was pretty sure of that. I had to think.

That's when I saw Argelia, picked her out a block away, saw her with the abstract clarity of a dream: the haughty swinging gait, the boredom and pathetic arrogance of every sweet young whore who ever walked the street.

TWENTY-EIGHT

She spotted me and the hard mask fell away, her step faltered, but she kept going. It took me a couple of blocks but I caught up and grabbed her arm. I was seething.

"Where are you going? I told you to stay in the apartment."

She kept walking. I grabbed her harder and she stopped and leaned back on the fender of a parked car.

"Look," she said. "Why don't you just wait for me in the apartment? I'll be back in a little while."

I was so angry I couldn't see straight.

"I want you to come now," I said.

She laughed grandly, head back, white throat exposed. She was stinking drunk.

"Oh my goodness. Such an *angry* man."

"I'm not leaving you like this."

"All of a sudden she can't take care of herself."

"Maybe that's right."

"Well, that's what *you* think," and she rocked herself off the car and started unsteadily down the street. I caught up and held her hard by the wrists. "It's ok for your gringa girlfriend to come see you anytime she feels like it, but this piece of shit can't go where she wants."

"What are you talking about now?"

"You're hurting me," she said.

"Are you coming with me now or not?"

"No."

She was shaking her head slowly, eyes fixed on the pavement, and I knew she meant it. Wherever she was going, whatever the convoluted scheme, I couldn't change it. Nothing I could think of was going to change it or her or anything at all. I let her go and walked back to the apartment. Maybe Thornby was right about the impressive dimensions of my stupidity. I felt nauseous. In front of the pool hall one of the regulars sat in a chair in her ratty green sweater and the sunglasses she wore through the night. She greeted me with her demented cackle—"Don't let the little soldier boys get you, Blondie!"—her nutty screech almost reassuring as I hurried into my building.

The janitor must have heard me coming. He knocked on the door right after I went into the apartment.

"Your *compatriota* came in the morning and asked me to give this to you. The *señorita* was home when she came."

"Thank you."

The note was on a single sheet of white lined paper, folded in half, torn from the notebook Laura carried in her bag.

Vos, I was hoping you'd be here, but I guess this will have to do for now. We know about Manolo and we're doing all we can, but things are getting out of control. I don't think it's safe even for you to stay now. If you can leave by tomorrow, and you should really try, take the 8 a.m. bus to Xela. I wish you'd been here. There's so much to say. I don't know where to start, so I'll stop—Love, L.

I was lucky to have gotten the note. That must have been an interesting little scene when she showed up here. It was almost a relief now having everything so clear, pieces of the puzzle coming together so even a moron like me could assemble them. There was nothing to think about now except self-preservation.

Xela was on the Pan-American Highway and more than halfway to the Mexican border. There wasn't much time to pack. I had a small suitcase for the trip and arranged with the janitor to ship the old steamer trunk back to the States.

I dug Manolo's envelope out of the trunk and put it on the desk. The envelope wasn't sealed. I unwound the cord from the tab that held the flap down and looked in. There were packets of mint $100 bills in Bank of America wrappers. I did a fast count. About half a million bucks. There was nothing else in the envelope. I tied it closed and dropped it into the suitcase I was taking with me on the bus and tried to calm down.

The trunk filled up quickly with my books and materials from the literacy study and rarely used clothes like the Brooks Brothers suit. I smiled at the thought of someone opening the trunk in New York and trying to decipher its contents, the way entire civilizations are deduced from relics in ancient burial sites: *Here lies a royal schmuck once engaged in vast scholarly pursuits*. Not flattering, but there have been worse epitaphs.

What remained fit into the small suitcase. I put the envelope on the bottom and threw in a few books and my type-written copy of the article. I wondered how Thornby had gotten it just the day after the publication date. I slid my portable typewriter next to the suitcase. This wasn't going to be so hard, I thought. Argelia could do what she wanted with the furniture and the refrigerator. I thought she would appreciate the gesture. We *are* generous, we Americans. Then I went to the bus depot and got a ticket for the 8 a.m. to Xela. That was it. There was nobody around that I felt like saying goodbye to. When I got back to the apartment, Argelia was sitting on the edge of the sofa. She was crying. I thought it was from seeing my stuff packed, but it wasn't that.

"I am deceived in the worst way," she said between sniffles. "He took me and screwed me and made a complete fool of me."

"Who?"

She looked up, her black eyeliner dripping, like a clown's huge teary eyes.

"She is very stupid. She injures someone she loves very much."

"What *happened?*"

"Fernando. That fat little piece of *shit*," she snarled. "He shows me his *Judiciale* card and says he can throw me in jail for what I'm doing." Her head sagged, her eyes struggling to focus. "And you even worse," she said quietly.

"You're lying again."

"I swear to God. He says you're in big trouble, some kind of spy, from Cuba or Russia—I don't know where." She threw up her arms, impatient with this geography of espionage. "He says, now dear, we both want to help him, but if you don't want your boyfriend to get his balls cut off, you do what I say. So I brought him some of those stupid papers." She nodded toward the desk I had now cleared off. "But he keeps asking for more and wants to know about what's his name, Manolo, and the gringa and who else comes to see you here. Things like that. But most of the time he just wants to do it, you know. I can't tell you how disgusting this creep is."

Things like that.

"What papers?"

"Do I know? Anything with writing."

I tried to visualize the sprawl of reports, notebooks, drafts, the names from my trips, addresses, phone numbers. It was impossible to reconstruct, no way of knowing who might now fall victim to the inept, paranoid suspicions of the security apparatus and my own unforgivable carelessness. She sat there waiting for me to say something, but talk seemed pointless if not dangerous now.

I went into the bedroom and tried to sleep but couldn't. I had certainly made a fine little mess out of my promising life. And it could get worse. What if I got stopped with that envelope? I tried not to think about Manolo. There was nothing I could do for him now. And that bastard Fernando, may he choke to death on one of his idiotic jokes. I had come to hate this place that had once seemed so interesting and filled me with such hope. I wondered why Laura had told me to take a bus to Xela, which was not too far from Santa Cruz. Maybe she would be waiting for me in Xela.

I picked up a book. I just wanted to go to sleep and wake up in the morning and leave. Argelia came in with a bottle of beer and sat down on the bed. She nodded heavily, her face plain and too weary to pose; the whites of her eyes were flawless, abnormally white.

"You think I'm drunk. Hah! You haven't seen anything yet."

"I don't want to see."

"What's that supposed to mean?"

"It means I'm leaving in the morning."

"With your darling gringa. Don't think I don't know you had it planned all the time. You really think I'm stupid, don't you."

"I'm just going, by myself."

"You expect me to believe that?"

"Believe whatever you want. I can't stay with you."

"Is that right?"

"I can't stay with a woman who" — I searched for the words, a woman I couldn't trust I probably would have said —

"Go ahead and say it! A woman like me. Well, you just wait and see how good I marry. You just wait."

"That's not what I meant."

"You just wait." She began to cry. "But what do I care? It doesn't make the slightest bit of difference to me, not from any point of view. It's time I saw my family anyway. My little guy who doesn't even know his *mama*." She shook her head. "I had it made. On my way to New Orleans with a guy who really cared about me. And what do I do? Fall in love with a communist gringo who thinks I'm a piece of shit. She really knows how to pick 'em." She forced a smile. "You really made me pay this time, you sure did."

I went back to my book, just wanting it to be over.

"Talk to me," she pleaded. "Talk to me."

She lowered her head onto my stomach and looked at me with those large sad eyes.

"Say anything. Tell me lies. Oh, excuse me, I forgot. You don't lie, do you? You are a genius and a saint. Please talk to me," she pleaded. "Those books. Always with a book. They make me sicker than all the booze I've drunk." She lifted the book delicately from my hands and tossed it aside. "Now talk, please, talk to me now."

"What's there to say, Argelia?"

"Oh my goodness, such a serious man!" She made a somber face and I grunted. She laughed and I tried not to smile, but she had picked up the scent of capitulation. She leaned against me, kissed me twice on the lips, dry testing kisses. "So serious," she said. "I've been thinking you're right. I've got to change. I've been thinking so much in the last few hours my hair is falling out."

She nuzzled under my chin, making herself comfortable the way I loved it, the perfect fit of our bodies still filling me with a terrible longing. But I knew now that she would bring me into her world before I would bring her into mine. I sensed her power to do that and did not want to see her or touch her or speak to her ever again.

In the morning, we barely spoke over coffee and rolls and left for the bus with time to spare. I carried the small suitcase and typewriter and she walked a step behind me with my raincoat over her arm. We stopped near the door of the bus.

"You really get me," she said, the words hissing through the gap in her teeth. "You really get me, you really do," through the slow tears and the sheer black hair that fell like a shroud over her face. I held her by the shoulders and we just looked at each other. Without make-up her eyes had a more oval shape, nearly oriental, tear-washed mascara still smudged in the corners. "I can't stay and watch you leave," she said. "I'll cry like a fool."

I let go and she turned away. The treeless plaza had its milky light of that early hour, smoke rising from the breakfast fires, the rattle of carts over concrete. She walked past the statue of the general, past a man asleep in his cart and then crossed the street. She wore the same cobalt blue slacks she had worn that day I met her on the coast. I could see her clearly until she passed from sight behind the old railroad station without ever looking back.

I took a window seat toward the rear of the bus and tucked my suitcase under the seat. Across the aisle sat an old woman whose face twitched like a rat but in her lap lay three stems of freshly cut, strong-scented roses, and as the bus pulled out and the storefronts flew past I thought about Laura maybe waiting for me in Xela and the long ride north and felt a little of the weight of the country lifting from my shoulders.

Then I saw the tall thin figure of Diego coming down the aisle, his nervous blue eyes taking in everything like that night we hid and waited outside the *pensión* in Santa Cruz.

He sat down beside me and as I started to speak he pressed his forefinger to his lips and then with the same finger flicked his earlobe. *Oreja*. Ear. Police. Nobody looked the part, not the lady with the roses or the man in front of her babbling to himself or the couple behind us hassling with their two kids, but then you could have said the same about me, that this role I had stumbled into seemed to be out of character with the person I was or thought I wanted to be.

I kept my mouth shut. Of all the virtues, the rich old maid of prudence arrives with the least fanfare.

TWENTY-NINE

The main road out of the city had a military checkpoint where vehicles were stopped and searched randomly. We bumped through the culvert that slowed down the traffic before the checkpoint. Diego slumped in his seat and pretended to sleep. A soldier came out of the booth and strolled around the bus, going through the motions of inspection. He climbed the ladder and poked at the crates and big suitcases on top. He circled the bus again, still barely taking notice of the passengers, and then with the same robotic movement lifted the mechanical arm and waved the driver through. Diego gave me a sly smile, pulled his hat down over his face and stayed like that for a long time.

The bus flew along the Pan-American Highway— two narrow lanes cut into the mountains at breathtaking angles. I would look down and see nothing but air as the driver took the blind curves, blasting his horn as passengers prayed aloud. After a while I stopped counting the little crosses along the side of the road.

In the early afternoon we stopped at a restaurant. Diego and I stayed in our seats until all the passengers left the bus.

He pulled a piece of paper out of his shirt pocket. "I was told to give you this," he said. It was the name and address of a hotel in Mexico City.

"This bus goes to Xela," I said.

He looked confused.

"*La Laura* said you're going to Mexico, true?"

"That is true." She's not in Xela, I thought. So this is it. I'm really leaving. "I'll be changing buses in Xela for Mexico."

"Yes, *La Laura* said you would be in Mexico."

"Have you seen her?"

"Last night."

"How is she?" He wobbled his hand.

"Everything is a little shaky."

"What about Manolo?"

"It was the *Judiciales* that snatched him. They're the worst."

"I was with him when it happened."

"Did he give you an envelope?" I reached for the suitcase under my seat; he put his hand on my arm. "No. We'd like you to take it out with you. They never search gringos."

"What am I supposed to do with it when I get to Mexico?"

He tore a one-quetzal bill down the middle and gave me half. "Whoever comes will have the other piece."

I knew it meant crossing a line I was not supposed to cross. I was still free to refuse and hand Diego the envelope and say I'm sorry. I certainly had no confidence in his assessment of how easily I could get through immigration and customs. How could they just assume I would agree to do this? Laura had probably come to my apartment the day before to deal with the envelope. Maybe she would have asked me herself to take it out. I could not see myself telling her no. Somewhere along the way, I don't know exactly where or when, or exactly how, I had already crossed that line. It had more to do with people than it did with politics.

I slipped my half of the bill into my pants pocket.

As the bus began to reload, Diego studied everything—the driver, the people coming out of the restaurant, the highway. There was an ice-cream vendor making last-minute sales through the bus windows. The woman across the aisle was insisting that the guy give her the change first, as a precaution against the bus leaving while he fumbled for the coins in his pocket. Diego put his hand on my knee.

"I've got to leave now, *compañero.*"

"Take care," I said.

He nodded gravely.

"Equally."

He slid out of the seat, spoke briefly with the driver and went into the restaurant. We pulled out a few minutes later without him. In Xela I caught a bus to Malacatán and from there early in the morning to El Carmen on the border. I had not slept in more than 24 hours.

The border crossing was an old wooden bridge over the Suchiate River. It ran so deep in the mountain below you could not see the water from where the bus stopped at the flimsy Guatemalan customs shack. The building on the Mexican side was new and much larger, a reminder that every poor country usually has a poorer neighbor. We had to leave the bus to go through Guatemalan immigration and customs and then walk across the bridge to do the same in Mexico.

I waited in line to get through immigration. The lady with the roses was in front of me. There was a problem with the immigration officer, who had her suitcase open and papers spread out. He didn't like what he saw.

"When were you born?" He asked impatiently. "On your *cedula* it says the 27th of November and here the 16th of December."

"I was born on the 28th of January."

"But it doesn't say that on either one."

"Look, I know when I was born. A person doesn't make a mistake about that."

"Do you have a birth certificate?"

"You have all my papers. They must have made a mistake in the office. You know how they are. You tell them one thing, they write down another."

She was putting up a good fight. I was getting nervous. It was too late now to try to conceal the envelope in the raincoat I was carrying, but that might have been worse than keeping it in the suitcase. I had no way of knowing. There was a reason you had professionals for this line of work. The officer directed the lady to step aside and waved me to the desk.

"Passport please." He studied each page, including the blank ones. "Your entry visa has expired."

"There's an extension."

"It's not validated."

I knew the passport was fine. I had spent two hours in immigration in the city and ran it past the embassy just to make sure. Something else was going on. He indicated a stamp with someone's initials as the problem.

"That's the way they did it at immigration," I said.

"It's not validated." He stood up. "Follow me please."

Through the window I saw two soldiers sitting on the rail of the bridge. I thought about Manolo. For an instant I saw myself bolting toward the door and across the bridge. I picked up the suitcase and the typewriter and followed the officer through the door into a small room with a desk and two chairs. There were bars on the window. He opened the passport on the desk and looked at it thoughtfully. "I can validate here," he said. "But there's a charge."

"How much?"

"Twenty dollars." He grinned. "Cheap."

I agreed that it was a reasonable sum, given the seriousness of the violation, and said that I appreciated his assistance. He put the 20-dollar bill in his pocket and said he hoped that I would return soon to his poor little country. Then he escorted me over the bridge to the Mexican side. He introduced an official who he said would expedite the entry process. This cost me another 30 bucks that I was happy to pay.

From there I got a bus to the train station in Tapachula and that night the train for Mexico City. I was exhausted and went to sleep. I awoke once in the dark when some soldiers came through on an identity check, looking for Guatemalan illegals. The low hills of the countryside were very dull in the early morning light but soothing after the spectacular angles on the

Guatemalan side. I could see mountains in the distance but they were just a wrinkle on the horizon. The fields were yellow and the trees stunted and far apart on the water-starved plain. It looked like another planet.

IV

Mexico City

THIRTY

The address Diego had given me was a little dive called the Hotel Mina just off the Alameda north of Hidalgo. The hotel faced a huge tract of land that looked like bombed-out rubble. A carnival had taken over one corner with its canvas booths and a scrawny Ferris wheel that turned only at night. This desolate vista had been the old red-light district before the bulldozers leveled it in one of those periodic spasms of civic indignation that are never without their strain of hypocrisy. I wondered where the trade had relocated and never did find out, though my new residence seemed to have picked up some of the displaced business.

For 30 bucks a week I had a big room on the roof, four flights up, with good strong light most of the day and a view of the ruins across the street. There the amenities ended. The old plumbing was noisy and unreliable and then there was the problem that came in literally with the wind. Because the common toilet for the five rooms on the roof flushed so anemically, guests were instructed to deposit their soiled paper in a basket next to the toilet. It didn't take much of a breeze to swirl some papers out of the overflowing basket and send them tumbling down the hallway and through the door I kept open to ventilate my hot boxy room. After a while I solved the problem by keeping the door mostly shut.

I had taped the envelope under a small desk in the room and arranged with the hotel to put my own padlock on the door and do my own housekeeping, which was not unusual for the place. I assumed that someone would come for the envelope sooner rather than later.

I was restless but didn't feel comfortable getting too far away for too long from my half a million dollars in hot cash. I did find a couple of good book stores on La Reforma and even street corner kiosks with all kinds of political literature, realizing first with puzzled curiosity and then pure exhilaration how restricted the flow of ideas and information had been in Guatemala.

I brought all kinds of magazines and pamphlets and a few books back to my room and was reading furiously. Here the "terrorists," "subversives," "communists," and what-not condemned in Guatemalan newspapers were called, sometimes respectfully, depending on the source, the *Fuerzas Armadas Rebeldes* — the name they had given themselves. Actions that had appeared to be random and spontaneous could now be seen as calculated and strategic. When I read an interview with a *FAR* leader, coolly enumerating the causes and justification and strategy of armed struggle, I could hear the subtext of conversations with Manolo. And of course the cause of the mutual misunderstanding with Diego in Santa Cruz now could not have been clearer.

So this was the organization, these the comrades with whom Manolo had leaped to seize the opportunity that history seemed to offer. They would wage a guerrilla war against the generals and the oligarchs and the American imperialists, just as the Cubans had done, and build a new society in which the wealth was shared, production rationalized, and justice prevailed.

I understood the allure of this appeal immediately. It was like what finding Laubach did to my perspective on the literacy campaign, but it was not exactly the same because I was still suspicious at how neatly everything fit into this grand theory of revolution.

Certain facts could not be avoided, however. The Cubans had indeed wiped out illiteracy in the space of a year. The government had sent high school kids into the hills and teachers into the slums and didn't stop until everyone could read and write. I wondered what the Christian missionary Laubach thought about the communists doing that. They were doing similar things with health and housing. Maybe the Cuban Revolution *was* the model for disasters like Guatemala.

A Frenchman named Debray wrote a book making exactly this point with the seductive logic for which the French are justifiably famous. It was a brilliant little book but got some important details wrong and a lot of good people killed. We all make mistakes. It's just that when you commit them to print the price tends to go up.

Sometimes when I thought about the envelope taped to the underside of the desk, I wondered what I would do if nobody came for it and had a lot of trouble getting my head around that. Or if the wrong person came? Or if somebody stole it? There were other questions, like the origin of these funds. The papers in Mexico were reporting that the *FAR* levied "taxes" on wealthy businessmen and ranchers, a form of quiet extortion that was sometimes resisted with the loss of life on both sides. There were other possibilities for the origin of the funds like plain old bank robbery or Cuban and even Soviet subsidies, all of which made me uncomfortable, but by then I had given up most of my illusions about getting out of this with clean hands.

These were increasingly practical questions. I had evidently gotten into the journalism racket myself with the *Times* article, which paid the rent and kept me eating—fortunately, because those last monthly checks from the grant that Thornby promised did not materialize at the embassy in Mexico City.

I began to think it might not be so bad, trying to figure out how to use all the dough in that envelope, assuming of course nobody came to claim it. What else was I supposed to do? Turn it in to lost and found at the local police station? But for now I didn't need it. When I picked up some freelance work for the *Nation*, I began to feel almost prosperous.

I started spending more time just walking around the immense city, drinking a little more than I should, waiting for some old sense of myself to return and thinking about what I would do next with my life. I would sometimes see a woman in the street I thought was Laura. I'd follow her, trying to get closer, once or twice even calling out her name and then feeling like a fool when the woman turned around. I told myself to stop, to think of her as part of a life left behind. I thought I could do that.

I loved the quiescence of those days, the reading and writing and walking, the leisurely meals, and sometimes at night a movie or splurging on a couple of drinks in a fancy hotel on La Reforma and then sitting in the plush lobby smoking my pipe, watching the tourist ladies strut past like exotic silvery birds. It was easy to get drunk on the strong Mexican beer and when that happened I would feel lonely and stroll back to my hotel with images of mysterious ladies cruising the city in limousines, on the lookout for a young man just like me.

The mysterious ladies bore a strong resemblance to Jeanne Moreau and María Félix. I went to many Mária

Félix movies, which seemed all that remained of the Mexican Revolution, this legend of the woman who would get her man, take him on any terms, the more violent the better. At the end of *Juana Gallo,* as the men ride into the sunset and the women, rifles in hand, stride behind the horses and Maria Felix swears to follow her colonel and lover, I could hear Argelia warning me about Mexican women and her brave talk about how if I thought I could dump her I better think again.

It was hard to figure how some things turned out the way they did, like the boy and girl in *The Umbrellas of Cherbourg,* a movie in which all the dialogue is sung, lilting and delicate but not operatic. Genevieve and Guy are very much in love but Genevieve gets pregnant and Guy gets scared and she marries an older man and then Guy gets married and they both go off and live their separate and plain, normal lives. You think that they are still in love and have made the wrong choice; then you think maybe not, maybe they have just grown up, and there is this perfect tension until the final scene when they meet many years later and she asks, *Are you happy?* and he sings, *Yes, yes, very,* and you want to grab him and demand that he explain how he could have ever turned his back on such sweet and tender love.

One night lying on my bed reading a collection of Sartre essays that Manolo had given me, I came across this underlined passage.

> *From the period when I wrote* La Nausée *I wanted to create a morality. My evolution consists in my no longer dreaming of doing so. I discovered suddenly that alienation, exploitation of man by man, undernourishment, relegated to the background metaphysical evil which is a luxury. Hunger is evil: period.*

That was Manolo, alright. But look where it got you, my friend. He had to be dead, I thought. I wondered if Laura or anyone else knew. She would take it hard. Even now, when I thought about them together, or the way they talked about each other, I sensed an intimacy from which I was excluded. I didn't want to think about that anymore. It seemed like I was forgetting her again, more like an idea in my head than the memory of a real person. Such resilience came in handy. I wondered what Sartre had to say about resilience, but my mind kept slipping away, tumbling off those formidable slabs of dialectical granite.

I shut off the light and listened to the clack of heels in the hallway below, each new set advancing a room farther, denizens of the old neighborhood filling the ark two by two. The plumbing erupted for a spell— belching, hissing, rattling, nothing even remotely like water gushing through pipes—and then the place hushed. Whenever a big truck went by, shifting gears at the corner, I could feel the building tremble. The next serious earthquake would probably demolish the old Hotel Mina. I heard thunder, muffled and almost purring in the distance. Then I heard what sounded like paper rustling against the door and I realized someone was knocking. I got up and opened the door.

It was Laura.

THIRTY-ONE

She stood in the doorway tilted in that same way she walked, a thin sweater over one of her loose plain dresses and that big old bag over her shoulder. As beautiful as ever.

"Can I come in?"

I turned on the light. She walked in and sat on the bed.

"What are you doing here?" I asked.

"I came to see you." She lit a cigarette and looked around the room, appraising its shabby spaciousness. There was so much I wanted to say I couldn't speak. Then her eyes locked on mine. "How's your life, *vos*?"

"I'm doing ok."

"I thought you'd be here with your girlfriend."

"It didn't work out."

"I read your article in the *Times*. It was good."

"I couldn't have done it without you."

"I think you could have," she said.

"Thornby loved it." I was trying to adjust to her presence, to shift her sudden appearance from the realm of the imaginary to the real. "Is there any word on Manolo?"

"Nothing good."

It was still a few years before "disappear" became a transitive verb, before the art of annihilating one's existence without a trace was perfected and that all you could do was wait for word to seep out of the security apparatus. Sooner or later you usually heard something, or a body would be found.

"Where are you staying?"

"With friends." She poked around in her bag and pulled out the torn half of the quetzal bill that Diego had kept. "Remember this?"

I got the envelope from under the drawer and gave it to her. She unwound the thin twine from the metal clasp, took a quick peek, rewound the twine and put the envelope in her bag.

"At least we got *this* right," she said, as much to herself as to me. She inhaled deeply on the cigarette and watched the smoke stream into the still air.

"What happened to your sugarcane?"

She shrugged.

"Haven't been able to find any here yet."

We sat there for a while without speaking. The thunder was coming closer. I watched her sitting there in the light of the single overhead bulb and I felt a terrible sadness, for both of us, then fear that she would leave as suddenly as she had appeared and I would never see her again.

"I assume this is a business trip," I said.

She walked over to the window and stood there. It was raining lightly. The thunder sounded again.

"You're still angry with me."

"I don't think angry is the right word," I said.

Rain ticked against the window. We listened to the thunder low and continuous. I went over and stood behind her. The only thing I knew with absolute certainty was that I wanted her more than anything I had ever wanted.

Lightning flared in the window and the thunder cracked very close. The rain was really coming down now. "I should be going," she said.

"It's pouring."

"Do you have something I can wear?"

"My raincoat."

She waited for the next flash.

"I mean like pajamas."

She doesn't know what she's doing, I thought, and then I thought just the opposite.

"Do you think that's a good idea?"

"*Vos?*"

"What?"

"Sometimes you ask too many questions."

I found her a shirt. She undressed and slipped into it quickly but I caught the sleek powerful lines of a Modigliani nude—the high breasts and long flat stomach and deep curve of hips and thighs. We lay on the bed listening to the wind-driven rain splatter on the tin roof like grease on a hot skillet. She propped herself up on her elbow, looking down at me.

"I really wanted to see you before you left," she said.

"Things were crazy."

"I didn't want to leave now," she said. "We're organizing in the mountains. It's a whole new stage."

"Does the Peace Corps know you're here?"

"I quit."

"They were going to kick you out sooner or later."

"I don't blame them. I never tried to hide what I thought about what's going on there. You should write something about it. People have to know."

"I'd like to."

"I know you will."

"How come you know so much about me?"

"Because that's who you are."

"I'll have to think about that."

"Always thinking." She tapped the side of my head and then ran her finger down along the line of my cheekbone. "You have an old-fashioned face."

"I'm an old-fashioned boy."

"I know."

She lowered her head, my mouth almost touching her neck, and there was this plain, fresh-scrubbed scent that tapped the frozen root of an old warm memory. I nuzzled her neck, breathing her in.

"Can't you get any closer?" she whispered.

"I don't know."

"Try."

It was like the other times when we could not get enough of each other, that hunger feeding on itself, but this time she didn't stop. She unbuttoned my shirt slowly, her mouth roaming over my body in little rhythmic circles like an animal pacing its cage, and then it was my turn, but I couldn't stop thinking that somewhere on the downy surface of her body was a hidden spot that could be pressed in just the right way and I who had found it would plunge into this awful impossible depth from which I could never be expelled. And then I could not believe that in a moment I would be swimming inside her but in a moment I was and then at last not thinking at all but stupefied by the absolute strangeness of those inner walls with their lining like warm mud, and then all the intensity at that exquisite point, the pressure building and then the blasting sweetness and her barely audible whimper.

When it was over we lay there in the heavy air, breathing hard, staring at the ceiling. My mind and my body felt empty and gorgeously calm.

"We're so *equal*," she said, mildly amazed.

THIRTY-TWO

In the morning I felt her drifting away again as she rummaged through her bag, busy making other connections. I didn't want to ask about what, didn't want to break the spell. We walked along La Reforma. It was a quiet Sunday morning with sunlight pouring through the monumental trees and church bells in the distance and the hush of side streets with a carpet of leaves knocked down by the rain. We walked past couples in the grass and the lines in front of the movie theaters with clusters of neon-bright balloons bobbing on strings.

"How do you feel?" I asked.

"Tired, and a little sore." She patted my arm. "I'm not complaining."

We went to my regular breakfast place, a tiny joint with French Impressionist prints on the wall and a few Formica tables. Felipe, the waiter, was always kidding me about coming in alone and I could tell he was going to say something now. He put on quite a show, seating us with such formality I could almost hear the violins.

"Good morning, Felipe."

"Good morning, Don Pedro." He bowed to Laura. "And to your beautiful friend."

She took the compliment in the ritualistic spirit with which it was offered.

"Good morning," she said with a slight bow.

This was all Felipe needed. He turned a chair around and sat himself down, straddling the seat with his arms on the back. He looked at Laura and then at me.

"Permit me one small observation," he said, pinching the air in front of his eyes. I liked Felipe but he was a wise guy and there was no way of shutting him up even if I wanted to.

"If it will get some food on the table," I said.

"The truth," he said to Laura, raising his right hand, "I have never seen this man so happy."

"With breakfast you will see him even happier," I said.

"But of course," he said, jumping up and readying his pen. We ordered the Chapultepec Special—orange juice, eggs, bacon, black beans, rolls and a pot of coffee.

"Will that be all?"

"Yes."

He looked at me sternly.

"I hope your intentions are honorable," he said.

"That goes without saying."

"You will invite me to the wedding of course."

"Felipe!"

He fell away laughing and scooted off to the kitchen.

"He's cute," Laura said. "You don't want to marry me, *vos*?"

"It's a lousy institution."

"You don't think you'll *ever* get married?"

"It depends. Do you?"

"I want kids."

"You can have kids without getting married," I said.

"Depends on what?"

"I'd want to be really sure."

"Sometimes you have to do things without being absolutely sure," she said.

"Is this a proposal?"

"No." She patted my hand. "Don't worry."

A slightly more businesslike Felipe brought us two glasses of orange juice and then the rest of the excellent breakfast. Laura tore pieces from her roll to dab into the yoke of her fried egg, assuring that not a drop of the rich yellow liquid would be left in the plate, a method that struck me as peculiar and idiosyncratic. It made me desperate, thinking how much more I wanted to know about her.

"All I can think about is you leaving," I said.

She gave me a worried smile.

"It won't be for a while," she said. "I'll be back to see you very soon."

"When's very soon?"

"If I can't get back tonight, tomorrow."

I walked her a couple of blocks to a bus stop near the Hilton. A man in a canary jacket went past accompanied by a lady in pink. Laura nudged me in the ribs.

"We need outfits like that, *vos*."

I went back to the hotel and stayed up late working on the article for the *Nation* about The Alliance for Progress and finally got into the unmade bed. It must have been about two in the morning. She was not coming back now, I thought, and began to think she would not come back the next day either. That was another reason I worked so late. It helped me not to think so much about her, but that was a lot harder to do now.

The sheets still had our scent. I lay there inhaling it with slow, deep breaths thinking this was absolutely the best and that I was incredibly lucky and that if I believed in God now was the time to recognize His beneficence. It seemed I didn't believe in God. A terrible thing to admit, like rooting for the enemies of your own country.

She came back the next afternoon, knocking lightly on the door the way she had the other night and tramping into the room as if it she had lived there for years.

"I didn't think you'd be back," I said.

"I told you I would." She sat on the bed. "You worry too much, *vos*."

"There's a lot to worry about."

"About us, or all the other things?"

"Both."

She smiled, looking at me in that direct, no-nonsense way.

"Do you think the *Times* would be interested in an article about what's going on in Guatemala now? You could get up into the mountains. You could interview the leadership."

"I could try them."

"I knew you'd like the idea," she said.

The next day I cabled the editor I had worked with on the literacy piece. He got back to me a few days later saying they wanted the article and would pay the same $600 fee.

With the passage of time I eventually came to realize that I preferred freelancing to working for any kind of institution and without a family to support could more or less survive economically. Having something to write that I cared about when I wanted to write about it has always been exhilarating. I couldn't know it at the time, of course, but in Mexico City in 1964 I prepared for the *Times* piece as I would for hundreds of others on similar subjects over the next 50 years.

I read everything I could get my hands on about guerrilla warfare and its contemporary Marxist manifestation. The successful British counter-insurgency program in Malaysia was one effective way to suppress these revolutionary movements. The British could be brutal when they wanted to, but the repression tended to be surgical and aimed at cutting the guerrillas off from their base of support. Another strategy was to crack down on the insurgents and their supporters ruthlessly, as they did in the Philippines. There were also a few places where the guerrillas won, like China and Cuba.

Laura would come back to the hotel almost every night and I would give her a summary of what I'd read that day and we'd talk about it. She would mostly

listen and ask questions that I could sometimes
answer, but I was alarmed by how little she seemed to
know about any of this history.

She had found a narrative that satisfied a deep
emotional need and seemed incapable of internalizing
anything that threatened it, least of all anything from
those same sources that had hidden the truth from her
for so long. I had a touch of the same fever myself.

It was a time of robust conversation in America's
governing class about how to deal with the
international communist conspiracy, even though a lot
of people, like Laura and myself, thought it was a
dangerously limited concept to begin with. Now with
this article it looked like I might have something to say
about the subject, which was exciting but also a
problem; because often as I read through the literature
I wanted the enemy to win, which I didn't think the
Times would appreciate. On the other hand, I had my
doubts. It was the conundrum of revolutionary
Marxism, so luminous in theory, so dismal in practice.

She said very little about what she was doing in
Mexico. A few stray remarks led me to believe there
was an office near the university and that she was
working with both Mexicans and Guatemalans. She
often had a railroad timetable that she would pull out
and study when we were alone. The first time it
happened, I asked her if she was planning on taking a
trip and she said no. I didn't ask again. I would learn a

lot more when news of the arrests in Mexico City hit the papers the following month.

The closest she ever came to explaining what she was doing was when we discussed a thick pamphlet she brought home one night — *The Theory and Strategy of People's War in Guatemala*. We talked a lot about it over the next few weeks. Scattered throughout were quotes from Marx, beginning with:

> *The ideas of the ruling class are in every epoch the ruling ideas, i.e. the class which is the ruling material force of society is at the same time its ruling intellectual force. The ruling ideas are nothing more than the ideal expression of the dominant material relations, the dominant material relationships grasped as ideas. Life is not determined by consciousness, but consciousness by life.*

Some of the language in the pamphlet approached the density of this quote, but the message was clear. In Guatemala the ruling class was the 20 families who, along with the fruit company, owned 98% of the land and controlled virtually all of the country's finance, commerce and industry. This was the same ruling class that, with its *Yanqui* masters, had installed the brutal dictators and crushed the democratic yearning of the Guatemalan masses. The solution was for the peasants and workers and patriotic middle class to build an army of the people to defeat the army of the ruling class and create a new government with the purpose of pursuing the interests of the vast majority of the Guatemalan people.

And then there was Vietnam.

In Mexico we had been reading of the early anti-war protests in the States and were curious, cut off from the anti-war movement but feeling a connection to it. Neither of us knew much about Vietnam. I spent a few days at the Lincoln Library in the American Embassy going through *New York Times* microfilm to get the history—Ho Chi Minh's long anti-imperialist struggle, the 1954 Geneva Accords that we violated, etc. I filled three small notebooks with quotes and commentary and one night we went over the material. We were both sort of shocked by the naked immorality of what our government was doing there.

"It's the same thing," she said.

"The same as what?

"Guatemala."

"I think it's more complicated than that."

"You always say that."

"It's usually the case."

"Look at Santo Domingo," she said. The Marines had just landed and two nights before we watched a torchlight parade down La Reforma to the Zócalo that ended with the burning of American flags and an effigy of Uncle Sam. "Do you think that's right?"

"Of course it's not right. But right and wrong and the realities of power exist in separate universes. Santo Domingo is not Guatemala and neither of them is Vietnam. For one thing, the population of Vietnam is four times more than Guatemala and Santo Domingo combined. That makes a big difference when it comes to guerrilla warfare. Even little Guatemala has an army of 50,000 soldiers who will shoot anyone they're told to shoot. How many fighters are there up in the mountains with the *FAR?*"

"You have to start somewhere," she said. "Look at Cuba."

You could argue that Cuba was the new revolutionary model or the exception that proved the rule. People smarter than me were convincing either way. Despite my intemperate remark to Fred Dubrow at Thornby's that night, I had no intention of crossing the line that Laura had crossed. Teaching people to read and write was as close as I cared to get to playing God: overthrowing governments was out of my league. All I knew for sure at the moment was how much I wanted this woman, wanted to begin a life together, to love and to be loved.

"They'll never let it happen again," I said. "That's why there are 42,000 American troops in Santo Domingo now."

"It could happen again. Why couldn't it? And even if it can't, isn't it something worth fighting for?"

"And dying for?"

"In revolution, one wins or dies." We were sitting at my desk in the hotel room. She lit a cigarette, exhaled and watched the smoke drift toward the door. "I think a basic way we're not alike is that I don't feel like an intellectual," she said.

There was that word again.

"I don't either," I said. "What does that mean?"

She tilted her head and took another drag on the cigarette.

"It's about being able to think abstractly, putting something together and making it grow abstractly. I know what's happening to me, what I think and feel about that, what I like and don't like. It's just the way my brain works—or doesn't."

"You did a great job on those revisions for the teacher's guide. It's hard work to think through certain kinds of questions, particularly when they're new. Didn't you have to do that in college?"

"I flunked Philosophy."

"Maybe you're being a little bit lazy about this."

"I'm not lazy. No one is. People are afraid, unconfident, anxious, depressed, but not lazy."

"And what are you?"

"Probably some variety of afraid."

"Of what?"

"Killing anyone."

"It's the nature of warfare."

"Maybe I'm a pacifist and don't know it."

"Then you shouldn't be doing what you're doing."

"What's the alternative, *vos*?"

"Educate people about what's really happening there."

"That's what *you're* doing," she said. "That's why your article is going to be so important."

THIRTY-THREE

She had such faith in this article. It would explain to the world what was really happening in Guatemala and so change the course of history. Having seen for myself the less-than-earth-shattering impact of the literacy article, I was not as convinced. I still very much wanted to do it for the same reason I did the literacy piece and what would become the meat and drink of my working life: tell what I thought was the truth to as many people as I could.

Laura had gotten clearance from the organization and was making the contacts for me to re-enter Guatemala. I had my Guatemalan tourist visa from the consulate in Mexico City and had a letter from the *Times* introducing me and requesting cooperation for a story I was doing, but the people in Guatemala kept changing the dates and routes. First I was to fly, then I was to go by bus; twice I had been packed, waiting for confirmation that never came. I began to think it would not happen and part of me did not mind at all.

These logistical problems also gave me a little better idea of what Laura was doing in Mexico. The hesitation and uncertainty from Guatemala reflected a movement under tremendous pressure. The armed units in the mountains apparently were no longer able to get everything they needed from inside the country.

"Things are going to get worse," she said. "We've got to prepare."

She would usually come back to the hotel at the end of the day and we would go to eat at the *torta* place across the street from the fronton courts. It was an old cathedral of a room with high Corinthian pillars and coarse red linen on the tables and very quiet except for the 20-minute break between matches when the place got hot and excited. It was fun then, too, to watch the gambling crowd, laughing, drinking, arguing, wolfing down the *tortas*, and then we would be alone again in the big muted space.

Some nights we walked through the *Alameda*, the treetops lit like green constellations, a band playing waltzes from the elevated wooden kiosk. At the far end of the *Alameda* was the ornate *Bellas Artes* building where the famous *Ballet Folklórico* performed, but that was like another world and we never went to see it. Our favorite place was a bench near the fountain with a naked stone maiden, refracted amber light rippling over her thighs. We sat there and talked and watched the people passing by.

We would go to a movie whenever we could. For no good reason other than a lot of publicity we went to see *El Derecho de Nacer*, one of those classics that somehow transcends its own clichés. It's about an abandoned baby who grows up poor but who becomes a very successful, kind and astonishingly handsome doctor. One day, out of the goodness of his heart, he treats an impoverished woman and so unknowingly saves the life of the mother who deserted him. The story left me cold, but I noticed Laura sniffling on cue along with almost everyone else in the theater. "It's very *sad, vos*," she whispered, her eyes never leaving the screen.

Walking back to the hotel she was amused but also disturbed at how the movie had gotten to her. The sentimentality was so obvious. It was propaganda against birth control, saving Catholic souls, etc. She analyzed it coolly and at length.

"But you were crying," I said.

"There was something believable about it. You felt this could have really happened."

"Only in a Mexican movie."

"Mister Toughie."

"You have a weakness for handsome young doctors."

We passed a restaurant with candles in the window and a doorman with three shiny rows of buttons on his coat.

"Why'd you say that?"

"I was thinking about Manolo."

"That's what I thought."

"It's not a crazy idea."

"Are you jealous?"

"Of course I'm jealous. I'm jealous of every guy you look at. You look at them the same way you look at me."

"That's not true."

It happened all the time. It was too innocent to call flirting, but it bothered me.

"Maybe you don't realize what you're doing."

"Or you're seeing things that aren't there."

"What about Manolo?"

We passed a restaurant with its door open. A woman's earring flashed green and from the bar came a deep American belly laugh.

"Are you sure you want to hear about this?"

"I'm not sure, but tell me."

"I was interested," she said, "but he had other priorities—and other girlfriends. I fell for him pretty hard. It was after I stopped coming to see you, after I heard from Paul. He came to Santa Cruz at least once a week and we'd spend hours talking. You know what a great talker he is."

Yes, I knew what a great talker he is, and I remembered that night he asked if I thought Laura had any prejudices.

"I didn't realize what was happening," she said. "I just liked him a lot, liked the talk and working with him and learning so much and feeling connected to something much bigger than myself, I don't know, it just happened."

"Did you sleep with him?"

"No. Not that I didn't think about it. I just knew it didn't mean the same for him. Just something convenient."

"Convenient for both of you."

"Don't be jealous, darling. Don't you understand by now how I feel about you?"

I thought I did, but I was also thinking about all the different ways love can die. Sometimes I would recall how I had been in love before and out of nowhere I would discover some odd imperfection in the object of my desire and how that would become the worm in the apple, the beginning of the end of what I knew as love. I kept waiting for this to happen with Laura, but this is not what happened.

Later that night we lay in bed listening to the footsteps advancing in the hallway below, doors closing, the Spike Jones music of the rinky-dink plumbing as it gasped and rattled to meet the sudden demand of a full house. Her hair fell across my face. It was heavy and smooth and sometimes I felt it might suffocate me.

"Do you like the way we make love?" she asked.

"What a question."

"Seriously."

"I love the way we make love," I said. "What about you?"

She turned onto her back and looked at the ceiling, as if the answer might be found in the flaking paint that was probably applied before we were born.

"It's like the 'Star Spangled Banner,'" she said.

"*What* are you talking about?"

"The rockets red glare, the bombs bursting in air."

"Such patriotic sex."

"We're living in sin," she said.

"Like everyone else in this joint."

"I don't feel guilty."

"Me neither."

"Do you think we should?"

"Absolutely not," I said.

"You're so sure of yourself."

"About some things," I said. "Others not."

"I'm sure about two things," she said. Ordinarily you would expect someone to say what they were, but this was a game we sometimes played. I had to guess what they were.

"About what you're doing politically," I said.

"If I had any doubts about that, I don't think I'd admit them even to myself at this point."

"But you have."

"When?"

"What you said about killing people."

"A moment of weakness," she said. "You should erase that."

"You're just interested in me for the article," I said.

"You *are* going to do it, aren't you?"

"Of course, if they can get it together down there. You also know I want you to come with me."

"I'm working on it."

She lowered her head to my chest and stayed very still for a long time. I thought about the movie and then the words of a song from high school that played one night when I danced with a girl I thought I would love forever as Frank Sinatra sang *"Fairy tales can come true, it can happen to you..."*

"What's the other thing you're sure of?" I asked her, my hand playing with her hair, tucking a strand behind her ear the way she would herself. Her face was buried in my chest. "You're not going to tell me the other thing you're sure of?" She lifted her head and looked at me. There were tears in her eyes. I asked her what was wrong.

"When we're together, I'm all here, not partly here," she said. "And it's beautiful to be with you."

THIRTY-FOUR

On Sundays we would treat ourselves to a big American breakfast at Sanborn's. The décor was more Swiss chalet than Mexican, but the tourists liked it and the price was right. You could also buy *The New York Times*. That morning there were two front-page stories on Vietnam. Malcolm X was making trouble again. Another mayor of Jersey City had run afoul of the law. It all sounded very far away.

We sat at the counter with the paper between us and ordered. Facing us along the curve of the counter was a woman with a nice tan and chalky green eye shadow.

"I'm not hungry," she said to the man next to her.

The man was paunchy and balding with curly black chest hair peeping through his shirt.

"Maybe a piece of pie?" he suggested. "Do you have any pie?" he asked the waitress.

"*Piña?*"

"Oh, they never speak English," the woman said. The man made a circle with his hand and then pointed to the pastry list on the menu. The waitress nodded. Then the woman changed her mind. "I want a cheese omelet. But fried in butter. Butter." She pointed to a pat of butter in front of Laura. "Damn it, Harry. She doesn't understand a *word*."

"*Tortilla de huevos fritos en mantequilla,*" Laura told the waitress, who gave her a big smile.

"Thank you," the woman said.

"You're welcome," Laura said and returned her attention to the paper.

"Oh, you're an American."

She elbowed her husband; it was a small world.

"Where you from?" the man asked.

"A little town near Kansas City."

The woman elbowed her husband again.

"Did you hear that, Harry? Isn't she adorable?"

"Where *you* from, son?"

"New York."

"City?"

"Yes."

"No kidding." He had a nephew in Forest Hills, a hotshot lawyer, maybe I knew him, which I didn't of course. Laura was turning through the *Times*. The woman got her omelet, folded it in half with her fork and sliced off a large mouthful. She gave me an approving nod.

"It's butter," she said.

Laura's hand dug into my thigh. I thought she was playing. I smiled at the woman and then looked at Laura. Something was wrong. She had my thigh with one hand and the other covered her eyes. The paper was open in front of her and she pointed to an article.

It was a brief article. A Guatemalan army deserter had turned up in Costa Rica and told the story there. Twenty-eight people missing for the past two months had been shot by firing squads. They had been tortured at police headquarters in the capital and then taken to the San José military base on the coast. The bodies were sewn into burlap bags and dropped into the ocean from a military transport plane. The soldier had the ID number of the plane. The article ended with the list of 28 names. Manolo was on the list. I didn't recognize any of the others.

Laura was shaking her head slowly. Her hand under the counter was still clamped to my thigh. I put my hand on hers. It was damp and cold and rigid.

The couple across the way had finished eating. The man paid the cashier and came back to where we were sitting. His rubbery stomach pressed against my elbow. "Anything we can do, son?" I shook my head and he put a hand on my shoulder. "What are a couple of kids like you doing so far from home?"

"Harry!" the woman shouted.

He ignored her.

"Well, the best of luck to you, in whatever you do."

"Harry! The limousine's waiting!"

We walked along La Reforma, the sunlight buttery on the green grass as people rustled past in the warming air, and under one of the great shade trees a boy and girl kissed as Rodin would have made them, except her eyes followed us as we walked past and a magazine slid from her lap.

"At least we know now," I said.

I thought about the road to the coast that went right past the barbed wire of the San José military base and over the canal built a long time ago by the fruit company and how calm the sea was the morning I swam there with Argelia. Then I thought about what Manolo told me in the ruins of Santa Cruz.

I waited for Laura to say something, but she didn't say anything.

We came to the circle where the Angel of Independence stood above the traffic, the golden angel offering her laurel wreath, her sun-tipped reflection clicking across the panel of mirror-black buildings as we walked along. I thought now was the time for a Sign, one of those cosmic jolts that illuminate the meaning of events, the ones outside and inside and their connections, so you knew exactly where you were and where you were going. But there were no heavenly signs that morning, at least none I could decipher, only Laura and the splendid sunlight and ordinary people and the awful news that was still not quite real. We had been waiting for word but not for this and yet this too served a purpose. It seemed like I kept getting blown off course and then blown back and still wasn't sure where I was headed, though for some reason I always knew when I had been blown off and when I was back on again.

I was back on again but it sure hadn't happened the way I had planned.

We sat down on a bench. An old man hurried over and before I could object began to shine my shoes: bent over, snapping the cloth, not speaking, *Justicia Social* embroidered on the back of his T-shirt. As he was finishing, he looked up with a big smile. "A real nice Sunday," he said, "first day of spring. And did you know it was also the birthday of our Benito Juárez, just a little Indian guy who really made something out of his life by working hard and struggling?" When he got up to leave he tossed us a cordial salute and said we could always find him right around here, same time every Sunday, rain or shine, and he picked up his shoe shine box and walked down the path toward some other benches.

"I have to go see some people," Laura said.

"You didn't know about any of this?"

"I knew there were problems." Her mouth tightened. "Didn't know how bad."

It fit together with all the delays and modification of instructions about how I was to travel, where and when to land, and what I understood to be at least one courier arrested here in Mexico and maybe talking too much.

"Maybe this isn't the right time to go," I said.

"We shouldn't have stayed here this long."

"What choice did we have?"

"I should have been back by now," she said. "I didn't really need to be here this long."

"You can't blame yourself."

Church bells erupted like an alarm, sending a wave of pigeons into flight around the Angel.

"I may not be able to come back to the hotel tonight."

I began to worry when she did not appear the next day or even Tuesday morning. She showed up Tuesday afternoon with a small suitcase.

"You had me a little worried," I said.

"You've seen this morning's papers?"

"No."

She pulled *La Prensa* out of her big shoulder bag and handed it to me—open at a story on page 2.

Yesterday Mexican police seized a large quantity of contraband arms destined for the red guerrillas in Guatemala. Federal Security agents captured Victor Hugo Martinez Pantaleon in the Express Service office of the National Railroads of Mexico as he was preparing a shipment of arms to Tapachula, Chiapas, where they were to be received by accomplices of the Guatemalan reds and smuggled across the border. It was he who led police to the house in Tlatelolco where six Mexicans and four Guatemalans were arrested in the operation. At least three other foreigners involved in the conspiracy are still at large.

"This is what you've been doing?" I asked.

She nodded. "How long will it take you to pack?"

"Not long," I said.

"Good. There's a seven o'clock bus to Guatemala."

I had practically nothing to take. I even left my portable typewriter with the desk clerk, telling him that if I were not back in a month it was his. He said that was very generous of me but hoped I would return. I hoped so too.

We walked the half dozen blocks to the bus depot. Laura said she had difficulty getting through to the organization, but somebody would meet us at the bus station in Guatemala City.

"Assuming we arrive on schedule," I said.

She patted my arm.

"We'll get there, *vos.*"

"Aren't you going to have a problem at the border?" I asked.

"Why?"

"That list. You're probably still on that *Judiciale* list."

"We've taken care of that."

She said it in that tone I had come to recognize: there would be no more discussion of this subject.

The sun had dropped behind the mountains, leaving a lone cloud glowing pink above the brown twilight of the city. On Avenida Juárez the thin scent of whisky hung in the air and buses went by shaking the ground. Over a loudspeaker in front of the National Lottery building they were announcing the winning numbers. They were singing the numbers, the soft androgynous voices of choir boys floating on the cool wind.

V

The Mountains

THIRTY-FIVE

We had prepared a story in case there were questions at the border. I had the letter of introduction from the *Times* and we had cooked up something about a harmless feature on the tourist trade. I was still worried about Laura's name on that list until I saw her passport. It was a new U.S. passport with her picture but not her name. The crossing was routine and nobody boarding the bus on the Guatemala side looked like an *oreja*.

When I think back to this return trip to Guatemala and the danger that awaited us there, I am still astounded by my innocent fearlessness. Maybe buried somewhere in my brain I did believe what Manolo had said about those things not happening to an American. Being with Laura was also part of it, the feeling of a protective aura cast over us both until this mission was completed.

So it did not take long to relax a little and content ourselves with the physical spectacle of the country: one minute cornered in a rocky canyon and the next soaring above a rich green valley or passing an adobe hut with resplendent flowers in the yard. The woman in front of us sat with her shoulder against the window and I saw how the colors of her bright shawl, colors I had seen before and always thought too rich to be natural, came from the hues and shades I could now see through the window: the vermilion of bougainvillea, russet from the freshly turned clay earth, the off-white of onions.

"How do you feel, *vos?*"

I thought about sharing my little insight about the woman's shawl but decided to let it simmer a while. I would tell her eventually, I thought. There wasn't anything I wouldn't tell her.

"Better than I should."

She smiled and patted the back of my hand.

"It's going to work out. You're going to write a great article."

"Then what?"

"Then we see."

"I want us to go back to the States," I said. "There's plenty to do there."

"I know."

Later in the dark we immersed ourselves in the changing air—cooler then warmer then dry cold—as the highway meandered through the mountains. There was a bright moon and snowy clouds and the mountains had a pale blue luster like the landscape of a dream. We would fall asleep for a while, Laura's head on my shoulder, the window open and the shifting sensations of the wind blowing in our faces, waking us up and lulling us back to sleep.

I thought about the time riding back from Santa Cruz with the little Sanchez boy going in for his eye operation. The kid was doing fine she had told me. She felt good about that, to the extent that she allowed herself to feel good about anything she had done in Santa Cruz. She was so hard on herself.

The bus rolled to a stop. Passengers stood up, straining for a view through the windows. A line of trucks moved past, headlights out, but in the ghostly light from the sky we could see the military insignia on the doors and the soldiers in combat gear sitting in the back of the uncovered transports, then the field guns bobbing on their trailers like enormous dark birds as the convoy crept along, the air clogged now with oil-scented dust. When the last vehicle was out of sight, the bus started up again.

With dawn we were rolling through the drylands, the soil a rust-colored ash and along the road giant cactuses hovering like twisted crosses. The drought had lasted longer than any but the oldest inhabitants could remember. A steel bridge sat ludicrously elevated, its massive cement pylons exposed on the piecrust of a riverbed. Entire villages seemed deserted, rows of adobe houses abandoned in the dust and baking heat.

The government had responded to the emergency with a well-publicized public works program. News accounts were sketchy but induced a kind of vague approval that at least something was being done. The first sign of its presence were the fences, miles of fences, branches stacked on forked posts with fresh white notches in the dark wood. But the fences served no purpose—no animals to pen, no crops to store, no property to demark—only idle hands to occupy. We came around a curve and suddenly the hills were swarming, boys and men, ragged and half-naked, with picks and shovels, digging holes, filling holes, moving earth in wheelbarrows, everything muted in the gray dust that heightened the illusion of having stumbled into another world, another time, like a panorama of slaves building the pyramids.

A man across the aisle shook his head.

"No rain," he said. "The sun kills everything. Not even armadillo left. The foxes stay, but with so much sun they chase their tails and die. The birds leave when they see there's nothing to eat."

"Like the people?" Laura suggested.

"The people are more or less like the armadillo. When they see the thing has gone completely to seed, they go. They move. Then the only creatures left are the buzzards and snakes."

As if on cue, we sped past a family of vultures dining on the glistening red carcass of a mule.

"Does it ever rain?" I asked.

"Oh yes," he said, "just enough to fool you."

We stopped once, at a barely inhabited little crossroads town. A poster on the walls showed a child with her face and body eaten away by Smallpox, a black band covering the eyes and bold print over the picture: *ERRADICAR LA VIRUELA—VACUNARSE.* Many of the posters had been torn down, considered perhaps a violation of the community's standards of decency. Here beggars overran the bus. Blind, hunchbacked, crippled, limbs gnarled or missing, a woman with running sores on her arms and legs, a leper with a flat sprocket for a nose. They scrambled aboard the bus, alone and paired, mother and child, sister and brother, grandparent and tot. Outside a man with his body cut off just below the ribs swung along on padded hands, charging back and forth in the street like a crazed dog.

The dust swirled up a little, there was a light ticking on the roof of the bus, and then it poured for five minutes.

THIRTY-SIX

We came into the city along *Avenida Bolívar* and pulled into a space behind the Central Market. It seemed that nobody had come to meet us. We sat on a bench, watching the bus unload, the crowd thinning out. A man lingered on the platform, glancing our way a few times, but then he left too. I felt the nerves tighten in my stomach. Laura lit a *Payaso* that flared and crackled and burned quickly.

"There's nobody here," I said.

"I know what you're thinking," she said.

"Am I wrong?"

"It wouldn't be the first time, *vos*. Come on."

We made one stop in the market where she bought a stalk of sugarcane. The woman chopped it into three pieces, each about a foot long, which she wrapped and that Laura put into her bag. We walked through the enormous indoor market, past produce covered with dirt and slabs of slaughtered animals still bloody, and through the portals into the noise and intense sunlight of the street that stopped you like a wall.

Then, behind us, a soft familiar voice.

"Good afternoon," Diego said. "We have a car."

He took our suitcases and we followed him around the corner. Yolanda sat behind the wheel of a

Volkswagen Bug. Laura and I got in the back and we pulled out. Yolanda caught Laura's eye in the rear-view mirror.

"We have to take him directly into the mountains," she said. "Things are too hot here."

"We saw something in the papers," Laura said. "About Manolo."

"Manolo and the others," Yolanda said. "Important people." She reeled off the names I didn't know. Victor Manuel, Leonardo, Bernardo, Clara ... names blurring into each other as the list grew, even though Yolanda pronounced each of them slowly: lingering over syllables as if seeing a face in her mind's eye or recalling some endearing trait, invoking their names now more for herself than anyone else. She concluded without anger or sorrow. "They didn't print a word of it here."

"It's true then?"

She slowed down to let a jeep pass.

"The truth is worse." We passed several more jeep patrols with their mounted machine guns. A tank blocked the road to the airport. "It's very tight. There's a curfew. They're sweeping whole blocks." She looked at Laura in the rear-view mirror. "Are you carrying, *compañera?*"

"No."

Yolanda nodded at Diego. I heard the clip of a handgun released and then slammed shut and the rattle of some loose ammunition. Then he handed

Laura the pistol wrapped in an oily piece of cloth. She found a place for it in her big shoulder bag and looked out the window.

We drove a couple of miles further along *Avenida Roosevelt* and then parked near the entrance of a new development, a bare track of cinder-block houses. There was nobody in sight.

"The contact's not here yet," Yolanda said.

We waited for what seemed a long time and then did a few turns around the perimeter of the development. The third time around Yolanda spotted the contact, a young man with a soft round face. When he stuck his head into our car, I saw that he was sweating.

"The white panel truck," he said nervously, "I think they've raided the house."

We all looked down the block and saw the truck in the driveway.

"Get in," Yolanda said. "We've got to get out of here."

"My wife's in the other car. She can't drive."

"Let Diego drive her."

"I want to see what's happening," he said. "Are you carrying?"

"Only pistols. You shouldn't stay."

"I have to see."

Yolanda was irritated.

"We'll meet you at the next corner in five minutes."

"Five minutes," he said.

He walked back to his car. We made a U-turn and drove away slowly.

"It's no good," Yolanda said to nobody in particular. "He gets too upset."

The contact was blown and they didn't know what to do with me.

"Maybe a hotel," Yolanda said.

"Or the house in Zone Two," Diego said.

"He needs a name," Yolanda said. She looked over her shoulder. "How should we call you?" she asked me.

I didn't understand.

"Pedro," I said. "Or Peter."

"No. A made-up name. Sometimes that is necessary."

It stopped me cold; I couldn't think of a name for myself. I ran through a few in my head, but none seemed right. Finally I said I would accept whatever name they gave me.

"Napo," Yolanda said.

Short for Napoleon. A sly insult, I suspected, which I decided to ignore.

"A great historical name," I said.

"Also the name of the police chief we recently executed," she said.

I looked at Laura.

"Napo," she said. "I sort of like it, *vos*."

A dark station wagon passed going the other way and a man inside looked hard into our car. Diego's voice jumped.

"It's them."

"Are you sure?"

"We have to get out of here," he said. "I think he recognized me. Take me where I can get a bus."

We dropped him near a stop that had some cover and drove back to the corner where the contact was supposed to be. He wasn't there and the white panel truck was gone. Yolanda stroked her chin.

"We have a little problem, Napo."

It took half an hour to get to the house in Zone Two. There were patrols everywhere. We drove down the Reforma, around the pint-sized Eiffel Tower in the traffic rotary, past the soccer stadium, across 18th Street—just a block from my old apartment—into the dense maze of the old city. I kept looking for someone I knew. It was all the same and it had all changed.

The house in Zone Two was on an upscale residential street behind a low wall and a yard thick with shrubs and flowering trees. The interior was the standard big open patio with all the rooms along two perpendicular walkways. The floors were expensive tile and the walls textured cement. It would have been a nice place to live, but the house was empty, not a stick of furniture.

Yolanda walked down the corridor along the patio checking the doors, some of which were locked. Then she came back.

"I'm afraid you'll have to stay here awhile," she said.

"How long's awhile?"

She gave me a long neutral look.

"I realize the accommodations are not the best," she said.

"That's not why I ask. I have a deadline."

This was not exactly true but close enough. She smiled faintly, with a glint of gold from those capped front teeth.

"We'll do the best we can, Napo."

Laura sat down on the floor of the living room and leaned back, her head flat against the wall. She looked tired.

"There's nothing to do now but wait," she said.

I went over and slumped down beside her. Yolanda had opened the window louvers a crack and was watching the street. The parka and slacks hid her frame, but she was tiny, maybe not five feet tall. She turned away from the window and looked at me.

"We can make you a little more comfortable," she said.

"It's alright."

"It will be difficult for you in the mountains."

Yes, I thought, and you would like me to say, that's right, it will be very difficult and perhaps I shouldn't go.

"I'll survive," I said.

"I certainly hope so." She turned back to the window again and after a moment said to Laura, "*Compañera*, may I have a word with you?"

The two of them left the room, an incongruous pair, the lanky American with her odd shuffling gait and her short compact companion whose every movement was a study in coiled efficiency. At first I could hear their voices from the patio but then it got quiet. I better get used to this, I thought. She was connected to them in a way that excluded me. She had accepted something that I evidently could not. This gave her access that I envied and feared. All I knew was that I had a job to do and I was going to do it if I possibly could.

Laura came back a few minutes later and sat down, her back against the wall, her arms clasped around her knees under the faded print dress. She would look at me and then at some random point in the room and then back again, her gaze shifting restlessly until it seemed to settle on the interior focus that she had been seeking all along. I waited for her to say something. I waited as long as I could.

"What was that all about?"

"She wanted to know if I was sure about you."

"Are you?"

She flinched, as if I had slapped her across the face. She looked at me for a long time, shaking her head slowly.

"How can you ask me that? How can you ask me that *now*?"

She leaned back against the wall again and stayed very still.

"I'm sorry," I said.

"I know you don't agree with everything we're doing, but I know you'll be fair. You'll do your best to tell the truth. We don't expect anything more than that."

"What do I say about killing police chiefs?"

"I knew that bothered you."

"How do *you* feel about it?"

"I don't like it, but I think about Manolo and twenty-seven other people and how they died."

"Revenge."

"Not revenge," she said. "War."

Diego showed up later that afternoon. He came with sandwiches and sodas and the evening papers. The junta had the guerrillas on the run in the mountains and were smashing terrorist cells right and left in the city. I asked Yolanda if it were true about the mountains.

"There have been problems," she said. "But they cannot destroy us. One dies, another takes his place. You will see."

When it got dark we discovered there was no electricity in the house. There were sounds from the street—dogs barking, the lazy whistles of watchmen making their rounds—alarming at first but then reassuring. The nocturnal routine of a well-off residential neighborhood with streetlights that also helped us get around inside the house. I sat on the floor, making notes. Laura came over and sat down beside me, resting her head against my shoulder. She didn't say anything. Her face was intense and lovely in the dim light and I wondered when we would be alone again.

She stood up.

"I'll be right back," she said.

"I'll go with you."

"I'm going to the bathroom, dear."

She walked down the hallway and I heard a door close. Yolanda was watching Diego clean his pistol. He had it broken down on a paper bag and she was studying him closely, following each step of the drill, ready to ask a question or point out an error. There was an unspoken camaraderie between them, a give and take that would have been unusual for the university student and the *campesino* in their normal lives. I asked Yolanda how old she was.

"How old do you calculate me?"

"Nineteen."

"On the nose."

The same age as Argelia, I thought. How could two women, growing up in the same city at the same time, be so different?

Yolanda turned on a little radio she kept in her parka and found some music. They were playing *"Themes From The Movies."* When "Maria" from *West Side Story* came on, she said it reminded her of her second year in high school when a boy would stand under her balcony and serenade her with this song. I didn't get the connection.

"But your name isn't Maria."

She glared at me and snapped off the radio.

"You're very clever," she said.

I realized what had happened.

"That wasn't my intention."

"It doesn't matter. Every other girl in Guatemala is named Maria." She got up and walked over to the window. There was a vacant lot on the corner, illuminated by a geometrically perfect cone of light from an old dish-reflector lamppost. "It is difficult to love in these days when dawn may leave one a widow," she said softly.

"One could avoid marriage," I said, and only then I remembered what Laura had told me about Yolanda's *compañero.*

"Who said anything about marriage? I said to love."

"There is a difference," I agreed.

She was still looking out the window when Laura came back.

"It's late," Yolanda said. "We should all try to get some sleep."

Diego dragged in a mattress. I wondered where he had gotten it. The place had appeared empty. I figured it must have come from one of the locked rooms. Yolanda and Diego left us alone, though they were still in the house, somewhere in the back, and I had the impression they expected others.

"Nobody's coming tonight," Laura said. "It's after curfew. Too dangerous."

A series of whistles sounded from the street. We were sitting on the straw mattress with our backs to the wall. It wasn't what I had in mind, being stranded in a dark house in the custody of strangers who could only survive by killing their enemies.

"We couldn't get out of this now," I said, "even if we wanted to."

"Is that what you want?"

"I want to get out of this house to do what I came to do."

"You have to be patient."

"I don't trust them. They don't know what they're doing."

"We have a lot to learn," she said. "We'll make mistakes."

"There are plenty of things you can do back in the States ," I said. "To help."

"I can't leave now."

She traced slow circles on the back of my hand, the same rhythmic circles that her lips had traced over my body in a time and place that now seemed very far away.

We made love that night on the thin straw mattress, but it was not very good. The floor was hard. Her body was hard. It was quick and silent and mechanical like she wasn't there at all.

Later we were awakened briefly by unfamiliar voices talking with Yolanda and Diego and then something that sounded like furniture being moved in one of the back rooms. I would soon learn there were 200 pounds of dynamite in our little safe house.

THIRTY-SEVEN

When I opened my eyes in the morning, Laura wasn't there. Diego was sitting across the room.

"Good morning," he said.

I had the feeling he'd been waiting for me to wake up.

"Good morning. Where is everyone?"

"In back." Then he read my look and added, "It's best that you stay here." He took a notebook out of his back pocket, glancing at me as he flipped through it. There was something tentative and vaguely familiar about his look. He was coming on like a beggar, the humble slant of the head, the needy eyes, this pathetic ritual of humiliation and superiority played out a thousand times a day in the streets of the city. He was working up his courage to make the touch and I felt sick that this was happening now, here, with this man. Then he asked, "I don't suppose you'd be interested in hearing something I wrote, would you?"

I felt like kissing the guy.

"Sure."

"You know, a commentary from a *campesino* for your article."

"Go ahead."

He began reading, the litany, how his people had suffered, had suffered for centuries, and now the time had come to fight. He'd pause to say something like "That's more or less it, you can change it of course, fix it up." Straight out of *The Theory and Strategy of People's War in Guatemala*, I thought. Our distinguished ambassador had been right about teaching them to read propaganda. This was dangerous stuff alright. One man's propaganda can be another's gospel, but I still didn't like it. I didn't like anyone spewing ideas that were not truly his own.

"The yoke of oppression," I said, a phrase he seemed particularly fond of. "What does that mean?"

He laughed uneasily. Laura came back into the room and sat down against the wall.

"I see you're not familiar with the *campo*," Diego said.

"No."

"The yoke is a wooden collar you put around the neck of the beast to keep it in line."

"You yourself did not wear a yoke," I said.

"Why are you doing this?" Laura interrupted in English.

"I'm trying to get beyond the rhetoric."

"It's not rhetoric," she said.

"There's nothing wrong with rhetoric. The question is what's behind it."

"I *did* wear a yoke," Diego said now, again with that embarrassed laugh. "I worked in the city for a few months with my own cart, transporting things. Actually, it was more like a harness than a yoke, but that isn't what I was talking about. I was talking about something else that I thought you should know." He sat there, chin in hand, eager to play.

They do have names. They really are the same flesh as yourself.

"So what does it mean, the yoke of oppression?"

He stroked his chin.

"Well, when you work for the *patron*, they call you in from the fields with a horn." He illustrated, tilting his head back, his hands cupped to his mouth. "The same horn they call the animals with. They kick you. They feed you slop worse than the pigs get. That's what it means."

He had finished.

"Did you get what you wanted?" Laura asked.

"It's a start."

"I'm glad you're doing this and not me."

"I don't think he minds."

She turned to Diego and engaged him with that tenderness that could still make me jealous, only now it did not hurt in the same way, and she got him talking some more, about a time when he had been cheated out of his wages on a road crew. I took notes as she gently coaxed the story out, a reproach, whether conscious or not I couldn't tell, to my abrasiveness. Yolanda appeared in the hallway, between the living room and the front door.

"There's someone here," she said.

Diego drew his pistol. Laura waved me away from the window and I moved closer to where she sat on the floor. She kept her right hand in her bag. Yolanda opened the door for a lanky young man who walked in without a word and then went down the hall, checking doors, windows, the wall of the patio, sight lines to the street from these different positions. Others arrived now at ten-minute intervals, four men, armed and very agitated. They sat in a circle on the floor, trying to figure out what had happened. Sometimes one of the men would illustrate a point or reconstruct the encounter by drawing a diagram with his finger on the floor. The *Judiciales* were raiding everywhere, people missing, documents seized. There were long pauses as they tried to steady themselves. Then Laura said something and there was more talk, but much lower and I couldn't hear. They all stayed there huddled together as I watched from the far side of the room.

Then Diego and Laura got up and took a position near each of the two windows in the front room. One had a view of the street and the other of the vacant lot next door.

Yolanda called me over and asked me to sit down next to the tall thin man who had come in first. They were all looking at me. Yolanda nodded toward him."The *compañero* would like to ask you a few questions," she said to me.

He sat cross-legged on the floor. A large 9-millimeter pistol rested flat on his thigh. He had a braided scar that ran from the back of his ear to his lower throat.

"I am told you have been here since yesterday afternoon," he said.

"Yes."

"The entire time?"

"Yes. I wasn't alone. Others were here. Why are you asking me this?"

"Just answer," one of the other men said.

"Tell us," the tall thin man said. "What will you do when you finish here? Will you go back to work for your government?"

"I never worked for the government."

"You worked for Robert Thornby."

"I didn't work for Thornby."

"You understand what he does."

"More or less."

"If you were still working for Thornby," he said, "we would have to think about executing you."

"I don't work for Thornby."

He asked me about reporters for different American newspapers. What did I think of this one? That one? Why wasn't I better informed about their work? I don't recall my answers but remember thinking they were not such good answers and then I saw him raise the pistol and felt the muzzle pressing hard against the side of my head.

"Now," he said, "we would like the truth."

I turned away with my eyes shut thinking if that damn thing goes off I don't want to see the mess. I don't know how long I sat there waiting for the bullet to smash into my skull. Then it was over. They were all talking about something else. Diego and Laura returned to the group and I was told to go back where I had been in the front room. I sat by the window. A boy and a girl were playing in the vacant lot on the corner. Trees blocked the view to the street, but something had distracted the two kids. A few more minutes went by and the meeting began to break up. I looked out the window. The two kids were running away.

THIRTY-EIGHT

"You should get ready, Napo." Yolanda said politely. "We'll be leaving very soon."

I was closing my small suitcase when Laura saw something and stopped me. She took out the shirt she had worn that first night in Mexico and held it for a moment against the lower half of her face and then gave it back to me.

"I love that shirt," she said.

"So do I. When are we leaving?"

"We have to leave in two groups. You're going first."

"I want us to leave together."

She shook her head.

"I already asked," she said.

I took her by the hand and led her onto the patio. It was bright but still cool in the morning air. All the plants were brown and dead.

"We should insist," I said.

"I'll be right behind you, darling."

The sunlight brought out a trace of rusty gold in her hair that I had never noticed. I wanted to be absolutely sure now that I saw her face as it really was—the faint saddle of freckles over the ridge of the nose that disappeared into the tight skin of those high cheeks, the wide smooth forehead and the green eyes like mine and her mouth warm in the cool air with the patio wall behind her and the treetops beyond etched into a pure blue sky, that wonderful mouth, weighted down now like the fruit-heavy limb of a supple tree until I disintegrate in that mouth and cannot think at all. I pulled back.

"Nobody kisses like that," I said.

"It's the only way to kiss you, *vos.*"

"Napo," Yolanda said impatiently. "We really must leave!"

I broke away following her and Diego out the door. We had gotten about halfway down the front walk of the house when she dove to the ground. Diego pulled me down.

"*Judiciales.*"

I couldn't see them, but Yolanda shouted over her shoulder.

"Three guys! Machine-gun! Across the street!"

Lying on the grass a few feet in front of us, Yolanda fired her big pistol on automatic, her arm vibrating like a jackhammer. Leaves flew off a tree across the street. I was flat on the ground with my heart pounding in my head.

"I'm going back," I told Diego.

He held me down.

"*Cálmate.*" He shifted his weight so I couldn't move at all. "They have the machine gun on the door."

The house spit a shower of concrete. They were walking a heavy machine gun from one end to the other. Somebody fired a burst from inside; the machine gun answered and a window fell apart. Then something ripped into the house, tearing a hole in the roof, and black smoke swirled out.

"We've got to move!" Yolanda shouted.

She crawled to the low wall along the sidewalk, braced herself with her back against the wall and pulled a grenade out of her parka. Another shell ripped into the house, blasting a hole in the side just below the roof. The firing inside stopped. The smoke was much thicker now.

Diego had rolled off me onto his belly but stopped firing when he saw the smoke behind us.

"*Madre de Dios,*" he whispered.

Yolanda pulled the pin and lobbed the grenade. There was a pop. She stood up and waved us forward. The grenade had misfired but one *Judiciale* was already dead next to the machine gun and two others were running down the street, one of them lugging the bazooka that had done the damage to the house.

Diego grabbed my suitcase and we bolted through the front gate. We ran in the opposite direction from the *Judiciales*. *I am going to get it when we turn the corner and there is another machine-gun instead of the car,* I am thinking; but the Volkswagen Bug was there, looking innocent and forlorn on this suburban street, framed by flowering flamboyant trees against a preposterously blue sky.

We had reached the car when the trees snapped in an invisible blast of wind and then a boom so close it shook the car. The sky went dark with gritty black smoke. We were driving away when Diego said it was the house. I rolled down the window. It was a strange darkness, the gray half-light of an eclipse, and a cloud very dense and smooth with a bruised color in the center.

THIRTY-NINE

As we drove away I kept thinking that maybe she had gotten out and then I would think of course she had not and I wanted to cry but couldn't. I tried to force it but heard the dry, shallow sobs of someone outside of myself and I wondered what had happened to the feelings that should have been there.

It was like that when my mother died. The heart freezes but you don't know it's frozen. You walk around for years or maybe even the rest of your life thinking you are perfectly normal until, if you are lucky, you are able to return to the scene of the crime, so to speak, and perhaps restore something of what has been destroyed.

We pulled into a parking lot behind some vacant storefronts to get the car off the road and wait for a prearranged contact to appear. When the contact did not materialize, we headed for another location on a roundabout route that kept us away from the military patrols.

Yolanda and Diego talked about the men who had also been in the house, but they were strangers to me and meant nothing. Yolanda tried to get me talking. I mumbled something about Laura knowing what she was doing, knowing the risks. The words came out but were not connected to anything. It seemed that any sound was better than silence and empty words better still and movement, simple movement, best of all.

We eventually changed cars and left for the mountains after dark. When the sun came up we were on a straight black stretch of highway with silky fields on our right and on our left mountains with their slopes pressed against the road. There was some military traffic. I asked what would happen if they stopped us.

"We have official identification," Yolanda said.

"What about me?"

"Tell them the truth. You're a foreign journalist. You have some kind of credentials, no?"

"Yes."

She made eye contact with me in the rear-view mirror. "You can change your mind, you know. We would understand that."

"I've come this far."

"Perhaps you should think about it."

But there was nothing to think about now except getting the story I had promised Laura I would get.

Late in the day we pulled off the highway and parked behind a store. Yolanda told me to take just what I needed from the suitcase. I took out a few pens and blank notebooks, a toothbrush and toothpaste and bought a small canvas shoulder bag in the store. Diego said he would lock the suitcase in the trunk of the car. I said ok but then on an impulse took the shirt out and put it in my bag. I never got the suitcase back but still have the shirt, along with a few other artifacts from those days.

We crossed the highway and began walking. Within an hour we could see the valley below, the river, the ribbon of highway flat between the green quilt of field and then curving behind the mountains. There was a last strip of scrubby hill above us and then a grove of brown pines tinted purple in the early twilight. The wind hissed like steam coming through the trees.

"The camp is just beyond those trees," Diego said. "We'll be safe there for a while."

The camp was in a cool glen with a high ledge on one side and a stream through the middle. The water in the stream was deep and very clear and slid past the boulders without a sound. On a field above the camp a ragged squad of older men and boys and women were drilling with sticks for rifles. They made their own gunfire sounds and were lighthearted. Yolanda explained they were members of a local support committee and would go back to their village when they finished the drill.

After dark we ate a meal of black beans and *tortillas*. We drank watery coffee and listened to the news on the radio. There was a brief item about several terrorists killed in an operation in Zone Two.

"That's it?" I asked.

"There'll be more," Yolanda said. "When they decide the information is of no use to us."

We moved at night and rested during the day. In the morning there was more coffee, beans and *tortillas* but also eggs sent by a nearby farmer. One morning we stopped next to a rocky pool that was well covered by trees and after breakfast the men bathed and swam in their underwear. I had seen two other women in addition to Yolanda, but they only went into the water after dark. Mostly everyone slept in the daylight hours.

But one day after lunch I noticed Diego with three other men and one of the women sitting in a circle with their rifles across their laps and books open in front of them. Yolanda saw that I was interested and came over. She seemed different here in the mountains. With the holstered pistol on her hip and in her khaki shirt and a red bandana tied loosely around her neck, the closest they came to a uniform, she looked very much the soldier.

"A literacy class," she said. "Would you like to observe?"

They were reading *Juan*. Diego was the instructor and knew his stuff, asking someone to talk about what had just been read, his tone always respectful. He lifted words and sentences from the page and used them in familiar conversation. He had not paid attention to Yolanda and me sitting just outside the circle, but toward the end of the class he pulled a copy of the teacher's guide out of his knapsack and introduced me, "the famous literacy expert," to the class. He made a lesson out of it, reading my name on the back page, reading Laura's name, "*La Laura*, a beloved *compañera* who cannot be with us today." He passed it around for everyone else to read and pronounce. This sudden invocation of Laura made me want to withdraw to some more private place.

"I am sure the *compañero* would like to say a word or two," Diego said.

I knew he meant well and so I gave the speech I had given I don't know how many other times as I traveled around the country. What a great thing it was to learn how to read and write; all the other people around the world who were doing the same thing—and they responded with the same murmurs of assent and smiles of approval I had seen everywhere else.

Of course there were some differences with this audience. They asked me about Vietnam, the struggle of *los Negros* in the United States and what I knew of our invasion plan for Guatemala. I don't think they found my answers satisfactory, but when we were done, each insisted on shaking my hand, thanking me for coming, complimenting my Spanish and asking where they could get other booklets. Diego made a big pitch for more booklets, so well honed that I suspected he had set up the whole thing with this in mind. Then they were gone, and Yolanda cracked a rare smile.

"You were blushing," she said.

Later that day a *campesino* came rushing into the camp to warn of army units nearby. A shot rang out from the sentry post and we took off and didn't stop for five hours.

FORTY

On the evening of my fourth day in the mountains, a man arrived from the city with some documents. He also brought a newspaper with a big front-page story about the battle in Zone Two. There was a photo of the blasted house with nothing left but the jagged remnants of walls. The roof had been blown off. The story had many details, including the 200 pounds of dynamite that were detonated in the firefight. Inside where the story jumped was a two-page spread with more photos and the names and ages of the three *Judiciales* and five terrorists—including an American, Laura Jenson, 23—who were killed.

The American made the story especially sensational. There was a photo of her taken in Santa Cruz that I still have and am looking at now. She's perched on the ledge of a street-level window with kids all around her and in her lap the Sanchez boy in his Superman T-shirt, the whole crew so goddamn happy I never know what to think except that someone made a terrible mistake. In the photo you see the curve of her calf below the hem of the loose skirt, a curve accentuated by the ankle strap of her sandal, like a dancer gracefully in command of her movement; but she was not graceful in the ordinary physical sense of the word, so the grace you feel is not related to the composition of cloth and bone and flesh, but to something else that radiates from the image.

The American Embassy identified her from the tip of a finger found in the wreckage. I thought of the strange cloud as we drove away from the house and of her dissolving that way, into the air I was breathing. That's how I will always remember it. I don't care if it's true or not.

Somehow I got my work done. I interviewed the young and angry leaders who explained how the movement was growing and what it would accomplish. Land to the landless, hospitals and schools for the sick and the poor. I interviewed farmers who brought food into the camp and soldiers who had deserted the regular army and students who spent long weekends in the mountains to breathe the pure mountain air of The Revolution and sometimes to be married by a rebel priest. I interviewed the priest who said that God blessed the struggle. I was methodical and precise. I had my story and felt good about that but on the inside I was numb.

Some of the young and angry leaders kept testing me. They would ask the same question from different angles to see if I would give the same answer. They tossed out technical information about their weaponry to gauge my interest and knowledge. They had Diego take me to bathe in a stream and afterward Yolanda told me this was how they had caught another gringo who said he was a journalist but had a Special Forces strangulation cord hidden under his shirt. She told me about his trial and execution.

Diego had been assigned to watch me. Sometimes he had his little notebook out and would ask for advice. He seemed embarrassed by my semi-captive status and so would pretend that our forced intimacy was coincidental or even natural.

"Nice night," he said, as we lay awake on the fern matting he had fixed up. "You warm enough?"

"I'm alright."

"It's cold. I've got an extra blanket."

"Thanks."

The blanket made a big difference. I began to relax in the heat of my own body. The sky was brilliant with stars.

"One of your satellites." He pointed out the dull close object moving like a planet through its man-made orbit. "It takes pictures, you know."

"Does it worry you?"

"We have to be very careful." He lay there with his hands clasped behind his head, looking at the sky. "What will you do when you go back?"

"Write this article."

"And then?"

"I don't know."

"You could stay here and help us," he said.

"I wouldn't be much help."

"*La Laura* was."

Don't do this, I thought. You have no right to do this.

"That was her way," I said.

"You will speak with her family when you go back?"

"I wasn't planning to."

"They should know the truth. They have lost a good daughter. Someone must explain."

"Yes," I said. "Someone should."

The next day a man came with a message that they had arranged to get me out of the country without returning to the city. The place we would meet the contact was only a half-day's march.

"You'll be leaving tomorrow," Yolanda said. She had taken me aside so that whatever she had to say would be private; we stood next to the massive ledge that had protected us for the night. "I assume you're eager to leave."

"I've got what I need."

She touched my arm lightly, but then kept her hand there a moment longer than I thought she would.

"I'm sorry," she said. "I truly am."

FORTY-ONE

Neither of us, nor anyone on Earth, could have imagined the sorrow that awaited this hard little country. Yolanda herself would die in battle two years later, mercifully spared the 30 years of conflict that claimed 200,000 lives and reached the height of its genocidal fury against the Mayan people in the early 1980s.

Of course in that sense Laura too was spared—from witnessing the horror inflicted on these people but also from committing the crimes she herself might well have had to commit in the course of this war. If you were so inclined, you might say God would never have allowed Laura Jenson to kill anyone, though it's not something I would say.

In the same file cabinet where I keep the newspaper with the photo of Laura is the 1999 report of the Guatemala Truth Commission that documents 626 massacres attributable to the government. The guerrillas were not angels and took innocent life themselves, but they were responsible for about 3% of the crimes committed, none of them characterized by the barbarity of the government-sponsored massacres.

The names of a few of these places in the report I recognize from those first field trips I took over mountain trails and across parched valleys and into lush tropical settlements to make the acquaintance of men and women teaching themselves to read and write.

The atrocities from one place to another are remarkably similar, which is logical since they were carried out by disciplined soldiers implementing the government's merciless strategy.

Here is one such account about a place I knew well:

In the early morning of December 6, 1982 a contingent of 58 elite Kaibiles commandos, whose training included killing animals and drinking their blood, entered Santa Cruz del Quiché looking for weapons they said the guerrillas had hidden there. Many of the men of the town who collaborated with the guerrillas had fled into the mountains, leaving behind the women and children and men who did not believe they had anything to fear.

The Kaibiles herded everyone out of their houses and separated the men from the women and children, placing the men in the schoolhouse and the women and children in the church. They found no weapons or guerrilla propaganda. The army officer in charge consulted with superiors by radio and then informed the Kaibiles they should begin "vaccinating" the inhabitants of Santa Cruz del Quiché.

They separated the children and began killing them. They held the smallest ones by the ankles and smashed their heads against walls and trees. The older ones they killed with hammer blows to the head. When they finished with the children, they began with the women. First they cut the fetuses out of the pregnant ones. Then they separated the very young women and took them to the pensión on the plaza and raped them and broke their necks when they were done. Then they began interrogating the women who remained in the church and, when they finished with each, took her into the plaza and slit her throat.

All of this with the women and children went on throughout the day and night of December 6. On the morning of the 7ᵗʰ they began interrogating the men in the schoolhouse. They hung the mayor and three others from a nearby tree, but they didn't kill any of the other men at that time. They brought them to the plaza to dispose of the dead women and children and wash the blood off the walls and trees and from the pews and floor of the church. The Kaibiles had ordered the men to drop the children into a well behind the schoolhouse, but the well filled up too quickly so the plan was changed.

In the late afternoon the men loaded all the bodies into wheelbarrows, pushed them up the smooth red path to the cemetery on the hill and then to the edge of the deep barranco where vultures circled above their feast. After each man had dumped the contents of his wheelbarrow into the barranco, he was told to wait there until all the others had done the same and then the squad of Kaibiles used their Uzi submachine guns to execute the remaining men.

The Truth Commission report, titled *Memory of Silence*, states that 203 people were killed in Santa Cruz in those two days—107 children, 70 women and 26 men.

I have traveled much of the world in the course of my working life and seen my share of the cruelty that human beings inflict on one another. Like most other educated people I am aware there is no shortage of barbarism any place on earth inhabited by our species, but I have never returned to Guatemala.

As I sit here in my little house above the sea, I am grateful for the departure of winter and the coming of a kinder season, when I hope what is left of my mind will be much less likely to drift back 50 years to those mountains.

FORTY-TWO

That last night there we stopped in a village and held a type of meeting the *FAR* called Armed Propaganda. They built a small fire in the grassy square and a patrol went house to house, informing people of the meeting. In the dark you could feel the cold mist rolling down the mountain. The heavy air felt like a tomb and I couldn't stop shivering. I hated these moments alone with my thoughts because everything was about Laura and was small and pinched and ugly. I thought she had thrown away something precious that belonged also to me and I was angry—at her, at Manolo, at all of them—and I took some satisfaction in thinking that if I couldn't have her at least now nobody else could either. I hated myself for thinking this but could not escape the pain and bitterness that obliterated anything generous or good or loving.

Then I saw the orange lights on the dark mountain, zig-zagging down, the same lights we had seen from her house that night in Santa Cruz. Now the men emerged from the darkness holding their flaming sticks of *ocote* that they threw into the fire.

They sat around the fire with us and told their
stories, how they had taken the land, sneaking in at
night, cutting down trees, clearing brush; how they
would scour the hills for a single breadfruit to feed
them for the day; how even now the land was giving
out, the second crop of yucca half as high as the first.
There was good land in the valley, fertile land, and
miles of it unplanted year after year. They could see it
from the village. They could taste it.

"Yes, that's why we are here," Yolanda said.
"Gather in closer to the fire where you will be warm.
Together. That's how we must be from now on." Her
voice was calm and strong but soft after the rough
angry voices of the men. "When I was a little girl I
remember my father looking down our street at the
mango and *manzanilla* and *cocos* and all the other fruits
that grow so abundantly in our soil, and he said, 'how
can it be? A country so rich with people so poor?'"
Murmurs of recognition rippled through the gathering.
She turned to the man beside her and touched his thick
white shirt held together with patches. She asked him
how many shirts he owned. The man laughed
nervously and held up one finger. "You work from
dawn to dusk," she said, "and you work hard, and yet
you have one shirt to your name. Is that fair? When
you bring your crops into town they tell you how
much they will pay, but when you buy in the store *they*
tell *you* how much to pay. You have no hospital, no

school. You work to make others rich and you have nothing. I ask you, is that fair?"

"We're alright," someone said.

There was silence around the crackling fire. A few of the men stole glances at Yolanda, who sat there and said nothing. Then an old man with a stubble of gray whiskers stood up and waved his hand contemptuously at the others.

"They're all afraid," he said. "Afraid of the army. Afraid of their own shadows, these people. I tell them, it's time to take land on the plain, like we did in '53. I tell them, we all go together, there won't be enough jails to hold us."

"Quiet, you old fool!"

"I'll say what I like. You're all cowards."

There was shouting as others jumped in for and against the old man. Yolanda studied each as he made his point, nodding whether she agreed or not. After everyone had spoken there was this kind of gravitational pull back to her again. She sat there with her back straight and legs crossed, presiding over the silence. The way she was sitting exposed a few inches of bare leg above one of her socks. The skin was smooth and brown and the leg itself almost dainty. A fine little body smuggled into those baggy clothes.

"That's why we are here," she said finally. "That army is the army of the oligarchy and opposed to your interests. We are the army of the people asking you to join. The struggle will be long. Many will fall, have fallen already. But can you really go on living like this?"

The men nodded pensively, their rough hands covering their mouths. A woman brought out a basket of *tortilla*s and we ate silently around the dying fire. Yolanda switched on the radio and found "The Voice of America." She said it had the best music and the news was amusing.

Another Italian government had fallen. A vote in Congress for the war in Vietnam. The Cubans up to their despicable tricks somewhere on the continent. Someone chuckled.

Then something about "An Hour Of The World's Finest Classics."

I reached for my pipe and discovered it was broken, a jagged break in the stem, snapped in two, and I felt a gnawing irrational anger needing the smoke and knowing the pipe was broken. It was my best pipe and it was broken forever. Even when I got another, which I would the first chance I had, it would not be the same.

It would never be the same, I thought, and it never was.

Someone threw a bundle of brush into the fire and in the flaring light I saw Yolanda staring at me with those small dark eyes and I began to cry, very quietly at first, and though I certainly knew *why* I was crying I did not know why *now* until I heard the music on the radio, that melody from "The Pastoral," when you begin to hear the horns clearly; then the crying just poured out and I tried to say *please shut off the radio*, my hand raised weakly, but only the uncontrollable sobbing came out from some place so secret and deep I could not tell you where, crying for Laura and I guess also Manolo and my poor dead mother and all the other casualties of life and war I knew and didn't know but imagined I knew in that moment of orgiastic grief.

Alarmed faces crowded close, wanting to help. Finally I managed to get the words out and someone shut off the radio. Yolanda put her arm around me, very lightly, formally, but also comforting, and we stayed like that for a while until I calmed down. The meeting broke up and we were about to leave when Diego came over, clearing his throat, his pale eyes working nervously.

"I've talked to the others," he said in that soft tenor that always sounded on the verge of tears. "We've decided. When you come, you know, with your Marines, you wear a red bandana here." He touched his throat. "That way we'll know you."

He stood there and for an instant I considered offering the same privilege of safe passage in the event of his country invading mine, but the absurdity of the idea was not humorous at all. I smiled and said nothing and he went back to the others. Yolanda was watching and did not seem to mind.

"You'll have to tell them not to send any more gringos like *vos*," she said. "You're bad for our morale."

FORTY-THREE

Moving over the trail that night we could hear people slip and stumble along the line. Some carried packs of more than 50 pounds. It was impossible to see the ground beneath your feet but in the starlight you could pick out the brightest object on the person in front of you, a hat, a sock, and from its movement get the lay of the land. I kept waiting for my eyes to adjust, but it stayed like that all through the night.

With dawn came thick gusts of fog. We stopped repeatedly to get our bearings. We were still high in the mountains but now I could see we were on a ridge running parallel to the highway below. The highway ran through a settlement where Yolanda said we would meet my contact. We had just begun moving again when she insisted that we double back to see something. We got to the place she wanted and then we all stood there, speechless and amazed.

In the distance were the sleeping volcanoes, smooth and blue against the burning rose of the sky, and below the volcanoes were miles of space and the tops of clouds rippled like tidal flats, clouds flowing from horizon to horizon or breaking up against the mountains so only the tallest peaks were visible like islands in a misty sea. The place had changed, had crossed that elusive line between the exotic and the beautiful, and I knew why.

"Is dawn always like this here?" I asked.

Yolanda smiled.

"You should see it later in the spring," she said. "When the flowers are in bloom."

*   *   *

Book Club Discussion Questions

1. What would you have done in Laura's situation, sent to this impoverished village and unable to improve the living conditions of the people there in any meaningful way?

2. Were you surprised by Peter's attraction to Argelia? Do you think she was in love with him?

3. Is Thornby a bad person or is he just presented in a negative light by Peter who does not like him? What if anything did you learn about U.S. policy in countries like Guatemala?

4. Was Manolo a terrorist? What is the difference between a terrorist and a revolutionary? Peter says the JFK assassination was the first time a political event affected his "interior life." What if any political event(s) have affected you in this way?

5. Peter says on several occasions that he does not believe in God. Do you think that's true?

6. What effect do you think Peter's experience as a young man in Guatemala had on the rest of his life? Does Peter blame himself for Laura's death? Do you think he should?

# # #

More books from
Harvard Square Editions:

People and Peppers, Kelvin Christopher James

Gates of Eden, Charles Degelman

Love's Affliction, Fidelis Mkparu

Transoceanic Lights, S. Li

Close, Erika Raskin

Anomie, Jeff Lockwood

Living Treasures, Yang Huang

Nature's Confession, J.L. Morin

A Face in the Sky, Greg Jenkins

Dark Lady of Hollywood, Diane Haithman

How Fast Can You Run, Harriet Levin Millan

Growing Up White, James P. Stobaugh

The Beard, Alan Swyer

Parallel, Sharon Erby

CPSIA information can be obtained
at www.ICGtesting.com
Printed in the USA
LVOW11s0358280617
539550LV00001B/13/P